THE VIRGIN AND THE BEAST

A STUD RANCH STANDALONE NOVEL #1

STASIA BLACK

Copyright © 2017 Stasia Black

All rights reserved. No part of this publication may be reproduced, distributed, or transmitted in any form or by any means, including photocopying, recording, or other electronic or mechanical methods, without the prior written permission of the publisher, except in the case of brief quotations embodied in critical reviews and certain other noncommercial uses permitted by copyright law.

This is a work of fiction. Similarities to real people, places, or events are entirely coincidental.

1

"You can't fire me!" I stare across the desk at my boss, shocked. When he called me in here this morning, I thought it was to talk about a *promotion*. Which, considering everything that's happened over the past two weeks, would be some very welcome news.

"I'm your top earning junior associate," I sputter. "I single-handedly closed the Johnson account."

"An account which we're about to lose because of your father's association with this company through you."

"I'm not my father," I say through gritted teeth. "I have nothing to do with his company." He made damn sure of that over the years. Van Bauer & Sons is strictly a male-only operation and has been for three generations. No daughters allowed. A thought which still rankles me even now, though I should be thanking my lucky stars I'm not caught up in the scandal and FBI scrutiny.

Dan shakes his head at me, the fluorescent light shining off his bald spot. "It just doesn't make for good optics to have a Van Bauer associated with our company right now, Melanie."

He can't be serious. "Look, I'm happy to change my name. Legally, if that's what it takes. But I just bought an apartment in Manhattan, I can't afford to lose this j—"

"Your father defrauded some of the most influential people in this city," Dan cuts me off, slashing a hand through the air. "Not to mention the thousands of regular Americans who lost their pensions to his scheme. New World Media and Design cannot and *will not* be associated in any way with Frank Van Bauer. You're out. Today."

My mouth drops open, ten rebuttals on my tongue. I glance down, momentarily distracted by the giant New World Media and Design paperweight Dan has on his desk. It's a horrible logo, created from a giant round-tipped arrow shooting up out of what I think is supposed to be a mountain range?—the whole thing just looks incredibly phallic.

In stressful situations, my mind likes to focus on *super* useful details like this. But really, what am I supposed to say to that? That it's completely unfair. I've spent my entire professional career trying to make it on my own instead of leaning on Dad's business connections. And I've done it, too. I've fought tooth and nail to climb the corporate ladder since I graduated early from Brown six years ago. To prove I could do it, that I was just as good as the son I know Dad always wished he'd had.

And now?

If this is any indication, I'll never be able to work in this town again. And Dad, he's facing jail time. As in, a life sentence.

I bite back the threatening tears, knowing if there's one rule above all others, it's never to let the bastards see they affect you. Any emotion, especially tears, in a corporate environment will be mocked as womanly weakness and held against you for years.

I stand abruptly and hold my chin high. "This is wrongful termination."

Dan looks at me disdainfully. "I already told you we almost lost the Johnson deal over this."

I can't help but swallow hard at that. Only weeks before Dan was falling over himself praising me for bringing in the multi-million-dollar contract.

"Your very presence at the company weakens our brand, which gives us perfectly legal means for termination. Not to mention that the CFO himself personally lost millions to your father's little scam. Be glad you're leaving with a severance package, *Ms. Van Bauer*."

He stands and leans over his desk. "Now remove your things immediately. Your ID badge will be deactivated at noon."

I grit my teeth together and start toward the door. *Take the high road, Mel. They go low, you go high.*

At the last second, I twirl around. "The company's logo looks like a penis and balls. Just an FYI." I smile sweetly and then stomp out the doorway.

∾

WHEN I GET DOWN to my office, all of my coworkers are eyeing me like I'm a contestant on the latest reality show about to head for the chopping block. God, did everyone see this coming except me? I knew it was bad when the news broke about Dad a week and a half ago.

Bail was set at one and a half million dollars. The bank froze all his assets. I was only able to pay it by not only using up everything in the savings Grandpa left for me but also by putting a second mortgage on the apartment I'd *just* bought. Not imagining that I'd have any suddenly dramatic life expenses, I'd put a lot of cash down on the place, so I had some equity in it… Which I then needed right back to get my father out of prison.

I bang into my office, ready to throw my things in a box and get the hell out of here as fast as possible.

But I stop in my tracks when I see a stranger sitting in one of the two chairs across from my desk. He's an impeccably dressed older gentleman. I was always around wealth growing up, but over the last few years especially, I've learned to pay attention to the small details that differentiate true wealth from the cheap imitation of it.

So I recognize the elegant tailoring and fine cloth that indicate this man's suit was custom made and expensive. And the fact that his cufflinks appear to be real gold, maybe an heirloom. Grandpa used to have some like that. The man's black wingtips are polished and expensive. I always check men's footwear when sizing up a potential client.

This guy is real money. The serious kind.

Too bad I didn't pay more attention when Dad started wearing knock-off Louis Vuitton shoes a few years ago after Mom died. She'd left him years before but he was always stupid over her.

I knew he was struggling. I just thought it was personal—I never dreamed the business was in trouble, too. Once when I dropped by to check on him, I caught him at home, drunk at eleven a.m., sitting on his couch in nothing but his boxers. It was obvious he'd been crying.

He yelled at me to get out, and Dad never yelled. Then he didn't talk to me for a whole month. When he finally invited me out to one of Manhattan's most exclusive restaurants for dinner—a place you go to be seen as much as for the exquisite cuisine—he was in his most expensive suit and smiling his salesman's grin. Business was good, he was hobnobbing with the rich and famous, and all was well in the world.

Or so it seemed anyway. He always put on such a good face. I had no idea he was digging himself deeper and deeper until it all toppled like a house of cards.

"Sorry," I say to the stranger, suddenly feeling the weight of reality like a lead weight on my shoulders, "All my appointments today are canceled." I lift my hands. "As of ten minutes ago, I'm no longer employed here."

"You are Melanie Van Bauer?" the stranger asks. When I nod, he stands and holds out a hand to shake. He's of medium height, maybe pushing seventy, with a full head of neatly cropped white hair.

"Yes," I say, drawing out the word as I reach forward and take his hand.

"You can call me Owens," he says with a pleasant smile, giving my hand a firm shake before releasing it. Then he gestures for me to sit behind my desk. "Please, sit. I have a business proposition to discuss with you."

I tilt my head sideways at him. "Look, I just told you I was fired. I don't know what kind of—"

"Your father is going to be imprisoned for the rest of his life," he starts with no preamble. "Probably for multiple consecutive life sentences once all the gory details of his Ponzi scheme are trotted out in the court of public opinion. That sort of thing is not supposed to affect the jury, but we both know this will be tried in the news for months before it ever makes it to the courtroom. The public is crying for blood and believe me, no one treats a man who steals the retirement pensions of nice little old ladies well in prison."

Oh God, not another one. I'm so not in the mood for this.

"Get out." I point toward the door. Dad and I have been harassed ever since the news broke. People camp outside my apartment, flinging accusations and worse—I got pelted with a tomato a few days ago. A bag of dog crap the day before that. We've been getting death threats over social media and in the mail.

I seriously don't need this bullshit right now. "I don't know who let you in here but I'll call secur—"

Mr. Owens holds his hand up. "What if I told you that you could spare him all of it? That it's within your power to help him?"

I pause with my desk phone mid-air, about to dial security. What the hell is this guy talking about?

Seeing my hesitation, he hurries to continue on. "I have an interested third party who can get him to a non-extradition country and set him up comfortably for the rest of his life."

I bark out a laugh and look around. "What is this? You have the office bugged and you're trying to get me on tape saying something incriminating? I told you bastards I had nothing to do with his company and no matter how deep you dig, you won't find me anywhere in the records."

I turn around and speak to the wall, carefully enunciating every word. "Daddy dearest didn't think a girl was good enough to work at his precious investment brokerage firm. So guess what? I never stepped one foot on that property or touched a single file on any of his computers."

"There's no trap, Ms. Van Bauer," Mr. Owens says calmly. "And there's no need to raise your voice. I'm happy to prove my identity, though at this time I cannot reveal the name of the party I represent."

I turn back around to him. And he really doesn't look like he's joking. In fact, this guy looks so stoic and serious, I'm not sure he's ever laughed at a joke in his life.

"Here are my credentials." He produces some papers from his inner jacket pocket and hands them to me. "Feel free to Google me, as they say."

I check out the fancy, embossed watermarked papers. They bear both his name, Francis Roger Owens III, and the company name, Owens, Jenkins, and Rosenberg Trust.

I take his suggestion and pull out my phone to look him up. A few taps later and it becomes clear that Owens, Jenkins, and Rosenberg Trust is one of the top New York wealth management firms. When I search images, I see the man in front of me standing at the Met Gala with half of New York's elite. There's a picture of him with Mark Zuckerberg. And one with the actor from that famous zombie show.

I look up from the phone, my mouth going dry. "What exactly is it you're proposing?" And why is such an obviously powerful man coming to the daughter of an infamous investment broker?

He smiles. It's the smile of a man who knows he's about to close a deal. Not kind or unkind, just the lift of both sides of his mouth and the glint in his eyes that say whatever deal he's about to offer, I'm in no position to say no.

"It's a small thing, really, when you compare it to saving the rest of your father's life. He had you when he was so young. He's only forty-nine years old. One hopes he has equally as many years left to live." Mr. Owens leans forward. "You can make all those years a gift to him. He can live a life of luxury instead of enduring God knows what in a super-max prison facility."

Oh shit. Why is he still pitching? It's not good when someone sells and sells the pitch without talking costs.

"Bottom line," I say, cutting him off when he looks like he's going to keep spouting BS about what a wonderful life Dad's going to magically have without paying any consequences for destroying the lives of all those people.

Mr. Owens smiles again. "All my client is asking for is what could be as little as a year of your life. A year of your life to give your father the rest of his."

"Doing what?" I demand, the hairs on the back of my neck prickling.

Mr. Owens drops the smile and pulls a contract out of his briefcase. He slides it across the desk to me. "My client needs an heir. You've been vetted as an acceptable candidate. You will stay at his residence and sleep with him until you come to be with child, then remain until you give birth. Then both you and your father are completely free of debt. In fact, you'll be well compensated for your time. And the federal government will never be able to touch your father for the rest of his natural life."

What the—

Sleep with?

Give birth?

He can't be fucking serious.

He gives me that let's-close-a-deal smile again, then pulls a pen out of his briefcase and holds it out across the table for me. "If you'll just sign here and here," he indicates two places on a long contract, "then we can get started."

2

I stand up as tall as my 5'6 frame will allow—well, 5'8 with my killer two-inch heels—and stare Mr. Owens down with every bit of haughty contempt bred into me by three generations of wealth and privilege. "Get the hell out of my office."

"I'll just leave this with you while you think it over. Here's my number." He produces a card, also from his inner coat pocket, and lays it on the contract. "But do call soon. My client is a man of..." he pauses as if looking for the perfect word, "peculiar habits. He doesn't like to be kept waiting."

I scoff in outrage and sweep both the contract and card into the trash beside my desk. Because while there's all that WASP breeding in my DNA, there's also my mother's Latina blood in me. "Well, you can tell your *client* to go stuff it because I'm not a prostitute or baby mama or whatever the hell you think—" I break off, shuddering at the thought of all of it. Having sex? With some disgusting stranger?

This is just fucking insane. How dare this man, however powerful he is, come in here and basically offer me a job as a prostitute? Dad being in the news so much has officially brought out all the crazies.

"Get out!" I shout.

Mr. Owens doesn't seem fazed by how upset I am. He just steps back from the desk and taps his wristwatch. "Tick tock, Ms. Van Bauer. Only forty-five minutes before security will come and physically escort you from the building. Better get packing."

With that, he turns and heads for the door. But not before tossing over his shoulder, "I look forward to your call."

∼

I WALK in the door to my apartment at a little before two in the afternoon. I couldn't find a box, so I had to stuff my large purse with all my belongings. It's bulging so much I have to hold it in front of me like a papoose to keep everything in.

Like a baby.

I shudder even at the thought.

I hate babies. I mean, that sounds bad, but I never want to be a mother. Lord knows my own mom was a bad enough example to put me off the idea forever.

God, that guy propositioning me like that was the most insane thing I've ever experienced. And that's saying something, considering I just learned two weeks ago that Dad tried to pull off the biggest Ponzi scheme since Madoff.

"Mel?" calls my dad's voice in a panic. "Melanie, is that you?" Dad rounds the corner of my foyer and his face crumples in relief. "Thank *God*. Why haven't you been answering your cell?" He's wearing pajama pants and a T-shirt stained with last night's spaghetti sauce. He looks like a shadow of his former self.

I stare at him confused. "My battery probably died. What's going on, Dad?" I drop my purse with a loud *thump*.

He rushes forward and grabs me in a crushing hug. "I tried your office line too, and no one answered. You don't know how worried I've been."

He squeezes me even tighter. *Okaaaaaaaay.* Dad and I are close but we aren't exactly the touchy-feely type. I can't remember the last time he hugged me.

"I got fired." No point in beating around the bush. Unlike him, I can't keep up a perfect sheen that everything's a-okay when in reality it's going down the shitter.

He takes a step back. "What? Why? You're the best damn ad account manager they've seen in years."

I just stare at him. I've never heard such high praise from him.

Then I heave out a sigh. "Daddy, I—" How do I tell the father I've always tried so hard to impress that I got fired from my dream job because of *him*? Because of the Van Bauer name?

He waves a hand but then the same hand is quickly raking through his hair. "None of that matters right now. We've got bigger problems. Everything's just—"

He's scaring me. All of this came as an insane shock when it blew up two weeks ago—*my* dad, the man I'd looked up to forever, defrauding all those people, lying to me, to everyone, for *years*.

He starts pacing back and forth in the entryway and finally heads into the living room. I follow him. All the blinds are drawn and the TV is muted, flashing some cable news show. Used plates and junk food packages litter the coffee table.

Seeing the mess only heightens the anxiety churning in my stomach. None of this is like my dad. Usually he's all about organization and he's a fitness nut. He works out more than me and he's forty-nine.

"Baby," he starts again, "the DA wants me to make a deal. You see, I got into business with some very bad men and—" He bites his lip and presses a hand to his temple like he can't bear to tell me the rest.

Okay, this is beyond scaring me. I've never seen him like this. He is freaking me out. I go over to him and grab his forearms to stop his pacing. "Dad. What men? What the hell is going on?"

It's then that I see just how bloodshot his eyes are. His breath doesn't smell like alcohol, but it's like he hasn't slept in days. I've heard him up at night but I've just tried not to think about it. My unspoken mantra has been: go to work and avoid, avoid, avoid.

The government seized all his assets, including the Upper East Side apartment where he lived. He's been staying with me ever since he got out on bail last weekend. And he's been... different. Not the confident man I grew up with.

But I've never seen him look so freaked out. So abjectly... terrified.

"We have to get whatever money's left together." His eyes shift back and forth wildly. "I have to get out of the country. I'll make a run for Mexico. Maybe find someone who can get me to South America."

"Dad, stop it." What the hell is he talking about? "You're scaring me. What's going on?" Growing up he and I were close. After Mom left us when I was a kid, I used to spend every afternoon after school in his office, coloring or doing homework in the corner and listening to him wheel and deal over the phone. I told myself that when I was older, I'd be just like him.

But then one day it all stopped. He said it wasn't professional to have his daughter at work like that even though he'd never had a problem with it before. He used to show me off to all his coworkers and brag about my good grades to anyone who would listen. But then a nanny started picking me up from school and taking me home to our huge and incredibly empty Manhattan apartment.

Most days Dad tried to get home in time for dinner and to help me with my homework afterwards if I needed it. We always still did the Sunday crossword together... but it was never quite the same. And then cue the pitched battles when I was looking at colleges and started talking about working at the family company. Which was when he dropped the big 'ole bomb that Van Bauer & Sons meant exactly that... *sons*. No girls allowed.

"Honey," he finally looks at me and devastation is clearly written all over his face—dropped brows, dark circles under his eyes, "you don't know how hard I've worked to keep this from ever touching you." He sinks down onto the couch behind him and clutches his head in his hands. "But no matter how hard I worked to keep it all afloat, I just kept getting in deeper and deeper."

Is he talking about the Ponzi scheme? I've asked him, of course I've asked him why he did it. How he could have been so *stupid*... well, I didn't word it like that, exactly, but still.

"Why, Daddy? What happened?" I sit down on the couch beside him and take his hand. It's a reversal of when we were little, of when I'd be afraid and he'd take my hand and all the monsters and scary things in the dark would disappear. That was his power back then. He was my hero. He could do anything.

He stares at the ground and for several long moments, I think he's still not going to tell me. I sigh and go to pull my hand back but he clutches it even tighter.

"After your mom left, I went through a bad patch. I started gambling. I almost lost everything." He squeezes his eyes shut and I can see how much it pains him to admit the weakness.

I swallow hard to keep back my shock.

"I pulled my head out of my ass eventually, but not in time. I borrowed money from some bad men to pay back my debts." He finally looks over at me, his eyes watery and red. "And then I had to borrow from my legitimate clients to pay *them* back. And it kept snowballing from there. I thought if the company just made enough money, if I could just float it for a *little* while longer, I could pay everyone back." He starts shaking his head. "But it got out of control."

His mouth tightens into a hard line and he squeezes my hand again. "But I swore none of it would ever *touch* you. You'd never be part of the business. You'd never be tainted by my mess."

A cry I can't keep back erupts from my throat. "So it was never because… because I wasn't—" I can barely get it out but it has to be asked, "a son?"

His forehead creases in a pained look and he shakes his head. "I hated that I had to make you believe that, but all that mattered was keeping you safe."

He pulls me into his arms again and I collapse against his chest.

Dad. Oh God. How could he?

"Why didn't you just tell me? Maybe I was too young to understand at first, but I'm a grown woman now. You could have confided in me."

He holds me to him while tears leak out of my eyes. His heart is thumping strong underneath my ear.

"I couldn't." I can hear how thick his throat is as he says it. "I was so ashamed. I'm a foolish old man."

I scoff as I pull back from him, swiping at my eyes. "You're only forty-nine, Dad. Hardly old."

He just shakes his head. "I've got to get out of the country, honey. The men I was talking about are dangerous—even after I paid them back..." His gaze moves toward the window like he can't bear to look at me while he talks about this. "I was never able to untangle the business from them. They're powerful men." He moves his palms down his pajama pants. "They wanted money... favors... The DA suspects their involvement and he's offered me a deal if I flip on them. I'm not stupid enough to take it." A haunted look comes into his eyes. "But it's obvious I'm a loose end they want tied up."

Tied up... does he mean, like—

"While I'm holed up in the apartment they can't get to me." His face crumples again. "But baby, now they're threatening *you*."

He walks to the attached dining room and comes back with a large envelope with several black and white photographs. All of me. All with a big red X marked over my face.

"I don't care if I die," my father whispers. "But I can't bear to let anything happen to you."

My gaze freezes on the pictures. Me in my workout gear—it could have been yesterday or any of the other Mondays, Wednesdays, or Sundays I go to my gym. But the second picture, I'm wearing a necklace that I rarely put on. I wore it yesterday in a sad attempt to jazz up my day and feel more feminine and pretty in my usual pantsuit and power blazer.

A cold shiver works its way down my spine. Someone was watching me? And taking creepy pictures?

Someone who wants my dad... *dead*?

"Who's doing this?" I whisper.

Dad shakes his head. "These men want me dead because of what I know. I'm not telling you or anyone else."

"What about protective custody if you did testify? Can't the police—?"

But Dad's already shaking his head. "You don't understand the power these men wield." He swallows. "My only chance is to disappear. Get south of the border and keep running." His gaze goes distant. "You should be safe as long as I'm gone."

I tug away from him and run my hands through my short hair. Holy crap. This is all real. My dad, he— I swallow hard against the tears.

And this whole time, he was *protecting* me, not shunning me from the business because I was a girl.

"Do you know someone who can help you? To disappear?" God, from all he's said and the pictures, they're probably watching the house right now. I look to the windows that he's shuttered. He must have had the same thought.

He reaches a shaking hand up to rub his chin. "That's why we need to get together whatever money we have. I'm sure we can find someone. For the right price—"

So that's a no about him knowing anyone who could help. Not surprising since he burned all his bridges by defrauding almost everyone he was in business with.

I look up at him, suddenly knowing what I have to do.

I walk over to him and squeeze his trembling hand. Then I head back into the foyer and lean over to grab my purse. I dig through all the crap I shoved in it and pull out the crumpled contract at the bottom. Then I fish around for the card.

Yes, I kept them.

Desperate times and all that—though, God, I didn't even know the half of it. My mouth goes dry as I withdraw my phone from the front pocket of my purse.

Now my hands are the ones shaking.

I look down at the card, thinking of how confident Mr. Owens would be that I'd call. Like there was no question that I'd be forced into this position.

Am I really willing to... *sleep with him until you come to be with child...* Mr. Owens words come back in perfect clarity and a shudder goes through my body.

I almost drop the phone back into my purse but then my eyes

catch on the photos of me Dad's still clutching in his hands. If what Dad's saying is true, this is life or death.

I dial the number.

Mr. Owens picks up on the first ring. "Ms. Van Bauer. How delightful to speak to you again so soon."

3

"No! Stop, wait! You didn't let me say goodbye!" I scream, fighting the grip of two men who drag me up the front stairs of a huge resort-type building in the middle of nowhere.

I look over my shoulder frantically at the small plane idling in a distant field and shout, "Dad!" even though I know it's useless and he can't hear me.

What the *fuck* have I gotten us into?

None of this is what I envisioned when the well-dressed Mr. Owens came over a half an hour after I got off the phone with him.

God, was that really only earlier today? As soon as I signed on the dotted line, Mr. Owens told us we had to leave immediately. That we couldn't bring even a single belonging with us.

When I explained the deal to Dad, glossing over the details and saying that I would be going to work for Mr. Owens's client in order to get him out of the country, Dad looked wary.

"What kind of job is it that they offered to help out your convict father, Mel? This doesn't sound right."

"So they color a little outside the lines. It's nothing bad or dangerous." I sat him down and spoke confidently. In truth, I had no idea *what* the hell the 'client' offering this deal was into, but if there was ever a time to sell a pitch, this was it. "You yourself said it. I'm one of the best up and coming ad agents in the business. Just think of this as very aggressive head-hunting. They want me for the job and they were willing to do what needed to be done to sweeten the pot."

Dad still looked dubious. Rightly so. But I could also see the spark of hope in his eyes. This was the only real way out of this mess and we both knew it. If what he said was true, we were sitting ducks in this apartment.

Mr. Owens arrived just then, tabling any further conversation. He said we needed to leave immediately. When Dad started to explain about some of the dangers of leaving the apartment, Mr. Owens cut him off, saying he was already aware of the threats against us.

So him showing up at my office today of all days wasn't a coincidence after all.

My stomach bottomed out. What if he was the very person who had sent those photos? Or his *client* was?

But then why come to me with such an insane and specific proposal? The very bizarre nature of it gave it some credibility—at least as far as Mr. Owens not working for the men who wanted my father dead.

No, my best hope was that he and his client were just taking advantage of my vulnerable situation. And wasn't that just awesome? That in the best case scenario this guy was preying on my weakness instead of actively trying to kill my father?

Dad and I exchanged a glance, then Dad said to give him a second while he went to change. He couldn't very well go out in his pajamas. I had no idea what was really going through his head.

Mr. Owens looked somewhat put out, but I didn't care. While Dad was upstairs I sat with Mr. Owens in my living room enduring the most awkward of silences.

Mr. Owens pulled out his phone and began checking emails. When I couldn't stand the quiet anymore, I finally asked. "Why *me*? Out of all the women in the world?"

He shrugged casually, not looking up from his phone. "You'll have to ask the client that. But I imagine it helps that you come from such a fertile family and that you are in a position of need regarding your father. Plus your good breeding and education."

"Fertile…" I scoffed. "But I'm an only child!"

He glanced up briefly from his phone before looking back at it and thumbing through something on the screen. "Your mother got a tubal ligation. But she's one of eight children and her father and mother both come from large families."

"Are you stereotyping Mexican families right to my face?" My back stiffened.

He shrugged again. "Not at all. I'm just a numbers man. And the odds are good you're fertile."

Enough of this crap. I stood up. "I'm going to go check on my father."

"Good. We need to be going."

It would be bad if I punched an old man, right? I jogged up the stairs and knocked lightly on the guest room door where Dad's been staying.

No response.

"Dad?" I pushed open the door and stepped inside. Light came from the ensuite bathroom where the door was cracked.

A sour, cold knot entered my stomach. I hurried forward and pushed open the door to the bathroom.

Which is where I found my father, dressed in a suit and freshly shaved, standing and staring down at three open bottles of prescription pills and a full glass of water.

"Dad, no!" I rushed forward and knocked over the pill bottles, scattering white and yellow circles all over the counter.

He tried to force me behind him. "Go back downstairs, Mellie. I'm not going to let you do this, whatever it is, for me. It doesn't feel right. Just let me end it here and now." He reached to start gathering the pills into a pile, but I knocked his arm away, scattering them again.

"No!" I threw my arms around his middle, both hugging him and pushing him away from the counter. He stumbled and when his back hit the far wall, it's like I could feel all the bravado leaving him. He hugged me back just as fiercely.

"Dad, swear to me you'll never—" My voice broke. "Never do anything like that again. No matter what." He was breaking my heart. Couldn't he see that? "I'm going to be strong, but I need you to be strong for me, too."

I felt him shake his head into my hair. "I'm supposed to be strong for you. This was never supposed to touch you. Just let me—"

I pulled back from him. "Swear," I demanded, brooking no argument. "Never again. If you love me at all, swear it!" I shook him and finally he nodded. I could tell it felt like a defeat for him to do it, but he did.

"I want to hear the words." My voice was harsh but I didn't care. There was no way I could go through whatever the next year would hold without knowing he would be safe.

"I swear I won't hurt myself. But, baby," he looked at me with anguish. "You swear that you'll be safe, too?"

I nodded. "I swear, Dad. We'll get through this. It's all going to be fine."

Just then there was a knock on the outer bedroom door. "I hate to interrupt," came Mr. Owen's voice, sounding anything but sorry, "but we are working under certain time constraints. If we could move things along?"

"I don't like this," Dad said, his head shaking. "If something seems too good to be true, it usually is."

I plastered on my brightest smile. "Everything's going to be fine. It's just a job, Dad. Trust me."

I took his hand and pulled him through the bedroom to his closet. "Get your shoes and let's go."

He did, reluctantly, and we went.

Yeah, so that saying Dad mentioned about everything seeming too good to be true? I've always known my father to be a very smart man—apart from the whole Ponzi scheme and getting involved with criminals thing.

Because the second Dad and I stepped into the black van Mr. Owens directed us to, two huge, burly men cuffed our hands behind our backs and shoved black bags over our heads.

They must have injected Dad with something because he stopped shouting almost immediately.

I freaked out, thinking they killed him, that the 'client' was actually the people who wanted Dad dead after all. But Mr. Owens calmly informed me, maybe from the front seat, "He's just taking a little nap but will feel right as rain once he gets to his destination."

"Wait, so you don't want him dead?" I asked in a confused panic.

"Of course not." Mr. Owens sounded perplexed. "We signed a contract, did we not? As long as you live up to your end of the bargain, your father will be perfectly fine."

Said as I was shoved in the back seat and one of the muscled henchmen sat beside me.

"The client doesn't want anything in your system," Mr. Owens continued in his calm voice as if none of this was out of the ordinary. "He's very wary of anything that might harm a potential fetus. Even though I informed him that was perfectly absurd and it was highly unlikely at such an early stage of development. Still," Mr. Owens sighed. "He was adamant. Well, this is where I leave you. Pleasure making your acquaintance."

And then I heard the sound of a car door opening and closing.

Fucking lunatic. I started screaming my head off and flailing every body part possible.

That lasted as long as it took for the muscle beside me to lift my hood and shove a gag in my mouth. Then he reached down and tied my ankles together.

I spent the hour-long ride in the van and then an even longer ride in what sounded like a small jet tied up like a stuck pig.

And now that the bag is finally off my head and my legs are untied, I find myself out in the middle of...

God, am I still even in the States? I blink and look around at the endless rolling grassy hills, mountains out in the far, far distance. It could be one of the... western states? I don't fucking know, I'm a city girl for God's sake. But those are definitely cows on the hills in the distance.

Fucking. *Cows*.

Where the *hell* am I?

I take one last desperate look around for any other sign of life and the phrase *no one to hear you scream* echoes in my head.

Two of the brutes who got off the plane with me drag me up the few wooden stairs to the doorway of the giant western-style lodge. The large three-story building stands starkly against the otherwise bleak landscape. There might have once been a façade with a sign over the door but it looks like it was torn down a long time ago. Now the wood over the door is just grayish and weather-worn.

The two men push it open and yank me inside.

"Dad!" I still call out uselessly, trying to look over my shoulder. I stop fighting the men carrying me but neither am I going to help them. I go limp, refusing to walk forward. The men on both sides keep me upright, dragging me through the entryway. Unlike my polished marble foyer in Manhattan, the interior of this place is wood, wood, and more wood. The walls are styled to look like it's a log cabin.

I've been kidnapped by Paul fucking Bunyan.

The toes of my pumps make a squeaking noise against the wood. I squeeze my eyes shut to all of it, wishing I could end this horrible nightmare but knowing it hasn't even begun yet.

Because I accepted the devil's bargain.

Will Mr. Owens actually keep his end of the deal? Or was that all bullshit meant to placate me? Are they going to toss Dad out of the plane somewhere over the Pacific Ocean? Or do I dare even believe that he'll be safe...?

We start up a stairway and the men dragging my lifeless body make no attempt to compensate for the fact the wooden stairs dig into my bare ankles with every step.

"Ow!" One of my shoes is knocked off, then the other a third of the way up the stairs. Son of a— Okay, so going limp was a bad idea.

"Just wait a second, let me get my feet under m—"

They don't wait.

Bastards.

I lift my feet up so they'll clear the sharp-edged steps and try to pull out of their hold again as soon as we get to the top of the stairs. I cry out after the man on my left roughly jerks me forward again.

"Let her go." The command is boomed from a figure down the hall. Even though the two men holding me release their grip, I can't help taking a step back with them.

The inside of the place is dark. There are tons of windows, but they're all covered with heavy drapes that create a dark, suffocating atmosphere. From the outside, the building was huge—far too big to be a single residence. My first thought that it's a resort seems to be correct. Downstairs I briefly glimpsed a huge open common room that might have once been used as a bar or for dancing. Up here there's a long hallway with doors at regular intervals like rooms at an inn.

In the middle of nowhere. Abandoned.

Just like in *The Shining*.

Oh God, I'm going to die with an axe buried in my chest.

Because at the other end of the hallway is a huge, hulking man who in the dim light is just a giant silhouette.

The size of him is enough to scare the shit out of me. But I don't know the half of it.

The next second he takes several steps forward. The light from the single wall sconce barely illuminates his face.

Just enough to see that if this is all a nightmare from hell, then he might be the devil himself.

4

Big. Huge. Monster.

Shit. Shit! This is the *client*?

His face. The left side is... the skin looks melted with angry pink lines spidering across his cheek down into his jaw that has a heavy five o'clock shadow. The skin of his left eyebrow is slanted across the corner so that he's eternally squinting and I'm shocked the eyeball seems still intact. Not to mention that his ear—he wears his thick, dark brown wavy hair long on that side but most of the ear is just —gone.

I can't help taking a step backward. He's huge. The hallway looks too small compared to him. He's got to be what, 6'4 or even 6'5, with shoulders so broad he looks like he might have to turn sideways to fit through doors.

I can't— I have to get the hell out of here—

"Leave," the giant, disfigured man barks. The two men behind me immediately flee down the stairs. I take another step backward, about to join them.

"Not you."

His booming voice freezes me in my tracks.

"There. The doctor's waiting." He thrusts an arm out toward the second door on the right down the hall.

Unlike the hallway, the room is brightly lit. It casts a rectangle of yellow light on the otherwise dark hallway.

There's another person here? Maybe they can help me? If I can just let them know that I'm being kept here against my will, they could—

But what about Dad?

Wait, so do I really think the deal is still on after they blindfolded and manhandled me here?

I still hurry inside the room. Anything is welcome if it means getting away from the terrifying beast in the hallway.

"Examine her," his low voice demands from behind me.

I startle forward even quicker into the bright light of the room.

The room, like everything else in the place, is all wood, but the window dressing and bedding is done in whites and grays.

My eyes quickly zero in on the petite brunette woman in her mid-forties, dressed in scrubs. She has a small table full of instruments and is standing beside the large bed that dominates the center of the room.

She looks past me and nods, I assume at the giant, then steps back and gestures toward the bed. "You'll need to remove your clothing for the examination."

My mouth drops open. And then I feel my cheeks flame.

Bracing myself, I turn back to the door. I keep my eyes somewhere in the vicinity of his giant chest. The dark-gray and blue flannel shirt he's wearing appears to be straining at the seams to contain his biceps.

Oh God, oh God, what have I done by putting my life in this man's hands? Still I manage to find my voice. "Is this really necessary?"

"Yes."

One word is all I get.

I steel myself. "Where is my father being taken?"

"To a place where he'll be free of the reach of the United States government. And anyone else who might wish him harm."

Mr. Owens intimated so in the car, but this seems to confirm it. He knows about the trouble my father is in... Or he's behind it. I can't help looking up, needing to see his face so I can try to gauge whether or not he's telling the truth. His voice is so... not monotone exactly. That's the wrong word. Just matter of fact. Like of course that's where Dad's headed.

I only manage to look at him for a half a second before I have to glance down again. That face... just *ugh*.

I couldn't tell if anything about him looked trustworthy or not. It's wrong and shallow of me. If we were out in polite society, I'd try to be more politically correct about someone with a disability or disfigurement, but considering the circumstances, I'm running a little short on empathy at the moment.

"How do I know you aren't behind all this?" My whole body trembles as I ask it. "That you aren't one of the very people my dad warned me about who wants him dead?"

"You don't," comes his grumble. "Not until tomorrow when he gets to his location. Then I can show you proof of life pictures of him with the local paper. You'll get regular updates every week throughout the year." There's a short pause. "Or however long it takes."

I swallow hard. Oh my God. If what he's saying is true, then it *is* all real.

A baby in exchange for my dad's life...

And all the things it takes to make a baby.

Holy *shit*. Is this actually my life?

"You can put this on while I examine you."

I turn around to see the doctor holding out one of those terrible, thin hospital dressing gowns. I go forward and clutch it like a lifeline.

"The bathroom's just over there." She points to one side of the room where there's another small door.

Yes, apparently this is my life, whether I want it to be or not. The giant at the door and those thugs with the black bags seem like no take-backs kind of guys.

IN THE BATHROOM, my entire body shakes as I slip off my Gucci pantsuit and underclothes, then pull on the hospital gown. I can't even look at myself in the mirror while I try to awkwardly tie the little tie behind my back and neck.

The wooden floor is cool underneath my feet. The bathroom is clean and what probably passes for high class around here—a marble topped counter with brass fixtures. An abstract watercolor painting of a cowboy riding a bucking bull hangs right behind the toilet.

So now I know.

Hell is cowboy chic.

Awesome.

I squeeze my eyes shut tight and then clutch the material at the small of my back. No way to stop your ass from hanging out of these stupid robes.

Holy shit, holy shit, holy shit. Ten hours ago I was waking up and heading into what I thought was just another ordinary day of work.

And now I'm...

God, I can't even think about my current situation too closely. Not if I want to make it through this and not freak the hell out.

I open my eyes and don't let myself consider it any longer. I walk back out to the other room, hand still firmly holding my gown closed behind me.

The giant is still standing right outside the doorway—that's the first thing I notice when I get back in the room. He's hovering just outside the sphere of light. I hope he's far enough away he doesn't notice the shiver that goes up and down my body. Oh God, oh God, oh God.

Maybe the exam will take the rest of the afternoon. Or rather, *evening*. I glance out the window at the setting sun.

Just how late is it? If it's nighttime, does that mean he'll expect... like, right away?

"When was the date of your last period?" the doctor asks, either totally ignorant of my obvious freak-out or doing a great job of pretending not to notice.

She continues with the preliminaries like this is any other check-up. Are my periods regular? Have I noticed any other irregularities or do I have any concerns I'd like to discuss with her?

The talking part is over far too quickly and then she's onto the exam. Just my luck, she's fast and efficient.

Her pronouncement echoes throughout the room while the speculum is still inside me.

"She's a virgin."

Even from the bed where I'm lying, my legs spread like the Thanksgiving turkey, I can hear his quick, heavy exhalation.

Relief? Surprise?

Mr. Owens said earlier that I was the perfect candidate. Was being a virgin part of the *client's* requirements? And if it was, how the hell did they know?

It's not like I wear a sign on my forehead, *no penises have tread here*. I'm a successful twenty-six-year-old woman. I work out, keep trim, and I get hit on plenty. At my age, it's weird to still be a virgin without, you know, religious reasons for it.

But all growing up, I'd watched my mother use her sex appeal like a weapon, luring in one man after another. She played up the stereotype of sexy Latina woman to the hilt, wearing tight, revealing clothing that highlighted her ample assets.

I hated it. Hated the admiring glances the boys in my classes shot her way on the few instances she actually showed up at my school functions. Hated the way my father was still broken-hearted over her years after she'd left him.

And I especially hated the fact that since I was her spitting image, everyone expected me to turn out just the same.

As soon as my breasts began developing, I started wearing the baggiest, most unsexy clothing I could find. I cut my thick, glossy brown hair short. I studied hard and focused on grades and avoided boys and parties like the plague.

When I got to college, I chilled out a little. I had hormones just like any other girl. Sure, I was curious. Touching and getting myself off took care of that a little bit, but I wasn't immune to romantic dreams.

My sophomore year, I got my first serious boyfriend. I met Brian in my Principals of Financial Accounting class. He seemed like a sweet, funny guy.

Until we were alone and all he wanted to do was reach under my oversized shirt to grab my boobs, which, in his words, he "couldn't stop thinking about titty-fucking."

Yeah, me and Brian didn't last long. I tried one more time, with a guy named Jeremy who was part of the group of friends me and my roommate hung out with. I told him up front I wanted to take things slowly. He said that was totally fine with him. We dated for several months. Which was when I walked in on him screwing my roommate.

Shocker that I was put off sex.

I didn't want to be labeled a cock-tease either so I just didn't go there. I tried dating a couple more times but ended up breaking things off fairly quickly. Mostly I just automatically friend-zoned guys. I kept my hair short and continued wearing clothes that covered up my curves.

My girlfriends told me all the time that I was nuts and that all these guys I thought were just friends were actually hoping for something more with me.

But then I graduated college and was still a virgin and it just started to be totally weird. How do you tell someone on the third or fourth date... so look, I want to mess around with you, but I'm kinda sorta a virgin and still a little terrified about sex, cool?

Yeah, I never found a way to bring that up in polite conversations and would just stop returning a dude's calls after the second or third date.

To my friends, I pretended I was waiting for some mythical perfect guy to lose it to, just to get them off my back about it. And then everything got intense with me working sixty to seventy hours a week and the last thing on my mind was a guy.

Now here I am and my virginity is possibly the thing that's put me in the running for the position of sex-slave/baby-mama to a complete stranger so giant that I doubt I'll be able to breathe if he lays on top of me.

And they say good things come to those who wait.

Bull *shit*.

My whole life has been about waiting. Playing it safe. Be the good girl, don't color outside the lines. Put in the hard work trying to prove myself to Dad, then to my college professors, then to my boss at New World Media. Just waiting for the day for it to all pay off.

And right when it was all starting to—I finally had the house, the job, I was even thinking about getting a cat—*boom!*—my life explodes and suddenly now I'm—

"All done," the doctor interrupts my thoughts, pulling off her gloves with a loud *snap*.

What? No. She can't be done. My eyes leap to her but she won't meet my gaze.

Instead, she speaks toward the door. "The rest of the information you requested will be in my report. I'll email it to you within the hour," she says, quickly packing up her tools in baggies and then replacing them in her black medical bag.

"Wait, that's it?" I ask, sitting up. "Don't you need to ask me more questions? Give me some vitamins or something? Draw some blood?"

"We already have the results of your most recent blood test," the doctor says, still avoiding my gaze. I might as well be a plastic mannequin to her. "And I've already recommended vitamins. It'll all be in my report."

And with that, she's walking out of the room. She gives the huge man standing in the hallway as wide a berth as she can. Then she's gone.

Leaving me alone with nothing but a thin little slip of a hospital gown between me and *him*.

I stare at his feet. He's wearing boots. Like, cowboy boots. They're huge black ones.

They say the size of a man's feet can indicate—

Oh God, now is *so not* the time for useless trivia, Mel.

I raise my knees to my chest, making sure to pull my hospital gown down over all the way to my feet so that I'm covered up in a little mini tent.

I avert my eyes to the white bedcover.

Silence.

No, that's not true—there's the loud *tick, tick, tick* of the grandfather clock on the far wall. And the anxious terror gnawing at my stomach with every second that ticks away.

Is this the part where he leaps forward and then savages me? Do I fight him or just let it happen? If what he's saying about Dad is true, if he's really going to be safe and free, then maybe it will all turn out okay. Just a year of my life...

But the sex. He's so *big*.

Oh God, he's going to rip me in two.

My breathing becomes erratic and I clutch my arms around my legs. If he just wants a baby, why can't we do this in a doctor's office, all nice and civilized? He can go make his deposit in a cup somewhere, then a doctor can spurt me full with whatever the medical equivalent of a turkey baster is. Wham bam, thank you ma'am, I'm knocked up the way God intended, in a clinic with no actual body parts touching.

No, no, no, there's absolutely no way I can do this, right? What the hell was I thinking earlier when I signed that fucking contract?

I wasn't thinking, I was reacting. Dad was so freaked and then there were those pictures of me and people wanting to *kill* Dad and—

Tick, tick, tick.

Why isn't he saying anything? Or making a move? Oh God, I'm going to scream.

The terror builds and builds until finally, I dare to look back to the doorway.

It's empty.

He's *gone*.

What in the—? He just... left? Now what?

First off, I scurry to the bathroom and change back into my own clothes. My black Gucci pantsuit, gray blouse, and matching blazer feel shockingly comforting if not exactly comfortable. But it's the only shield I've got.

Right, Mel, a whole one-millimeter thick fabric shield that Mr. Beast-dude could rip apart with one good yank if he wanted to.

So... it would be cowardly to just lock the door and hide in here as long as possible, right?

Screw cowardly.

I run forward and flip the flimsy lock on the bathroom door.

Then I stand there in the brightly lit bathroom for about five minutes until I realize that a stupid bathroom lock isn't going to be much more of a hindrance than my Gucci suit to a guy as big as that.

So I rush out into the larger room and lock *that* door. Then I run to the huge mahogany dresser and try to shove it over in front of the door.

It won't budge.

Goddammit. I lower my center of gravity by crouching low and try again.

Still nothing.

That doesn't make sense. Sure I might not be winning any girl's heavyweight titles in the near future, but it didn't even *budge*.

Which is when I lean over and see it's freaking *bolted to the ground*.

Holy crap. Did he anticipate me trying to move furniture to try to block him out of my room? Are his plans for me that horrible?

What the hell am I doing?

I can't—

This is too—

What was I thinkin—?

I jerk the bedroom door open and fly toward the stairs. I take them two at a time, stumbling and only managing to keep upright because of my death grip on the stair railing. I jump the last three steps and then I'm over to the door, one hand on the knob.

I jerk it open, only to be greeted by the vast, empty landscape I saw earlier.

"Leave and our deal is done."

Out of nowhere, his voice is suddenly booming so close it's all but in my ears. I whirl but don't see him. I turn frantically left, then right. Finally I locate him at the top of the stairwell. The sound must have carried off all the wood since there isn't a lot of other furniture in here.

"I'll not only bring your father back into the country," he leans over the balustrade, his body just a silhouette in all the gathered shadows, "but I'll drop him right on the doorstep of the men who are looking for him. The blood won't be on my hands. He made his own bed." His voice is cold.

Damn him.

I slam the door, wrapping my arms around myself and backing against the wall of the large foyer.

"Good choice. There's a whole lotta nothing for thirty miles in any direction. You wouldn't have gotten two miles before I dragged you back here."

I expect him to come storming down the stairs but the next time I look up, he's gone.

∼

I LIE awake the whole night in bed. Waiting, on edge, sure each moment I'll hear the click of a key unlocking the door as he comes to claim his prize. Because, duh, obviously he probably has keys to all these rooms.

But he never comes.

He doesn't come the next night either.

Or the next.

I've given up on hiding in my room and wander the giant house freely now. He's gone all day. Each morning out my window I see him leave out back, looking like a cowboy, big hat and all. I didn't go exploring until the second day of no activity. He stays out all day doing... whatever he does. Ranching? All I've seen are cows. He disappears around the side of the house and I have no idea how big the property might be.

Even though he was gone all day yesterday, I'm still tentative as I head downstairs. Maybe I can find a computer or a phone?

Not that I know exactly who I'd email or call or what I'd say if I could. In a way, I'm an accessory to helping Dad jump bail. It would certainly be very easy to frame it that way. And the people who were after Dad… would they still try to harm me if I suddenly popped up again? How long does Dad have to be gone before they accept he's *gone*?

God, even thinking about Dad makes my chest hurt. Where is he? Is he okay? He's got to be freaking out worrying about me. And then I start panicking all over again because what if he hurts himself? But no, he swore. And he has to know that at this point, it wouldn't do any good. I've already been taken. The deal is done.

Please, Dad, just be okay.

Turns out it doesn't matter who I'd email if I could because my captor is either allergic to all technology or he has it locked up tight. There are landline phone outlets, but no phones. No TVs either. *No freaking TVs.*

The first floor of the lodge is pretty stripped down. There's a well-stocked kitchen, which I raid freely. In the main lodge area, there are just a few tables and a big leather couch left in what was obviously once meant to be a big bustling common area for a lot of guests.

Both the first and second floor have fireplaces in the central guest areas, which are sparsely decorated with random furniture. While the lodge is in good shape, some rooms on the third story are completely empty of furniture altogether. I've only peeked up there. There's one locked door that I suspect is the giant's room. I didn't pay it much attention, frankly.

Once I find the library on the second story, I keep blissfully busy.

Books. Reading. You know—that thing we all used to do before YouTube videos and Pinterest ate up all our time?

I was frankly going a bit nuts trying to play Nancy Drew and discover clues about my captor while waiting for him to decide he's done toying with me.

Shudder.

No thank you. Escaping into other people's drama is far more preferable to living my own.

There's another big couch in the library by a big window. I throw back the curtains to let in the light and then cozy up to lose myself in Jack Reacher's latest adventure for the afternoon.

That's where he finds me several hours later when he finally comes for me.

After all that waiting, ears perked for any noise at the door, eyes strained for any movement of shadow for hours on end, when he actually comes, I'm so engrossed in the book I don't notice him until he's standing over me.

I let out a small screech of shock and drop the book, my hand flying to my chest.

I look up at him in my surprise and immediately wish I hadn't. With the curtains drawn, the room is bathed in mid-day light. I can see every monstrous melted inch of the top left half of his face.

Meanwhile, his squinting eye seems to see straight down into me, measuring my disgust for him. My whole body tenses as I sit up straight on the couch.

His hair is sweat slicked and he's pulled off the work shirt I always see him go out in each morning. He's just in a tank top and jeans, exposing acres of muscled, bronzed skin. He's as big as a fucking ox.

"Oh, hello." I sit up on the couch, backing as far away from him as I can. "I was just—"

"It's time," is all he says. He holds out a smart phone. I blink and it takes a second to make out what I'm seeing on the screen. But then my eyes focus.

There's Dad, standing on the beach, blue ocean behind him. He's frowning and has dark circles under his eyes, but otherwise looks fine. He's holding up a paper. The giant zooms in on the picture and I see today's date on the paper. The writing is some kind of South Asian script. My hand jumps to cover my mouth, a sob catching in my throat.

I try to grab for the phone, wanting to zoom out again and look at Dad, but he pulls it away and puts it back in his pocket.

Still, it was enough. Dad looks good. No bruises or black eyes. He looks healthy.

Safe.

There's no time to process though, because the next thing I know, the giant has leaned down, picked me up like I weigh nothing, and swung me over his shoulder in a fireman's carry.

Then he starts jogging with me up the stairs.

To his bedroom.

5

"What? Wait, if we could just talk for a second—"

He doesn't stop or even slow at my continued protests.

No, he just continues up the stairs, my body jolting with each step.

Holy crap, what if he drops me on my head? Without thinking about it, my hands drop to his lower back to steady myself. The iron hard muscles there do nothing to assuage my escalating terror.

Damn, this guy is built like a Mack Truck. He's thick around the waist like a boxer and from what I can tell, it's all pure muscle. He's inhumanely big. Like a normal human except he comes in an extra-large size. His back is broader. Neck is thicker. Thighs are more massive. He takes the stairs two at a time like he's not carrying a hundred-and-thirty-pound lead weight over his shoulder.

He pulls out a set of keys from his pocket, unlocks his door and then we're inside.

I have an upside-down view since I'm still over his shoulder and at first I'm afraid to look around. What if there are, I don't know... huge pentagrams painted on the walls or sacrificial altars set up?

But when I finally peek it looks... well... normal.

Except, you know, for the huge giant who's holding me essentially captive. And the fact that there's barely any light up here. Just a small lamp above a mantle that casts the whole room in shadow.

There's a large desk pushed up against one wall. It has two large monitors on it with a laptop hooked up between them. Both screens are dark now.

Well, that answers that question. He's not anti-technology, he just planned well in advance and doesn't want me having access to the outside world. Awesome. That's not super creepy at all.

And the other major feature of the room is a bed.

A huge king size bed. God, the thing looks *bigger* than king size. Do they make them bigger than king size?

"So what's your name?" I ask, my face still inches away from his jean-clad ass. "I'm Melanie. I mean, obviously you know that. But you know, we never really did the whole introductions thing."

The next thing I know, I'm flying ass over ankles as he tosses me on the bed.

He looms over me like the monster in some movie.

Oh God, oh God, just keep talking. Humanize yourself to your captor, isn't that what they say? Besides, I always chatter when I'm nervous.

"You have a really beautiful library." I try for a smile that I'm sure comes off more as a pained grimace. "I thought at first it was just lots of old books, like, for decoration. But then I found the contemporary section. You really like mysteries, huh? Lee Child books? He's great, one of my favorites, I—"

He reaches back and pulls his t-shirt off over his head.

Holy bulging muscles, Batman.

I gulp and without really thinking about it scramble backward on the bed.

He's just so exponentially *large*.

He reaches down and grabs my ankle, yanking me back to him in one swift tug.

"Xavier," he says. "My name."

And then he reaches into the drawer beside his bedside and pulls out a knife.

Giant psycho's going to kill me.

I'm about to die.

I screech and try to roll away from him but his huge hand clamps easily around my ankle yet again.

"Hold still," he growls.

And then I hear the sound of fabric being cut. I look down wide-eyed to see he's slicing my expensive Gucci pants off me, starting at the ankle. Once he gets to the knee of each leg, he starts to rip, his muscles flexing.

He has to use the knife again to cut through the top where the belt loops are. I lay panting in terror.

"You could have just asked me to take them off," I whisper as he pulls the ruined fabric from around my body. I want to drop my hands to cover myself, but God, it won't do any good, will it?

This is happening and there's no stopping it.

"I didn't like them," is all he says.

My favorite gray silk blouse is the next to go. He doesn't have to use the knife. He just rips it open and the buttons all come off in a consecutive set of explosive *pops*.

Then he flips me over on the bed so I'm face down.

Ridiculously, I wonder: Does he just expect me to go around the mansion naked all the time now? Because *that* will be comfortable.

Gotta love my knack for worrying about the really important things.

Next he's slicing through the straps of my bra—which yes, is very worn and has definitely seen better days. But still, it was one of my last barriers to him and now it's gone.

I'm still face down on the bed as the contraption holding my mid-sized breasts comes free.

And then—shit, shit, *shit*—he cuts off my underwear.

I lie here not sure if I'm glad I can't see what he's doing now or if I'm more terrified because I want to watch his every move.

Before I can decide, though, one of his huge hands drops to my back.

My eyes squeeze shut.

I expect him to be rough. To grab me like he did my ankle earlier. To take what I'm here for him to take.

I don't expect the tentative touch.

I don't expect the soft exhale as his other hand comes to my skin and he caresses down my back from my shoulder blades to the top swell of my ass. He stops just short of touching it, though, and massages back up again.

I feel the bed dip as he gets on, springs squeaking. I imagine his huge body taking up the whole bed, larger than life. Just thinking of that, his body crouched above me, is enough to have me tensing and ready to scramble off the bed and running for the door.

His hands pause on my back. He felt the sudden tension in my body.

Dammit.

This was the deal, Mel. There was never going to be any getting around this part, you know that.

But God, I only made the deal a few days ago and between then and now I've done everything possible to *avoid* thinking about this moment.

Still, it's here now. I squeeze my eyes shut tighter and try to force myself to relax. Everything I read online over the years said it would go easier if I relaxed.

Yeah right.

You try relaxing with two hundred and thirty pounds of muscled beast over you while you're buck naked.

His hands rub down my back again and this time when he gets to my ass, he doesn't pause. Before I can even take a full breath, both his hands are full of my ass cheeks. He squeezes them in his massive hands, first one handful, then the other. I might not be anything to write home about in the bosom department, but I'm not lacking when it comes to junk in my trunk.

Just my luck, because apparently he's an ass man.

He leans down and his cheek traces the same path his hands just took, down my spine until his stubble brushes my ass.

He's been unexpectedly gentle the past few minutes.

So I don't expect the bite.

It's not hard, just a nip of his teeth on the round of my ass—but it's enough to have me yelping and looking over my shoulder at the top of his dark head.

Like he can feel me looking, he growls and glances up at me.

The left side of his face catches me off guard just like it has each time I've looked him full on. And then he's moving—far quicker than it seems like a man his size should be able to.

He whips open his night stand. My breath catches until I see he's only holding an eye mask.

"Oh really, that's not necessary. I'm sorry. I won't look if you don't want me to. You just took me by surprise there with the—" My voice breaks off because what am I going to say—with the ass-biting? With your scary monster face?

He doesn't wait for me to finish anyway. He's already slipped the eye mask around my head and is adjusting the strap.

Alrighty then. Guess he's not big on talking things out.

Then I'm being flipped again, now to my back.

Everything's happening so suddenly, I'm not prepared when his weight comes down on me and his mouth suctions on my right breast.

I—

Wait, he's just going to—

To jump in like this— I mean, what—

I blink underneath the blindfold, my eyelashes fluttering madly against the silk fabric of the mask.

I don't—

I mean, I just—

That feels—

A high-pitched breathy little gasp escapes my throat.

And then I'm mortified. What the hell was that?

He's going to think that I—

He abandons the first breast and moves to the second. What he's doing with his mouth— I try to get a full breath, but my lungs aren't working right. His hand lifts and starts to massage the breast he was just suckling while he keeps at the other. He plucks and tugs at the nipple and holy crap, it's like it's connected to a live wire straight to my—

My whole body jolts and without really thinking about it, both my hands fly to his head. I don't know if I'm trying to encourage him or yank him away.

What the hell am I thinking—yank him away, definitely yank him *away*.

But I barely register the feel of his thick, wavy hair before he grabs both of my wrists in one of his hands and pins them above my head.

I struggle in his hold. The sensations he's pulling out of me are so foreign.

It's all so much, so fast. My whole body just feels restless. I need to be moving. To be doing something.

Or maybe not. God, what am I even thinking?

I should just be lying here, taking whatever this bastard has to do to me. Right? That was always my plan for my first time, even before this insane scenario.

Close my eyes, pretend really hard I was somewhere else, stare at some spot on the wall and let him just rut and get it done with. That's how a some friends in high school and college had described it—at least that's how you got through the pain of the first time. A couple of girlfriends loved sex. But even they admitted their first times were awful. Definitely something to just be survived.

But now here is this man—no mere *guy*—making me feel such crazy, intense, oh my *God* things.

This is all wrong. Not at all how it's supposed to go. Most especially because I'm being *forced* to be here.

This is not some romantic fling with a man I've finally decided is the *one* that I trust to try this with. This is some monstrous stranger, taking something he has no right to, except for the fact he basically *bought it* by helping my Dad and—

The hand not holding my wrists traces down between my breasts and grips my hip. And dammit, I can't even be bothered to disguise the fact that I'm all out panting now.

My legs twist underneath him. When did he sling one of those jean-clad legs over mine? His leg is huge and heavy and it acts as a clamp. To try to keep me from getting away? Or to keep me from grinding against him like a tramp in heat?

Oh God, the thought washes me in shame and I try to still all my restless shuffling as his fingers grip and knead the flesh at my hip. What am I doing? Why is my body reacting this way?

My breath hitches as his hand reaches around to my ass and he pulls me up and into him. He's hard. I can feel him through his jeans.

The thought should terrify me.

And I am.

Terrified, that is.

But I'm also damp between my legs.

Oh who the hell am I kidding?

I'm drenched.

I'm so goddamned wet my juices are probably going to make a wet spot on the front of his jeans.

My face heats in utter humiliation.

But then his hand that was just gripping my ass caresses back around to the front of my body, dipping down between us.

My first thought is that I want to howl in embarrassment because he'll feel exactly how wet he's made me.

And then I want to just howl because *holy hell*, his fingers immediately seek out my engorged little bud and he starts to press and circle with perfect pressure and—

It feels both so wrong and *so* right. My stomach clenches as he continues to rub and rub.

All I can do is *feel*. Sensations cascading over one another: The rasp of his slight beard against my breast. His tongue and teeth torturing my nipple so exquisitely.

And those talented fingers. Taking me higher and higher.

Without meaning to, my pelvis arches up into his hand. The

rising ache of needing release—it's so much higher than those rare occasions when I've nervously touched myself in the dark before.

I've never felt anything like this. His large, blunt fingers are nothing like my thin ones. I always tease myself with the gentle press of my middle finger but he uses his thumb, rolling and pinching, alternately gentle and rough. I would have thought I'd hate this... this lack of control. This giant stranger taking what he wants like this. It's so wrong. But that very thought seems to amp my pleasure even higher.

"Need to taste," he mutters and then he shifts himself off of me. The next second his fingers and hands and mouth are gone.

I stop the whine of protest right before it crosses my lips. Still, I can't help the brief moment when my whole body arches in the direction he seemed to go.

And then I'm flooded by both shame and relief. Maybe he'll stop now. Maybe that's all I'll have to endure for tonight.

I flop back against the bed, squeezing my eyes shut underneath the mask. But there's no time to try to get my head on straight before I realize that the noise I'm hearing is that goddammed nightstand drawer being opened and shut again.

Oh no. What now?

He takes my wrists and then I feel something looped around them. Rope? A belt? Holy shit, he's tying me down.

Oh God, no. No no no no no.

He's.

Tying.

Me.

Down.

Somehow it's finally hitting me in a way it hasn't before. I'm out here all alone with an obviously *crazy* person. A very large, very muscled crazy person who wants to tie me down and do... God knows what to me.

"You know, we really haven't gotten to know each other yet. Don't you think that might be nice? They always say communication is key." I laugh shrilly. "Take you for instance. Xavier's such an interesting name. Did your mother or father think it up? Is it a family name? Do you have any brothers or sisters?"

Especially any sisters, I think but don't say. Some nice little sister I might remind him of? Then I remember I'm naked and where his mouth and hands just were... okay, so scratch the sister image. But still, okay, how else can I humanize myself?

"I was an only child but that's just because my mom got her tubes tied after me. She didn't really like kids. She was one of seven children and it kind of burnt her out on the whole thing. But I always wanted a little sister or brother."

The constraint—I'm almost sure it's a belt for how sharp the edges feel cutting into the skin of my wrists—jerks tight as he pulls it taut and then ostensibly ties off the other end, probably to the thick wooden rungs lining the headboard. Terror makes me light-headed. I give an experimental yank but nothing gives even the littlest bit. I remember how sturdy the wooden bed frame looked and my breathing gets shallow.

Where was I? Oh right. Trying to humanize myself so I don't die in some virgin sacrifice my third day here. I know he theoretically brought me here to pop out a kid for him, but what if that was just so I'd get in the damn van and really he's a psycho killer and—

Rough hands shove my thighs open.

Oh God, this is it.

Brace for impact.

Here it comes.

Devirginization in three, two—

I about jump out of my skin at the feel of his warm breath and the touch of his silky-soft tongue tracing up my inner left thigh.

Receiving pleasure when I expected pain is a shock to my system. I don't know what to— I can't even—

"Um, yeah, so I— I—" The last word breaks off in a gasp as he grazes his stubbled cheek along the inside of one thigh, pausing at the apex.

Is he—oh God, is he *smelling* me? And then his lips join the scrape of his jaw, a soft torture of lips and tongue that creates such an agonizing contrast I'm not sure if I'm in heaven or hell.

When he tongues up the center of my slit, I shudder and gasp with pleasure so sharp, I feel like I might pass out.

Just moments ago I was clear-headed and sure I was about to be murdered and now—oh *God*, with the simplest of touches, he has me limp as a mewling kitten underneath his searching tongue.

Again I'm horrified by my body's lusty reaction to him. How can I be turned on right now? How can this be happening to—?

Oh, oh, oh God— My whole body spasms as his tongue reaches the promised land and he sucks on my clit. *Yes*, right there—

Then he pulls back so that just the very tip of his tongue teases my clit, up and down, then side to side.

Holy— Oh shit, oh my *God*— I've never— I didn't even know it could feel like—

He pushes my legs open even further and it's only with the most feeble resistance that I try to keep them clenched. I shouldn't. This is so, so wrong. But when he elbows my knees further apart again, they fall slack. He takes advantage and presses my legs open wide with his arms, moving between my legs as he continues eating at me like a man starved.

A groan of pleasure wrenches from my chest. I shake my head, biting my lip against the rising tide of desire and need. No, I don't want this. Even as the other half of my brain screams—*Just yes. More. Please more.*

I yank at my arm restraints in futility and frustration and *need*. God, I've never felt so needy for it in my whole life.

He sucks my whole clit into his mouth again and a high-pitched whine escapes my throat. But then after sucking and eating at me like I'm everything he needs to survive in the world, he pulls back with lazy kisses.

No, wait, I—

Rational thought dissolves. I'm so close, riding that blissful edge. So much higher and brighter than ever before. Oh God, I need it. It's *right there*.

I try to lift my hips up to his mouth because God, he can't give me that and then just take it away again. My nipples are hard as rocks but I can't move because he's holding my hips to keep me in place.

Then his mouth dips to tongue inside my pussy. A long, deep thrust of his tongue that makes my limbs quake. My eyes pop open again and I cry out in shock and pleasure at the intrusion.

His thumb takes up where his mouth left off at my clit. Oh God, if I thought he was eating at me hungrily before, it's nothing to how crazy he goes when he gets at my little virgin pussy.

He thrusts his tongue in and sucks and kisses at the swollen, sensitive lips of my sex. And then a finger from his other hand joins his tongue, slipping inside my sopping hole.

I cry out, not in pain but because *yes*, oh God, *yes*. I didn't even realize how empty I was there until I've finally got something solid to clench at.

And clench I do. My whole body contracts around the digit he presses further and further inside me.

He hisses, pulling away from me just long enough to mutter, "Fuck," before sucking me even more earnestly. His mouth goes back to my clit as his finger continues to explore inside me.

First to a knuckle, then deeper until I feel the base of his hand at my pelvis.

I let out a breath as he moves his finger inside me, first pressing against one wall and then another. Exploring. Or stretching? I don't know. It feels strange and wonderful and—

A second finger teases at my entrance and I bite my bottom lip to keep from crying out. I can't stop my quick, huffing breaths though.

Is this when it will start to hurt? Will he just jam it in?

But no, he works the second finger in as slowly as he did the first, probing and stretching as he goes.

And then he does this thing with his teeth, nibbling at my clit while he presses upwards with his fingers and holy—

A high-pitched wail escapes my throat.

It's *so good*.

So high.

Fuck. Oh God, *yes*, more.

More. Oh—

My back arches off the bed as I come.

I'm blindfolded but the light is so bright behind my eyelids as I hit the peak. He keeps suckling me through it.

I'm still panting, barely coming down when I feel him shift. He's moving.

That was so good, so freaking insane—

But then, all of the sudden—

Cock!

He's sticking his cock in me!

Holy shit!

My brain blinks on again. There's no warning, no nothing—he tricked me by giving me the best orgasm of my life and now his huge body is covering mine and he— he's—

I can't see. I have no idea what's happening. Oh God. I yank against my wrist constraints and try to pull my legs together but the head of him has already pushed through the lips of my sex.

So much bigger than his fingers.

"*Christ*," he mutters, his voice low.

I should say something. Like, *how about we do this tomorrow? Or never?*

Oh God, it's going to hurt. I'm going to bleed. He's a freaking giant. He's going to tear me in two. Oh God, oh God, oh God, oh God—

He tries to push in more and doesn't budge. He's at the barrier and I clench even tighter as my terror amps to an all new high.

"Relax," he says. It sounds like an order.

I wind even tighter.

"Christ, even your teeth are clenched."

At his words, I realize he's right. My jaw aches with how tight my teeth are gritted.

Awesome, so he'll realize what a bad idea this is, pull back, and we can forget about this whole thing. Maybe he'll come to see that I'm the wrong girl for this whole ridiculous plan and go find someone else much more accommodating and—

His lips drop back to my breast.

I'm so surprised at the move and the spark of reignited pleasure that for a second, my body relaxes.

He takes advantage and thrusts in.

The pain makes me yelp and my legs come up reflexively. Where I encounter his body. Still, my legs strain against him, clutching him to me since I have nothing to grab except the leather strap of the belt holding my arms over my head. And I need everything possible to ground me in this moment.

I can't help but be terrified of the expected pain.

But... it was little more than a sharp pinch, not the sustained pain girls have so often talked about. And it's already fading. The fact that Xavier hasn't let up his attentions to my breasts is certainly helping distract me, too.

And then there's him between my legs.

Inside me.

Holy shit, he's *inside* me. Having sex with me. Even though at the moment he's just still, like he's allowing me to become accustomed to him.

I hold my breath. He's over me. He's everywhere. I can't see him because of the mask but that almost makes it worse or, I don't know, at least more intense. With every breath, I inhale his foreign, male scent. His chest hair brushes against my breasts, our bellies are mashed together, and then there's his, *his*— I swallow. He's lodged so deeply inside, like he's piercing straight through my body.

It's too much to take in at once.

And then he starts to move. Not thrusting himself in and out exactly, just swiveling so that he's rubbing against that part of me that's so sensitive from his earlier attentions.

My legs clench reflexively around his hips as all the sensations from earlier roar back to life.

What. The. Fuck.

Not again. Surely not again, not while he's—

His large hand clutches my ass suddenly, kneading the flesh before tracing down and hiking my leg even higher around his hip.

And my fucking traitorous body moves with him, my foot notching behind his back and unwittingly positioning myself so that his cock settles even deeper when he pushes back in.

It's just, the more he swivels, the more that liquid sensation in my stomach starts to go molten again. He gently rocks more and more until his cock slips in and out of me in small micro-thrusts.

At first there's discomfort. But even that is countered by the rising tide of pleasure he's managing to wring from my body again.

Eventually he starts pushing for more, thrusting his cock deeper inside me. And to my everlasting shame and confusion, my legs have come up and wrapped around his hips.

His huge chest brushes against my chest and his scent is everywhere. Leather and soap and man. His warm body over mine. Skin to skin. And his hard cock pressing inside me where no one has ever been before.

"So good," he mumbles, "So tight. So good."

He slips one arm underneath my back and grips my shoulder from behind, bracing himself on his elbow. His other hand grabs my ass so he can drag me on and off of his cock as his thrusts become more frantic. The position has us so close our chests are cemented together. He buries his face in the hollow of my neck as he pumps more and more furiously.

The pain is gone and all that's left is the rising tide of pleasure and this man fucking me like his life depends on it.

And his cock.

He's hitting so deep, in places I never imagined—

And the way it feels. It's— I can't— It—

All the while he grinds his pelvis up and against my clitoris.

Then his cock hits that spot deep inside and he's clutching me so tight, closer and with more desperation than anyone's held me in my whole life.

I can't help but buck against him with every thrust as our bodies play out the most primitive act between man and woman.

He starts to suck and bite at my neck like he can't help but to devour whatever part of me he has access to and God, *oh God*, it's coming again, higher and deeper than before, harder and more soul-shaking than anything I've ever felt in my life—

If I thought I screamed earlier, it's nothing to the screech that pours from the top of my lungs now. My legs spasm as they clench around his body. Oh— oh, oh *ohhhhhhhhhhhh*—

He pumps into me, more ferocious than ever, once, twice, and then a third time he thrusts deeper than I would have thought possible. He stills and clutches me to him.

For a second the world stops spinning and time stops ticking and everything is completely still except the pleasure exploding like a thousand fireworks lighting up our bodies.

The pulses of the orgasm just keep going and going and *going*.

He thrusts in and out lazily several more times and then pauses another long moment, head still buried in my neck. As rational thought returns, I wonder if he can even breathe there.

And then all the other thoughts come back.

Holy shit.

I just had *sex*.

This stranger who's barely said three words to me just took my virginity.

And I... liked it. I *participated*, even. Shame and confusion choke me as I squeeze my eyes shut. What happens now?

Is this the part where he pulls out a cigarette and casually smokes? Isn't that what they do in movies? At least in old movies. Now movies are just excited about the sex part—they all fade to black somewhere in the middle of it. Then it skips to the next morning or something. You rarely if ever get to see what happens *right after*.

Like, when the guy is still half-hard inside you and you're blindfolded and tied up and have no idea what the hell you're doing.

But then he quickly pulls out and withdraws completely from my body. It's so startling after having him so close, after having him *inside* and surrounding me on the outside, that I'm immediately cold. Chill bumps rise all over my body.

I want to ask, *what now*? I want to ask, foolishly, *was I any good*? I want to start chattering a million miles an hour to fill the horrible empty silence that's taken over the room in place of our moans and pleasured gasps from minutes ago.

I draw my legs together, feeling horribly exposed laid out like I am, my arms still tied over my head, body on display. Is he looking at me or like, busy checking his phone to see if he got any pressing emails while he was screwing me? What does he even do for a job that he's able to afford this fancy house and all the land that must go with it? And what kind of connections does he—

"Don't shower or bathe. I want you still smelling like me when I come for you in the morning."

With that, he releases my hands. By the time I've scrambled to a sitting position and pulled off my blindfold, he's gone.

6

He had to be kidding about the shower, right? I wander back to my room in a daze and spend the rest of the evening like that.

I'm a woman used to being in charge. I see what I want and I take it. But this afternoon with him, God, that was like nothing I could have ever—

I mean, sex was something I was afraid of for so long and then for it to turn out like *that*. It wasn't bad at all. It was sort of... wonderful.

My mind rejects the thought even as I think it.

No. I do *not* want to be here. This is all *against my will*.

...Isn't it?

Because it didn't seem like it when I was howling with pleasure earlier. What if I am my mother's daughter after all?

Slut. Whore.

I heard the words people in the country club whispered about my mom behind Dad's back. Because of her heritage, she was never warmly accepted in Dad's wealthy circles—they were married in the nineties, after all, and women from Mexico were supposed to be serving the food or cleaning the place, not on the arm of one of the wealthiest members. It wasn't fair and Dad tried to shield her from the worst of it. But then, of course, Mom went and made sure to live up to all of their worst expectations.

Still, what does it say about me that I could enjoy sex with a stranger who all but kidnapped me? How could I respond like that?

I wrap my arms around myself and drop my head. And that's when I smell him. His scent is all over me. It's as if he marked me as his, like an animal might. I don't even know exactly how to describe the scent. I close my eyes and try to pick out distinctive elements. Some sort of manly scented body wash and... is that hay? Leather, too, maybe.

And the earthy smell of sweat and sex.

I want you still smelling like me when I come for you in the morning.

I shiver.

Screw that.

I can't stand smelling like him for another second. I speed walk to the bathroom and flip the shower to the hottest I can stand it. Then I step in and scrub hard at my entire body as soon as I get under the spray of water. When I go to wash my hair, my hand stutters after grabbing the bottle. It's the same brand of shampoo that I use at home. What the—?

I take a step back out of the shower spray and look at the rest of the items in the bathtub. It's my brand of body wash and conditioner, too. All in full, brand-new bottles.

How could he—? Did he have people break into my apartment to figure that out? Or watch me shop?

Just how long has he been watching me?

I look around the shower and up at the ceiling. Are there cameras on me right now? I raise my arms and cover my breasts.

Because that matters when the man had his mouth all over them just an hour ago, Mel. The thought makes me cringe in shame and embarrassment.

I can't believe I just... *gave in* like that. I mean, yeah, I knew that sex would be expected of me in coming here. I'm not naïve.

The second I signed the contract, I knew I was basically prostituting myself for my dad's freedom. But somehow it seemed like a noble sacrifice or some BS back when it was just an idea and not a reality.

And none of my ideas of how this would all go down *ever* involved enjoying myself or getting off.

I grab my body wash and spurt a generous handful in my palm. Then I get to work scrubbing at every inch of me he touched. I rub especially vigorously between my legs, ignoring the sensitivity and soreness of the area. The shower has a detachable head and when I turn it on my lady bits, it immediately feels good against the aching flesh. I wash up and down, making sure I'm extra clean.

And then the stream of water strays back my sex.

Did I bleed? I didn't notice any blood, but then, I wasn't hanging around to examine the sheets. It barely even hurt.

I remember his skilled fingers. How he played me so expertly. My own fingers stray there.

My eyes snap open and I jerk my hand away from myself. I replace the shower head back in its place high on the wall to finish the rest of my shower as quickly as possible.

Then I get out of the shower, towel off, and get into bed. Skipping dinner is a no brainer. I'm ready for this day to be over.

Sleep is still a long time in coming but eventually, blessed unconsciousness takes me.

∽

"How hard is it to obey simple instructions?" His voice is a roar that jerks me from sleep.

I sit up in bed, my heart pounding as I look around me frantically. The room is completely dark. Still nighttime. Where am I—? What—?

"You washed me off you." While slightly quieter, I can hear anger barely restrained in his voice. Xavier. I'm at his lodge in the middle of nowhere. Effectively captive.

"I, I'm sorry—" I stutter. "I didn't think you—"

"You didn't think!" he thunders. "You didn't think you needed to obey orders? You know what happens to soldiers who don't obey orders? They *die*."

I scramble away from him on the bed, but he grabs my ankle and yanks me back, just like he did yesterday.

Oh my God. This guy is crazy. Like *crazy* crazy. You'd have thought the whole locking a girl up in an abandoned resort thing would have tipped me off, but it really only becomes clear in this moment. This guy just might be certifiable.

I wasn't kidding when I said we're in a place so remote no one will hear my screams.

I scream anyway.

7

"Let go of me, you psycho!" I scream.

Xavier doesn't say anything else, he just flips me over on the bed so that I'm face down on the comforter. The next second he's lifted up my nightgown—the only kind of sleepwear provided and nothing like I would wear at home—and pulled down my panties. He grabs both of my wrists and pins them at the small of my back, forcing my face even deeper into the mattress. I thrash and turn my head enough so that I can at least breathe.

Oh God, is he going to rape me now? So was earlier just some fluke? Like, he had to wait till full dark to do it how he really likes? Psycho fucker. Well, I'm not going to make it easy for him. I don't care if I agreed to be here. No always means *no* and—

A resounding slap on my ass startles all my thoughts momentarily quiet.

"Count," he demands. "And ask, please Sir, may I have another?"

My mouth drops open. I crane my neck to look over my shoulder. I can only make out the barest outline of him. It must be a new moon outside because there's barely any light coming through the curtains. He's just a looming shadow at the edge of the bed behind me. "Are you fucking kidding me?"

He lands another punishing slap to my ass, this time on the other cheek. "Language," he snaps.

"Fuck you!" I spit, yanking even harder to get away from him.

He spanks me again. I yelp in outrage, at the same time noting that his hand landing just feels like a sharp sting. It doesn't *hurt* hurt. But, still, this whole thing is just getting more fucked up by the second. Who the hell does he think he is? I haven't been spanked in... well, *never*. It was frowned upon by the time I was growing up. And the fact that this man has the *gall* to spank me now when I'm twenty-six years old is just—

He lands another blow.

"We'll keep this up until you learn your lesson." He sounds calmer now. "As soon as you start counting, you'll only have ten more."

I grit my teeth. If this asshole thinks he can get me to humiliate myself with one little spanking, he's got another thing coming.

He spanks me again, landing it on a spot he's hit previously. It stings like a bitch, but I don't make a sound. I do flinch, though, and he chuckles, sounding even more relaxed. "You're stubborn. Good. You're here to be a breeder, and I want my child to have good, strong, stubborn genes."

Oh my God, I've been trying so hard to forget that whole part of the deal and he has to go and remind me of it *now*? Like this?

When his hand next comes down, it's not with impact, but a caress. His voice is likewise caressing. "But it's just as important for stubborn people to know when to give in."

His hand dips lower and underneath to my sex where he starts to play with my pussy. And even though I barely know him, it's like my body is already trained to his touch. Within seconds I'm softening and moistening for him.

No. *Stop that, body*. Enemy! He's crazy. He came in here yelling about soldiers and acting nuts and reminding me he expects me to be his baby mama and—

His middle finger starts to rub circles round and round my clit while his thumb teases at the entrance of my pussy.

My breath hitches and almost immediately his hands are gone.

Another *smack* lands on my ass.

"It's easy," he says, totally calm now. "*Sir, may I please have another?* Then the punishment will be done and we can return to your pleasure."

Punishment? I am *not* going to play his screwed-up games. "What the hell does that have to do with anything?" I say, desperate to try to get back to some vestige of sanity. "You need me here so I can make you a baby. So just fuck me and let's be done with it."

Thwack. His palm lands again, jarring my whole body into the mattress.

And then his hand dips to my sex, teasing me even more thoroughly than he did before.

"Language," is all he says. I hear the rustle of a buckle and then I feel the hot, smooth weight of his cock lying against my ass. He presses against me, his long, thick rod caught between us. My sex immediately contracts upon feeling it.

The next moment, his thick, bulbous head is pressing against my netherlips. I gasp and unlike earlier, he doesn't hesitate. He just pushes right in. Not a shove, but there's no hesitation either.

I'm drenched and other than some brief discomfort, his passage is smooth. Still, I can't help my uneven breathing at the foreign sensation.

Does this mean he's going to dispense with all the other nonsense and we can just have sex like normal people until his swimmers do their job and I get pregnant?

I can't believe I just had that thought but seriously, the sex is enough to handle. I can't deal with all this extra shit he's throwing at me.

"So goddamned tight," he mutters once he's bottomed out inside me, his hips pressed against my ass. He's coming from behind this time, and it feels different than when we did it chest to chest earlier. I clench around him reflexively at his words and he groans.

The breath I haven't even realize I've been holding expels at the sound because it's like it finally sinks in—he's having sex with me again for the second time in 24 hours.

I'm having *sex*. Right now. This is what sex feels like. The fullness is still like nothing I could have described before feeling it.

He pulls his cock out halfway and I can't help but to concentrate on every inch of him as his cock drags along my inner walls.

And then he spanks me again. *While* he's inside me.

It shocks my concentration loose as I cry out in frustration.

Especially because by this point, with Xavier's fullness inside me and, I don't know—maybe in part because of how screwed up it all is —I am *so turned on*. I press my forehead to the bed in humiliation.

He grabs my hips in his large hands and fucks me with long, slow plunges. He hits a spot so deep inside it makes sparks light behind my eyes.

Still, this is all just so screwed up. I try to pull my hands out of his grasp at the small of my back but his grip is unrelenting.

He spanks me again. "Just ask, please Sir, may I have another?" His other hand comes around my body and whispers over my pulsing clit before he pulls away again.

"Wait!" I gasp, trying to twist my body to chase his hand. But he's gone. Instead, his hand goes back to my hip. He abandons slow and starts pumping away, hard and fast. I imagine the muscles of his ass as he thrusts and withdraws from my pussy. He's so huge, all those tanned muscles flexing with every—

I'm disgusted with myself even as the thought makes me gush over his cock. I feel so dirty and wrong and—

"That's right," he murmurs. "Christ, watching my giant cock disappear in you. You have no idea what I want to do to you. The hundred ways I want to desecrate your tight little body."

The hand on my hip clenches tighter and then lifts before coming down hard on my ass in a resonating smack.

I cry out a high keening noise of pleasure.

"Listen to the sound of that." He seems so awed by it. He fucks me twice as fast for a few moments before slowing down again. "You want it. I know you do. I'm going to finish inside you and plant myself so deep. But you don't get to come."

What? No. I have to. I'm so close. I jam myself down on his cock. Oh God, it's so close. I need that insane high. It will make all of this disappear, just for a second if I can get free and—

"Not unless you beg me. Not until you learn how to obey, little pet. It's so easy." He spanks me again. "*Sir, may I please have another.* That's all you have to say, ten times while you count, and I can give you what you want. What you need."

His hand comes back around to my clitoris.

Yes. Yes, fuck *yes*.

Tears well up at the release that's *right there*. It's going to burn me up from the inside out. I've never needed anything so badly in my life. The wave is climbing, climbing, climbing, and then finally it starts to crest—

My mouth drops open right at the very moment.

But. Then. He. Pulls. His. Hand. Away.

Immediately the high drops.

I cry out in devastated loss at the denied peak.

He clucks his tongue in disappointment and spanks me again.

And oh God, it's on the tip of my tongue. *Please, Sir may I...*

Pleasure and oblivion are right there. So close. Just *there*— My whole body strains toward it.

But the slight dip in consuming pleasure without his hands on me allows my brain to finally catch up with my runaway body.

And no!

Holy shit, *no*.

What the fuck am I thinking?

I will *not* be reduced to some pathetic little girl, begging her *captor* for pleasure. Even if I am the one currently captivated by him. He's speaking so much more than the bare monosyllabic phrases I've heard him utter before now. I'm getting more of a peek at the man himself. Even if that man is a filthy, sex-fiend control freak.

"Last chance," he lands yet another smack on my ass, which has to be red as a ripe strawberry by now.

I bite down on my bottom lip. Rational mind wars with sex-starved body.

"Stubborn little pet," he growls, leaning over and biting at my neck as he thrusts in and out of me. Each time he bottoms out I'm teased by a pleasure that threatens to light me up but never *quite* does.

Then he thrusts hard and stills inside, clutching me to him.

And I don't know how I can be so totally full and yet feel so empty at the same time.

8

I wake to the heavenly smell of frying bacon. I'm famished, I suddenly realize as I sit up in bed and clutch the covers to my chest. I barely ate a thing yesterday and *God,* that smells good.

In spite of my hunger, I linger in bed a moment. All the memories of yesterday run on an unforgiving reel in my brain. My body's absolute lack of self-control.

I can't believe I... that I was like that.

My hand drops down between my legs and I wince slightly at the soreness there. I squeeze my eyes shut and force all my confused thoughts away.

Thinking about all of it won't help anything. There's just today to face. One foot in front of another, one day at a time.

I take a fortifying breath and then get out of bed and head for the dresser. I know from my exploration on the previous days that all I'll find inside are lacy underthings that are nothing like the no-nonsense supportive undergarments I usually don.

I hold up a see-through red lace demi-bra with dismay. But then my nose catches the scent of bacon again and I shake my head and put the damn thing on. It's better than nothing. I slip on the matching underwear and head to the closet.

Here is another crime against Melanie Van Bauer's personal aesthetic: Dresses line the rack from one end to the other. And not just any sort of dresses—flowy, pastel, floral print dresses. Did you hear me? I said *floral print*.

I'm a woman who wears power suits. Black is the only color in my palette, I've often joked. It makes up most of my wardrobe, interspersed with the occasional gray.

When you're a woman striving to be taken seriously in a man's world, you have to go to certain lengths to make them forget about the fact that you're actually female. Not that it ever actually works. It still always felt like a boy's club. But I was used to chopping my brown locks short and maybe it felt good to continue being the opposite of everything my mother had been. I abandoned any color even remotely feminine—aka, *all* color.

This closet, though? It positively drips with color. And the dresses are the most ridiculous little frilly things. My first day here, I slammed the closet shut with a gasp after one glimpse.

Now that my Gucci suit is shredded, though, there's no choice but to don one of these—I pull out the least offensive dress—*things*.

It's a dark-blue A-line dress that reminds me a bit of every dress Maria ever wore in the Sound of Music. A lot of the dresses in the closet have a similar shape. So maybe Xavier has a thing for the 50s?

Awesome. 'Cause that was notoriously a great time for women's lib.

Well, Mel, he did spank you.

I stare at the dress for another second, debating with myself. The only other option is to go out with no clothes on at all. And what message would showing up for breakfast in nothing but red lacy lingerie send? Or I could just skip breakfast altogether and stay up here in my room under the covers?

My stomach rumbles with hunger.

I swear the bacon is calling my name. *Mellllllll*, it calls. *I'm delicioussssss.*

I slip the dress over my head. I catch the briefest glimpse of myself in the mirror but turn away before I can see my girly reflection full on. There's just no need to see the complete effect.

Let's go get stuffed with some over-salted, fatty meat.

Bacon makes everything better.

I exit my room and hurry down the stairs.

The kitchen is large and must have once served the whole resort. It's dim with light only filtering in through the heavy drapes. I briefly explored it during my initial wanderings. It feels much more intimate than some of the industrial kitchens I've glimpsed when my friends waitressed throughout college.

The floor is a warm, brown, Spanish-type glazed tile, and the grill, stove, and oven take up one wall. Xavier's set up a small six-person wooden dining room table off to the side that, like his bed, looks handcrafted.

At the moment, however, my attention is stalled out by the man himself. The dim light is still plenty to see Xavier standing in front of the counter, flipping golden pancakes from a griddle onto two plates already loaded with eggs and bacon.

He's shirtless, wearing nothing except some loose-slung jeans while he does this—not even any socks. It brings back vivid memories of all the things he did to my body yesterday and heat burns my cheeks. I cross my arms over my chest as I enter the kitchen.

The good side of his face is turned to me as he flips the last pancakes on the griddle, and with a shock, I realize that Xavier is actually extremely good looking.

When I first met him, all I could focus on was the ruined half of his face. But from this angle I can see him as he once must have been.

Ruggedly handsome. He has strong, angular features.

"Do you like syrup on your pancakes?" he asks and I immediately look to the floor, hoping he didn't catch me staring. He transfers the pancakes to the plate.

"Sure," I say, toeing at the floor nervously before glancing back up at him.

He's younger than I first thought, too. Maybe in his early thirties, if that. He wears his hair a little too long. Is he self-conscious about the bad part of his face? The one mostly missing ear? What happened to him anyway?

He pours a light dribble of syrup back and forth over the stack of pancakes and then holds out my plate. I'm not sure when I last had pancakes. It's not a very New York meal.

I take my plate and turn to the table.

And then I realize there's only one chair.

Xavier doesn't seem to notice that anything's amiss, however, as he brushes right past me and sets his plate down in front of the single chair. Then he pulls his phone out of his pocket, clicks a few times and hands it to me. I hold my plate to my waist so I can grab the phone.

There's Dad, standing by the railing of what looks like a resort right on the water, which is so blue it's almost turquoise. My breath hitches. "It looks like paradise."

"Not a bad place to retire," Xavier agrees.

Dad looks anything but happy, though, as he holds up yet another paper. *Daddy*.

"Does he know I'm okay?" I look up at Xavier anxiously. "Can I talk to him?"

Xavier's mouth tightens into a line. "That's not part of the deal. No contact while you're here." He takes the phone back, leaving me holding my plate awkwardly.

I sigh, my stomach churning as I think of Dad going crazy worrying about me. With the way we were taken... which God, was so freaking *unnecessary*. I grit my teeth, though. Exploding at Xavier isn't going to get me what I want. "Well can you at least get him pictures of me, too? Showing that I'm okay?"

He studies me for a brief moment, then nods once. I barely have a second to breathe out in relief and utter a quick, "thank you," before he's gesturing beside his plate. "You can set yours down here."

I look around as he sits and, without ceremony or preamble, begins to eat.

"Um, is there another chair or step stool I could use...?"

I mean seriously, I get that these aren't normal circumstances, but it's not like he didn't know I was coming. A modicum of hospitality might be nice. He certainly didn't forget to stock up on all the other items in his bedside drawer. Remembering to make sure there was an extra chair in the dining room might have gone a long way toward showing me I'm not just an expensive sex toy/baby incubator.

Ugh. *Baby.* Shudder.

No, not thinking about that right now. Not thinking about that *ever.*

Turns out that's easier than I would have thought, because Xavier levels me with a cold stare and snaps his fingers at me, pointing downward. "On your knees at Master's feet. That's the only way you'll get any food."

"What?" I half laugh.

I mean, of course he's got to be joking.

That was a joke.

Right?

Right???

But Xavier just keeps up his icy demeanor, both the good and ruined half of his face immovable as he watches the confusion that's no doubt playing out on my face. His intense focus makes it twice as hard to think straight.

He's apparently *not* joking. And I note that while he's got a fork and knife, he hasn't provided me any.

Fine. Screw him.

I'm a grown woman perfectly capable of finding my own cutlery. My stomach rumbles and I look down at the bacon that has been continuing to sing its siren song ever since I stepped into the kitchen.

I reach down and grab the most delectable looking piece on my plate. But before I can lift it to my mouth, Xavier's hand clamps down around my wrist like a shackle.

"No food goes in that mouth except what *I* place there. And no pleasure is allowed except what *I* give you. You will learn to submit to me in all things. Including trusting me for every bite of nourishment."

I glare down at him, sitting so casually in his carved wooden chair with an inlaid leather cushion. I don't know if it's having been so intimate with him yesterday or even just seeing him today as more of a man and not a monster, but I don't feel afraid of him so much anymore. At least, not afraid that he'll hurt me.

Through my teeth, I manage to grit out, "Let go of me."

With his other hand, he plucks the bacon out of my fingers, and then he lets my hand go. My mouth drops open in outrage and I try to reach for another piece. His large arm blocks me from the plate.

"Stop being ridiculous," I say, and try for another grab. Again I'm blocked and absurdly, I feel like I'm back in kindergarten fighting over who gets the last piece of birthday cake. I refuse to be humiliated like this and I fold my arms over my chest, infuriated.

Xavier, on the other hand, picks up the morning paper beside him on the table and starts reading as though nothing's wrong, completely unruffled.

"You can have everything on this plate," he says calmly and conversationally, eyes still on the paper. "As long as you take it from my hands."

"With you feeding me like I'm a dog?" I bite back.

His cool eyes lift to mine and for just a second, they flare when our gazes connect. "Exactly like that, Pet."

I let out an infuriated huff and turn my back on him. I start to stalk out of the room, but not before I hear his warning. "You'll go hungry until you accept food from me. I'll have you licking my fingers, you'll want it so bad."

I ignore the fact that his words send an absurd flare of lust through my lady bits and stomp back up the stairs to my room.

Later when the house is silent and I see out my window that he's walking out toward… wherever the hell it is he goes to spend so much of his day, I hurry down stairs and make a beeline for the kitchen.

Only to find it locked. Solid oak pocket doors I hadn't even realized were there have been pulled out and locked securely on both entrances to the kitchen.

"Son of a bitch!" I mutter, rattling at the doors uselessly, knowing they won't budge.

I'm hungry all day, wandering the house and fuming. Xavier stays out until dark. The only interesting room on the third floor is locked, so there's no exploring up there. And no matter how long I fidget at the kitchen door locks with my bobby pins, none of them magically unlock like they do in the movies. If I just had access to my iPhone so I could google how you break into locked doors. There's obviously some trick I'm missing.

It's a little before sundown when I hear the front door jangling and know he's coming back in. I hide behind the library door, peeking through the crack to watch him go by. He's drenched in sweat and as he passes by, he pulls his white t-shirt off over his head.

And holy muscles.

Everywhere—huge, glistening, bulging muscles. I don't know, I thought maybe I'd been overexaggerating how big they were in my imagination.

Nope. They're just as inhumanely large as I remember.

Suddenly the door I'm hiding behind is swung open and I'm exposed. Then that huge chest is right in front of me, wide as an ox and probably just as strong.

The scent I was so eager to wash off me assaults me all over again—body wash and animal and sweat and hay and man and sun. That's not the reason I'm holding my breath when he backs me into the wall I was just hiding against, though.

"Watching out for the Big Bad Wolf, little pet?" He presses his sweaty, glistening chest against my breasts and almost immediately I can feel his thickening erection through his work pants.

I close my eyes against the hundred sensations his touch immediately evokes. The mint of his breath that's combining with his scent and the pressure of his body—all of it drives my senses wild for some *stupid* reason.

And he can tell. Goddamn him, he knows.

"If I reach between those pretty little thighs, I'd find you drenched for me, wouldn't I?" he rasps, rubbing his stubbled chin over my trembling lips.

And then, him being him, he drops his hand beneath the skirt of my peach, floral print dress. He easily pushes past my tiny excuse for panties and plunges his thick finger inside me.

He hisses low when he feels *exactly* how wet for him I am, and I drop my head back to the wall in shame.

"Come join me in the shower," he demands, pulling his finger out and withdrawing from me. I blink my eyes open at him and set my jaw.

The nerve of this bastard. "Unlock the kitchen."

He grins at me and it's a dazzling sight. I'm so shocked by it, I forget to breathe for a moment. It's then that I realize that even though it's been just four days, I'm already becoming accustomed to the ruined upper half of his face. After getting over the shock of it, it's not actually that gruesome. The skin is just kind of flat and smooth. Yes, his eye droops and while the top half of his ear is missing, his hair mostly covers it.

After realizing how good looking he actually is earlier and with the brilliant smile he just flashed me, my brain almost automatically maps out the corresponding structures on the other side of his face underneath the burned part. Though, is it a *burn*? Is that what happened? What about those streaky bits that extend down his cheek where his stubbly beard won't grow. Maybe some kind of explosion or shrapnel?

"I'll unlock the kitchen later for dinner when you show me you can be a good pet who submits and takes food from my hand. In the meantime, I suggest you come with me now to take a shower and be fucked like you've never been fucked before."

Oh right. It doesn't matter what he looks like. He's still an asshole.

My mouth, probably perpetually half-open in a state of shock around this man, drops open even wider.

Eventually, I find my voice again. "You can't just starve me."

He shrugs and as he pulls back, his face goes neutral like he's indifferent on the subject one way or the other.

Outrage wins again. "You brought me here to pop out a baby for you. I didn't agree to the rest of this bullshit. We've already had sex. I could be pregnant right now." God, even the thought makes me want to run screaming out the door, but dammit, I have a point to make here. "And what—you're going to starve the mother of your child? You're really willing to risk harming—"

In a millisecond, he's got me pinned up against the wall again, his body flush against mine. "Don't you *ever* dare accuse me of risking the health of the baby." His voice is dangerous.

"I'm doing all of this for the baby. You will be walking around with my son or daughter in your belly for nine months but you're unruly, undisciplined, and untrained. I won't stand for it. A few days without food won't hurt you as long as you have liquids and vitamins. There's something far more important at stake. The woman bearing my child will obey and submit to me in all things."

"*Obey* you!?" My head is literally going to explode.

"Yes." He nods decisively. "Obey."

"Let me tell you something, buddy," I pound his rock-hard chest with my pointer finger. "I am a woman in the twenty-first century. We don't have to meekly *submit* and *obey* anymore."

"Oh really? Haven't you figured out by now how pleasurable obedience can be?" His good eyebrow arches imperiously and the next thing I know, I'm on my back on the library floor carpet. My lace panties are yanked to my ankles and Xavier's head is buried between my legs.

I want to stomp my foot and scream, "no fair!" But at the same time, I don't dare do anything that might make him stop.

Because in a few days, he's apparently turned me into a sex maniac.

It's just that, when his mouth latches onto the bud at the top of my sex, I can't even— It feels so…

Everything else is crazy, but then there's *this*. I close my eyes and my body takes over. I don't have to think— It's just— *So… Oh…*

He sucks and sucks so hard I see stars. I reach down to bury my hands in his curling locks but at the last second he catches my wrists and pins them to my side near my hip.

I buck against his mouth.

Oh God, he's barely been at it two minutes, but I'm already almost there.

So close.

Muffled cries of ecstasy groan from my throat as he takes me higher and higher.

It's almost there.

I'm frantic with it. I need it so bad.

Everything's been crazy and insane, but this need is so pure and clear and—

My stomach bottoms out even as I jerk my pelvis up into Xavier's face, ready to ride out my climax when he suddenly pulls away.

"Wha—?" I blink in confusion as he stands up, leaving me in a useless puddle on the floor.

He wipes his mouth with his forearm, face placid. "Follow me into my shower and we can continue. Then at dinner I'll feed you like a good little pet." He holds a hand down to me to help me up.

So I can be his *pet*.

Goddamned-mother-fucking piece of—

"Fuck you!" I shout again.

"Language," he says with a frown, turning on his heel, "But I *will* be seeing you at dinner." He tilts his head sideways, eyes focused on my still exposed pussy where he flung up my skirt. "I want to eat you out again for dessert after the filet mignon."

He ignores my scoff of outrage and leaves to shower.

When I try to beg off dinner an hour and a half later, Xavier lifts me over his shoulder—so goddammed annoying he can toss me around like that!—and deposits me on my feet by the dining room table. Where again there are no chairs other than his own.

He proceeds to eat the most juicy-looking filet in front of me. Both the cut of beef and Xavier himself look mouthwatering. Xavier's freshly showered and changed into a blue Henley and a worn pair of jeans.

Every so often he'll hold out a bite of meat on his fingers to me. Not even on a fork. Each time I turn away in disgust even though the rumbling of my stomach echoes loudly in the mostly empty common room.

Xavier finishes the last bite of his steak with a satisfied burp and I glare at him. I have no idea how I can both be so attracted to him and repulsed by him at the same time. He's *starving* me and for what—just to prove some dumb point?

And you're refusing to eat for the same reason, an annoying inner voice argues.

Shut up, I snap back. *He started it.*

Glad to know I've got the mature high ground here. Sigh.

Especially since I don't know where the hell I'm standing when, after Xavier finishes his meal and downs half a glass of red wine, he declares it's time for dessert. He stalks toward me where I've hovered at the opposite end of the table.

I thought he was joking about that.

Nope, apparently not. He grabs me and hikes me up on the edge of the table, then rips my panties off before going to town on my pussy as voraciously as he attacked his meal.

Which is to say, in minutes, he has me straddling the same edge he had me on earlier in the day. I grab the tablecloth with my hands, knowing if I reach for him at all, he'll just pin my hands down. I bite my lip and try to muffle my cries.

Oh God, I'm so close.

The waves are shattering. Higher and higher.

So close. Almost there.

If I don't make a noise, maybe he won't realize and I can climax before he pulls away.

I try to stay still. So achingly still when all I want to do is shove my pussy against his face until he's sucking down all my honey. So hard, never stopping and—

Oh, *oh, God, yes*—

The bastard pulls away right before the sweetness hits.

"Wait—no, please don't—!"

He pauses, wiping his mouth with his forearm, eyes glittering.

"Did you have something to say? Are you hungry for Master to give you your dinner?"

He reaches lazily up with his thumb and gives my pulsing clitoris a caress.

I bite down on my lip because, oh God, just say yes. Let him give you what you need. It would be so easy. Stop fighting it. Bliss is *right there*. I try to press into his thumb but he retracts it, leaving me whining and panting for him.

"Just say the word, Pet."

Pet.

Fucking *pet*.

The word stings and cuts through the haze of lust. God, would I so quickly give up my self-respect for one little orgasm?

I don't need this asshole for those anyway. I can take care of it all by myself, thank you very much. He said no pleasure is allowed except what *he* gives me. But he leaves all day to take care of his farm or ranch or whatever the hell it is he does all day.

While the master's away, the mice will play.

I am *not* his pet. I am my *own* master. Always have been and always will be.

I turn my face away from him stubbornly, shove my dress down, and scamper off the table. I ignore his dark laugh behind me as I run up the steps toward my room.

∽

He knocks on my door and invites me to breakfast the next morning, but knowing it will just be more of him taunting me with food I can't have, I ignore him and stay under my covers. For once he doesn't drag me down to torture me with the smells and sights of food I can't eat.

I stay in bed until I hear the *boom* of the front door closing that signals he's left for the day. Then I throw off the covers and run to the window just to make sure. And yep, just as I thought, he's headed out, a wide brimmed hat on his head and tight-fitting Levi's hugging one truly *fine* ass—

I jerk my eyes away from my captor's backside and go back to bed.

Time to remind myself that no man has control over me or my body. I've never been a super sexual person—or at least, before now, I've never allowed sex to consume so much of my thoughts. And I've certainly never let it influence my actions.

I just need to regain perspective and take back my power. Remind myself there's nothing Xavier has to give me that I can't take care of all on my own.

I dip my hand underneath the covers. I touch myself and try to let my mind wander. *Okay, time to pull out all my best fantasizing material.*

Except all the fantasies I used to use to get myself off seem pale and vapid compared to what *real* sex is actually like.

And my only experience with the real thing is with Xavier.

Who is the *last* person on earth I want to be thinking about right now.

But when I close my eyes, it's his firm fingers I imagine roaming up my thigh and teasing my pussy lips. When I slide my own fingers inside myself, I can't help imagining they're his. With my other hand, I pluck at my nipples the same way he did.

I arch and cry out under my ministrations.

I think of the way his eyes glitter with dark lust and how it felt when he shoved that huge cock so deep inside me, again and again and again—

I come with a piercing cry, my whole body spasming with pleasure.

The orgasm is quick and sharp, and all too soon over.

It was okay, but nothing like the full body fire that erupts when he touches me. When his cock penetrates me.

I shudder even thinking the phrases and I start touching myself all over again.

And then again.

And again

It's one day-long masturbation session.

I masturbate in the shower. And afterward when I'm drying off, laying on my bed. I masturbate while I'm trying again with the bobby pins at the kitchen lock, pausing to drop to the floor and shove my fingers roughly in and out of myself while I rub my raw clit hard and deep until I scrape yet another orgasm from my exhausted body.

It's barely pleasurable anymore, but if this is what it takes to break free from Xavier's strange hold over my body, I'll do it every day while he's out.

Still, I'm done for now. I'm so tired. Something they don't warn you about when you try fasting—it's so tiring.

It makes sense if you think about it. Without any calories going in, you've got nothing but your own stores of fat to burn for energy. I'm no dainty little flower—there's plenty of extra to burn, but I'm still plenty tired just drinking only water for two days straight.

I drag my worn-out ass back up the stairs for a long afternoon nap after the orgasm-a-thon. I only wake up when my door bangs open.

I blink sleepy eyes, confused when I notice dim light shining through my windows. Is it already evening?

But I jolt upright when I see the tall, hulking silhouette standing in my doorway.

"I hope you enjoyed yourself this afternoon." Xavier does not sound happy. In fact, he sounds pissed the hell off.

I scramble back on my bed when he stalks toward me, his boots thundering against the wooden floor with each step.

How did he even know? Deny, deny, deny.

"Xavier, I don't know what—"

"It's *Master* to you," he bites out. "I tried to do this the nice way. To let you freely roam the house. But I should know that to break a mare, you can never give them any head."

Like he has before, he picks me up and swings me over his shoulder. He's just come in from outside and his intoxicating scent is stronger than ever.

Damn him. I smack against his muscled back as he heads for the stairs. "Let me down! You fucking bastard, put me down this second!"

"Language." He gives my ass a sharp *smack*.

I make an outraged noise and kick out. He wraps one of his huge arms like a band across my thighs, holding me in place.

"Let me down!" I scream again.

Down the stairs we go and damn him, it's so scary I have to grab hold of his hips. Once we get to the bottom floor, though, I go back to smacking at him. "Let me go!"

When we go through the kitchen and he kicks open the back door, my breath catches—it's the first time I've been outside since I got here. But then I go back to hitting and kicking out considering what limited space I have with him holding my legs down. "Let me go, you crazy bastard! Put me down!"

He ignores it all and keeps going forward.

"You want down? Fine." The next second, I'm flying through the air and landing with an *oof* on a smelly bale of hay. I roll sideways and topple to the ground, then scramble to my knees and finally to my feet, looking around to get my bearings.

I'm in a 12x10 foot shed. The only light comes from the open doorway and cracks in the ceiling. But I can see enough—and smell enough—to know an animal must have lived in here at some point. What looks to be a couple of dog beds are set up in the corner and the whole place *stinks*.

"Why did you bring m—?" But I barely get the words out before Xavier cuts me off.

"Last owner used to keep a couple pigs in here." He's standing in the doorway, arms crossed, an easy smirk on his face. "Kept 'em as pets but didn't like them destroying the house. I inherited them along with the property. Problem was, they kept getting out. So I reinforced the walls last year." He knocks on the wall and it does indeed sound solid. Then he glances upwards at the ceiling where several shafts of sunlight come beaming down from above. "Kept meaning to get around to the roof but," he shrugs, "I ended up just selling the pigs off."

Son of a mother-fucking— If he thinks for one second that he's going to leave me here in the goddamned *pigpen* of all places—

I rush toward him but he slips out the swinging door and shuts it in my face. Then I hear a heavy-duty padlock in place.

"What the fuck do you think you're doing?" I scream at him

through the surprisingly heavy wooden door. I rattle it but it doesn't. I ram my shoulder against it but there's still barely any give. I ram it again, even more furiously. "Let me the fuck outta here!"

"Language," is his only reply.

"Fuuuuuuuuuuuuuck!" I shout at the top of my lungs, grabbing hold of the door handle and jiggling so hard the metal starts to cut into my fingers. I kick at it but that does little better. "Son of a bitch!"

I spin on my heel, unwilling to give him the satisfaction of watching me flounder with the stupid door for another second. But God. I look around and then clutch my head in my hands. He's just locked me in a pig pin.

In a fucking *cage*.

I've been living in some sort of fantasyland the past few days. This is what this was all really leading to. A dude who locks women in sheds like animals.

"No more lies," he says through the door, sounding firm but calm. "No more hiding."

I squeeze my eyes shut against the low rasp of his voice.

"Order and discipline are all I ask."

I'm not going to say a goddamn thing to that. That is, until I hear his footsteps walking away.

"Wait, you can't just leave me like this!" I turn and call after him. I'm wearing just a light summer dress. Night is coming. Sure the shed is better than nothing, but is he really just going to—?

I peek through a crack between the door and the frame. Just in time to see his back as he nears the corner of the house.

"Son of a bitch!" I yell after him.

No reaction.

And then he's gone.

I scream another long stream of expletives. Nothing but the noises of the wilderness answer back.

9

I'VE EXPLORED EVERY INCH OF THE SMALL SHED BY THE TIME NIGHT falls.

There's a bale of hay that smells sour with mildew. More hay is scattered all over the ground, so there's no real good place to sit. The dog beds—which I guess the pigs slept on?—are completely ruined. Like Xavier said, the roof is in obvious need of repair.

I pace back and forth for hours. He wasn't lying about the walls either—they're obviously new and durable. I tested each one, thinking I'd find a weakness somewhere and be able to kick through and escape. Don't people get rushes of adrenaline in extreme situations, like when moms lift cars off of babies and shit? Where's my magic adrenaline rush?

But nope. I can't get even one damn board would budge.

How long does the insane bastard intend to keep me caged up in here? If he thinks I'm going to stand for this, he— he—

What, Mel? You'll yell at him some more?

Yeah, that'll show him.

I wrap my arms around myself as I peek through crack at the door.

As the sunlight drops behind the mountains, it's impossible not to feel my spirits sink with it. At least it's not very cold since it's May. But it's dark. So dark inside the shed I can't tell if the moon is out at all. Through my little crack by the door I can *just* make out that a few lights are on in the house.

Is he really going to leave me here overnight? So what if he is. It's not like I'm afraid of the dark, come on, I'm a grown wom—

A howl breaks the quiet.

I shriek and jump backward, almost stumbling and falling on my ass.

A second howl joins the first.

Holy shit—are those wolves? Like, legit *wolves* wolves?

I keep backing away until I'm in the center of the shed, turning first one way frantically and then the other. Christ, now am I hoping the walls *are* durable?

Breathe. Just Breathe, Mel. But I can only seem to gasp in air in tiny little pants.

"How are you doing, Pet?"

I shriek again at Xavier's voice, so close he sounds like he's right at my back. I swing around and find him standing in the doorway, holding up a flashlight that's also a stand-up lamp.

Holy shit, how did he open the door without me even hearing him?

He's holding blankets and a basket. As if he *does* mean for me to spend the night out here. Son of a *bitch*.

"Did you fantasize about me when you were being so disobedient and fucking yourself all day long?" His voice is sharp as a whip.

My mouth drops open and I step back as he steps inside the shed. And let me just reiterate, it's a very small shed and Xavier is a very large man.

Maybe I should have tried to run at him and get through the door the second I saw him there—but really, it'd be like running at a brick wall. I imagine myself bouncing right off him like in some cartoon. Either that or I'd get a concussion.

Not to mention that no matter how truly screwed sideways this is all getting, he's still got my dad's life to hold over me.

And there's what he just said. I've had the past few hours to think about how he knew what I was up to all day. The only thing I can think of is that he had cameras set up in the house. Watching me.

Like he can hear my thoughts, his next words echo and confirm them, "Watching your hands all over my cunt, taking what's only mine to give." He sets down the blankets and basket, advancing toward me.

"Maybe she'll come to her senses, I thought. Realize just how much what she's doing will displease her master. But then I realized—" One of his hands grips the short hair at the back of my skull. He yanks my head backward, baring my throat and forcing me to look him in the eyes, "—she doesn't acknowledge me as Master yet. Which means she and possibly my baby inside her aren't safe."

His jaw tenses and his dark eyes burn with that dangerous glint he sometimes gets. "Do you know how it makes me feel when things I own aren't safe?"

I swallow hard and his gaze focuses on my throat.

"It doesn't make me happy, Pet. I need to keep my things safe. And to do that, I need order. Discipline. A horse that's not broken is a danger to itself and everyone around it."

Every word coming out of his mouth is terrifying. He's talking about me like I'm a possession. An animal he owns.

I want to lash out at him. Scream obscenities I know will infuriate him.

Another part of me is far too terrified by everything that's happened over the past few days. Being dragged out here in the middle of nowhere to a place where I don't know any of the rules. Then there's the sex. Now being locked in a shed. Not to mention everything else about the confusing man holding me in such a vulnerable position.

With his hand still gripping my short hair, his head drops and then he's kissing and biting his way up my exposed throat. I gasp at the sensation because I'm infuriated that he would dare take such liberties after locking me up like this.

And because for one exhilarated and confused second, I think he's going to continue up my neck and finally kiss me on the mouth.

Instead he sucks long and hard on my throat right above my collarbone, sure to mark me in the place most visible no matter what I wear.

His lips finally let go with a loud *pop*.

He moves his mouth to my ear. "Submit," he growls low. "Accept your place on your knees at my feet."

My whole body goes tense at his words and I jerk back, my gaze shooting to his. In the lamplight, his eyes flash a brilliant blue-green.

He seems momentarily startled by the eye-contact. Or by the probably mutinous look on my features. And then his face lights up and I see the second of his rare grins.

"I knew I chose right with you. The finest mares have fire. They don't break easy." He pulls me to him so that my entire body is flush against his. I can clearly feel how hard he is. "But, honey," he whispers, again right in my ear, "they always break for me."

And then he lets me go.

"Blankets." I can only stand there, a little stunned as he walks over to the basket. "A gallon of water. A small bit of broth."

He levels his gaze on me. "That's all you'll get until you submit."

Then he leaves, taking the lamp with him and leaving me in the suffocating darkness.

10

I last three days in the shed.

It's the late afternoon rainstorm on the third day that does me in. It starts raining so hard that there's nowhere to stand in the shed without standing in a puddle. And, oh yeah, the rain brings the moldy, mildew smell to an all new high. Along with the residual smell of pig stank.

I myself am fairly ripe by this point, too. I finally gave up and slept on the hay bale last night, but with the rain soaking everything, it would mean tonight I'd have to sleep either on a wet bale of hay or freeze by curling up on the concrete floor in one of the puddles.

And this is all without taking the bathroom situation into consideration. Or rather, the lack there of.

Because when a girl's gotta go, she's gotta *go*. Nothing you can do about it. Naturally, Xavier neglected to provide even a bucket.

So, while shivering in the corner, arms clutched to my chest, teeth chattering so badly the clacking is giving me a headache, and squirming back and forth because I *really* have to pee but the idea of heading over to what I've dubbed the 'bathroom corner' of the shed has me depressed beyond words, a question comes to me.

What was it that I was so hot and bothered about that led to all this?

I think it was something about being worried about losing my dignity if I let Xavier feed me by hand?

I look down at my grimy skin and the dark smears of questionable origin I found this morning on my once sky-blue dress after I pulled one of the dog/pig beds over myself as a blanket last night when I got cold.

Cause I'm doing so *awesome* in the dignity department right now.

Not to mention, God, I thought the hours passed slowly when I could wander the house and read book after book?

Ha.

Hahahahahaha.

Try sitting in a 12x10 square cage for sixty hours straight.

There's nothing to do but strain to listen for any little sound.

I heard horses, I think? That makes sense since Xavier keeps using horse metaphors. Maybe he trains them? Or boards them?

Mainly there's just the unending drone of crickets that kept me awake all night last night. During the day, there's nothing to look at but peek through the one crack by the door. Then there's the bug and mosquito swatting to look forward to when the sun goes down.

Have I mentioned how much I *hate* nature?

There are only so many times you can think out elaborate revenge murder fantasies in exquisite detail before even they start to lose their luster.

Thankfully, the lack of food makes me sleepy so I nap a lot.

Which worked well enough when the sun was out, but now that I'm soaked through and stinking so much I can barely stand to be in my own presence? Yeah, not so much.

Staring out at the rain-drenched landscape, it hits me what an absolute fucking idiot I've been. It's Hostage Basics 101.

I just have to *pretend* to go along with what the lunatic wants. I only need to make it *look* like I'm submitting. He doesn't have to know that in my head I'm secretly whispering *fuck you fuck you fuck you* every time I eat the food he's hand-feeding me.

Then bam, I can be comfortable while I get through this whole thing. Get pregnant. Pop out a kid. Get back to my old life.

Maybe that sounds harsh. But you have to understand, I'm not the maternal type. I never was. Blame it on my mom who always referred to me as her 18-year shackle. She couldn't tell the story enough times about what a difficult baby I was and how by the time I was two months old, she'd already made the appointment to get her tubes tied.

She realized what a mistake she made, she'd say, but by that point it was too late to give me back! She said it laughingly to friends like it was all a huge joke. My existence, the great bumble of her life.

But that was fine. I had Dad and we were as close as two peas in a pod. He said Mom just wasn't ready for kids. She had a hard life growing up in Mexico taking care of her seven brothers and sisters. She hated anything that reminded her of that. Aka *any sort of responsibility whatsoever. Aka, me.*

Dad loved her so much, though, he never saw her for the user that she was. It was somewhat taboo, marrying outside his wealthy WASP circles. Maybe it was love between them at first, I don't know. He met her when she was waitressing at a bar near Harvard. My grandparents never accepted her—some intruder in their lives from south of the border—but Dad loved her beyond all reason. To him, she would always just be the most beautiful woman he'd ever seen in his life, who for a time had chosen *him*. Even after she left him and went on to become a richer man's trophy wife. Then she died in a car wreck and became forever enshrined in his memory.

She had that way about her, though. A way of making people love her. The only other person who saw her for the narcissistic, spoiled woman that she was was her older sister Mariana. Not as pretty as my mother, Mariana is still an attractive woman living in Mexico. I was able to visit her a couple of years ago. It was such a relief to finally be able to talk about the real woman I'd known my mother to be. Like I could finally be sure I wasn't just making it all up in my head. But no, that was how Mariana remembered her, too. She was a kind, calm woman with a passel of children who all seemed to adore her.

It was already too late for me, though. I was the spitting image of my mother, if a shade lighter in skin tone and with a short bob instead of her long hair that she always paid such meticulous care to. And I'd also inherited her aversion to children.

My college friends had babies and I'd visit them from time to time. I felt nothing. No biological ticking clock. No yearning to hold the babies. They screamed a lot and it always got on my nerves.

So, while I might be my mother's daughter, I always swore I wouldn't make her mistake. I'd never have kids. Not something I thought too much about because, well, at least until several days ago —*virgin*.

But now I have to have this stranger's baby.

Well, fine. Women are surrogates for people all the time. That's all this is. I have no motherly instincts, obviously. I can barely handle *thinking* the word baby much less saying it out loud. So yes, I'm just the surrogate for Xavier's baby. It doesn't make a difference that the egg making up half the baby happens to be *mine*. Women also donate their eggs all the time. So what if I'm doing both parts, the donating *and* the surrogating?

It's no big deal. At the end of this year, Dad will be safe forever. He's already starting his new life in whatever island paradise Xavier's settled him. Yes, he's upset right now because he doesn't know what's happening to me but Xavier said he'd send pictures letting him know I'm okay... I look around me. Well, God, so at this particular moment, I'm not awesome but I'm going to fix all of it.

Just a year of pretending and then I'll find a way to start over, too.

I can legally change my name.

Move out of New York and go somewhere no one knows me. Maybe Chicago. There are some great ad firms there. I'll have to start from scratch and yeah, it'll take a lot of work. But I'm stubborn and—

My stomach cramps with hunger.

Right. I've got more immediate problems.

If Xavier keeps to the same schedule he did the other days, he shouldn't have gone in for dinner yet. Whether he'll hear me is another matter. I open my mouth and yell at the top of my lungs.

"Master? Master! May I please have dinner?" Maybe he has a camera on me out here, too?

The sun is dropping near the horizon even though it's probably another hour before sunset. But I suddenly can't wait another second.

And lucky me, through the crack I see Xavier come ambling around the house toward me just a few minutes later. He's in his work gear, giant hat and all, like I caught him mid-cowboying. What the hell does a cowboy *do* all day anyway, other than, I don't know, feed animals?

Internally I roll my eyes. Right now, the only animal I care about him feeding is *me*.

He doesn't seem surprised that I'm finally giving in. His expression is the same calm, placid one he usually has. Like this is all business as usual.

God, has he done this sort of thing before? The thought makes my stomach sour. But no, he obviously hasn't done *exactly* this thing before, because there aren't any kids running around the place. Then heat flushes my neck—what, am I weirdly excited to be special in this fucked-up dude's world? I shake my head at myself.

The door swings open and he steps in, gaze zeroed in on my soggy form.

I want to snap out something snarky like, *enjoying the view*? But instead, I bite my tongue and lower my lashes. "May I have dinner, Master?" Ugh, the words feel like acid on my tongue, but I manage not to gag on them. Barely.

I keep my gaze averted, but it's difficult, especially when Xavier doesn't say anything in return. After what feels like an endless silence I finally hear his heavy steps coming toward me over the soggy hay.

His large hand drops underneath my chin and he lifts my face up toward his. He searches my eyes. "You'll accept food from my hand like a good pet?"

Don't react, don't react, don't react.

I nod and apparently do a good enough job of not showing that what I *really* feel like doing is punching him in the balls. The hand underneath my chin pushes a lock of hair behind my ear. He continues to caress around the back of my neck where he squeezes in a gentle massage. Then he pulls me in against his chest, continuing to rub my back in soothing circles.

"Good girl," he murmurs. "Shh, that's my good girl."

And absurdly, the gentle touch after the uncomfortable, stressful, and occasionally terrifying days outside makes me want to cry and cling to him.

The fact that his warm body feels like safety is super screwed up. I know that, logically.

My body on the other hand? God, all I want to do is curl up against him.

This is how Stockholm syndrome starts screams some rational part of my brain.

It's just that in spite of the sun coming out after the rain, I'm so cold. Cold and wet and miserable and *tired*. Most of all tired. I swear I might collapse at Xavier's feet I'm so tired.

And wouldn't that show him, the cruel jackass. He's no more the good-hearted hero than I am Cinderella. This is no fairytale. It's real and ugly and fucked up.

And you just have to play along and see it through to the conclusion while trying to keep your sanity intact.

No biggie.

I'll just ignore the swell of emotions that rushes when he picks me up into his arms. Not in a fireman's carry this time. No, he swings my legs up and puts one of his huge arms underneath my knees, the other securely under my back. My arms shoot around his neck for lack of anywhere else to hold onto. He heads straight for the house. I'm weak from the days without food and I clutch onto him with the little bit of strength I've got remaining.

Once we're inside, he doesn't head upstairs to get cleaned up like I think he will. No, instead he heads toward the kitchen.

He sits me down on the single dining room chair, then swiftly walks out again. Almost immediately I lay my head down on the table, staring after him in the direction he left.

Okay, so food will come first. That's good. Very good.

He returns a couple minutes later, carrying one of the large arm chairs from the den. The chair is piled with towels and blankets. It barely fits through the door to the kitchen, but he sets it down and shimmies it through sideways. Then he hauls it so that it's right beside the stove.

Without a word, he comes back to me, picks me up, and carries me over to the plush chair. When he deposits me on it, he wraps me in the blankets, tucking them around me like a parent might a child.

I can only blink up blankly at him during all of this. I don't really know how to handle this side of him. The man who tosses me into an pigpen for three days is easy to hate.

This incarnation who caresses my hair and whispers, "Shh, you're doing so good, everything's going to be easier now, just rest while I make us some food."

Him, I don't know what to do with.

He curls up one of the blankets like a pillow against the wingback chair. "There, rest your head," he urges, helping me settle my head against it.

I don't even flinch at his touch this time. I feel strange and almost numb. From hunger? I'm not sure. I just know I don't feel like myself.

I pull my knees up and curl into the chair, watching Xavier as he pulls a small kitchen towel out of one of the drawers and runs warm water over it from the tap. Then, without a word, he comes back to me and washes my face. The rag is warm as he scrubs in long strokes from my cheeks down over my neck to my throat. His motions are slow and unhurried. Soothing even.

He finishes quickly. Then he silently fires up the gas stove and pulls eggs and bacon out of the fridge. He fries the bacon first and it smells so good that it makes my empty stomach cramp. I briefly wonder why he's making breakfast food even though it's almost nighttime.

Xavier still seems perfectly at ease, though, pulling the bacon out of the pan with a fork and then cracking eggs into the sizzling grease without looking over at me once. He washes his hands while the eggs cook then flips them with the fork at the end to scramble them. He piles them onto two plates and peels a couple of tangerines before setting the plates at the head of the table. Guess it's breakfast for dinner tonight. Apart from the tangerines substituted for pancakes, it's the same meal I refused that first morning.

Only once he's set the plates down does he look my way again.

Maybe he'll let it slide tonight because I'm so tired and I can just eat my food like a normal person? We can start up the whole charade tomorrow and—

Then I see him retrieve a large square pillow from inside the bottom cupboard and lay it on the ground beside his chair.

Or not.

He comes over to me and reaches both hands out. I'm not sure if it's better or worse when he doesn't just manhandle me. Holding his hands out to me like this, it's a request to do what he wants. Like I can choose to obey or not.

But no, my foggy food-deprived brain tries to remind me —*appearing* to comply on the outside doesn't mean that I'm actually giving in. I'm just being smart and getting some goddamned sustenance.

There's no point in starving.

Or spending another night out in the shed.

I drop my feet to the ground, lift my weary arms, and grasp his big hands. He hefts me to my feet and wraps a sturdy arm around my waist as he leads me over to the pillow beside his chair, where he helps me lower to my knees.

Again, everything in me rebels. Except my stomach. My empty stomach is very on board with whatever will get it food the fastest.

I crouch down on the little pillow, jaw tight.

I'll do this but it doesn't have to mean I like it.

I arrange myself on my knees and Xavier's hands immediately press on my shoulders so that I'm sitting even further down, folded ass to calves. Then he arranges my hands the way he wants them. Last but not least, he pushes my head down to the appropriate angle so I can see only his bare feet and the bottom of his jeans.

"This is the submissive position. It's one I want you to become familiar with."

My back stiffens. Is he freaking kidding? It's bad enough that I'm sitting here at his feet, but he thinks—

"I can tell how much you like that idea, Pet," he laughs, stroking my short hair and then scratching down to my scalp.

Then he settles a blindfold over my eyes. Wait, where did that come from? Did he already have it on the table and I was just too out of it to notice it?

"Eventually it will become second nature to you."

At what no doubt is my stunned expression, he continues, "I am your Master and you are my pet and you will learn your true place starting *now*."

He snaps his fingers. "Open," he commands.

His hand drops from my hair and one of his fingers settles with the barest pressure on my bottom lip.

I'd love to tell him to go to hell for snapping at me like a dog, but the next second, the smell of eggs hits my nostrils and my mouth falls immediately open.

His fingers return, placing a small bit of eggs into my mouth. I bite into the warm, soft, slightly moist food, having to suck it from his fingers at the end to make sure I don't waste any of it.

For a second with the blindfold, I was afraid he'd try to trick me and put something gross in my mouth as additional punishment for not giving into him right away—but no, it's just eggs. Perfectly cooked, salted, delicious eggs.

My mouth is open and waiting when his fingers next descend. He pops the second bite of eggs in my mouth. His other hand lingers on my head, stroking my hair while I eat.

Petting me.

The realization should be humiliating, but screw it. It's just the two of us here, and besides, I've already decided I'm the one playing *him* in all of this, so none of it really matters.

I open my mouth again, but this time, nothing meets my lips.

"I've got some bacon right here. Would you like some of that?"

I nod my head up and down.

Xavier tuts his tongue at me. "What do you say, Pet?"

Oh my God, I'm definitely crushing his balls when all is said and done. "Yes, Master," I manage to get out through my thick throat. "Sir, may I please have the rest of my breakfast?"

"That's right," he says soothingly, his hand returning to my head. "That's a good girl." The next thing I know my taste buds are exploding with the flavor of maple-smoked bacon.

Next comes more eggs, then bacon again.

"Suck my fingers," he orders. "Suck every last piece of juice off."

He shoves his thick fingers in my mouth and obediently, I suck.

He pumps them slowly in and out, eventually pulling them out with a pop and shoving his thumb in instead.

It's just a show, I tell myself as I suck greedily at his thumb. I just need to make it look convincing or he might decide the meal is over before I'm ready.

"Now for something a little sticky and sweet."

Why does every word out of his mouth suddenly sound like the dirtiest thing in the English language?

He sticks several slices of tangerine in my mouth.

"Bite down," he instructs.

The slices are a mouthful and when I comply, juice spurts out and down my lips. I duck my face and lift a hand to wipe at the juice, but Xavier's swats me lightly. He grabs my hair and exposes my throat in that way he's so fond of doing. I chew and swallow some of the tangerine pulp, but juice continues dripping down over my chin.

I startle when I feel Xavier's tongue on my neck, licking upward to catch the trail of juice. He must be down on the floor with me. Up and up his tongue traces, all the way to my bottom lip.

My breath hitches as he licks the last of the juice from the corner of my mouth. Then he nuzzles his cheek against mine. "That's right. Shhh, you're doing so, so well."

When he sticks another piece of egg in my mouth and his finger lingers after I finish the bite, I suck without him even asking.

By the end of breakfast when my formerly empty stomach feels full to bursting, I'm near to crying with the confusion of needs he's stirring up in me.

He hauls me up from the floor. I stumble unsteadily on my feet, unused to sitting in a position like that for half an hour. His strong arms set me aright. I think that he'll take off my blindfold and let me go up to bed.

Of course nothing ever goes like I expect with this man. The blindfold stays on and when he hefts me into his arms again and takes me upstairs, we don't stop at my bedroom on the second floor. My head falls against his shoulder as I feel him carry me up to the third floor.

Oh God, what now? I'm finally full but no less tired. If I could just sleep for a week, that'd be *awesome* right about now.

He pushes open the door to his large suite and I brace to be dropped unceremoniously onto his giant bed again. I squeeze my eyes shut underneath the mask.

It only makes sense, though. I'm here for a reason and we haven't been up to any baby-making activities for almost three days now.

But he keeps walking once we're inside the room. Then I hear his boots on tile. His room is carpeted. We must be in the bathroom.

He sets me down on my feet and I stumble a little, disoriented.

"Lean against the wall for balance," he says, and then I hear the sound of a faucet being turned on and the echo of rushing water.

A bath. He's running me a bath.

My body sinks against the wall he indicated beside me. Oh God, a bath does sound divine. I don't even want to think about the layer of dirt and grime and God knows what else that's coating me. Ugh, I shudder just thinking about it.

Even when Xavier was stroking my hair earlier, his fingers kept getting caught in tangles. My hair is barely four or five inches long—there's not that much to get snarled. Still, personal hygiene hasn't been at the top of my list of priorities the past couple of days.

The bathwater turns off a few minutes later and Xavier's hands return. From behind, he starts low at my knees and his fingers skate up my outer thighs, higher and higher until he lifts my dress up over my head. Without him asking, I lift my arms to help him get it off. He murmurs approving noises—not even words, just positive vocalizations.

My bra comes off next. Then his warm hands are on my body again, starting on my hips and caressing down as he slides my panties off.

He leads me with an arm around my waist like he did earlier.

"Step," he says. "Careful." He holds my hand as I step blindly over the rim of what I'm guessing is a bathtub. My foot sinks into warm water. It's deeper than I expect and I have to clutch Xavier for balance. God, is that the point of the blindfold? So I have to depend on him for absolutely *everything*? My food? Every single step I take? I mean, is that some sort of deeper lesson I'm supposed to be getting from all this?

Or am I making too much of it and he just gets off on having chicks blindfolded?

"Steady," he says, holding me up.

More splashes. He's getting in with me. Just how big is this bath? And when did he take off his clothes? I guess he could have taken them off when the bathwater was running and I might not have heard him.

With slight pressure on my shoulder, he urges me to sit down, keeping me stable while I go down on a knee, then settle into the warm water.

He drops with me, sitting as well. Which is when I realize it must be a specialty bath or jacuzzi because both of us fit easily with room to spare. A second later, jets turn on, confirming my thought. Churning water immediately starts to relax my aching muscles.

Xavier settles himself behind me, legs spread on either side of my body. In the second it takes me to wonder if us being naked in such a confined space is affecting him, I feel his hard length pressing against the small of my back. *Yep*, he's affected all right.

He must feel me tense because his hands immediately come to my shoulders. He begins massaging, up to my neck and all down my arms. "Shh, relax," he murmurs.

Said the spider to the fly.

He slips the blindfold off my eyes in the next moment and I blink, expecting a rush of brightness. But the sun has gone down, so even though there is a large open window and a skylight, the room is dark except for a single flickering candle on the counter near the doorway.

Xavier prefers the dark. Because he doesn't like people seeing his face, or for some other reason?

Either way, I don't turn back to look at him. For a while I strain to make out details of the bathroom as my eyes adjust. The bathroom is large, like his room. I can make out a shower in addition to the jacuzzi bath. There's a high, wide window that's actually uncurtained and open to the moon and a scattering of what seems like a million stars.

The bubbling jets drown out all other noises but I smell the sweet scent of my body wash in the moments before Xavier lifts my left arm and starts rubbing the soap up and down into my skin. My arm feels small in his large hands as he soaps my forearm and then down to my wrist, then to my hand.

He pays particular attention to each individual finger. Momentarily our fingers lace together as he works the soap and my breath hitches stupidly at the intimacy.

Then his other hand joins the first and he begins the most relaxing and amazing hand massage I've ever received. I have to fight against groaning and going limp against him. The struggle is real. Especially when he gives my right hand the same treatment as the first.

Between his gentle, expert ministrations, my full tummy, and the warm, soothing jets, I feel like I might just drift away on a pampered bubble.

I might even actually drowse for a few minutes while he continues washing me. He uses a washcloth to wash my face and neck again, then down to my chest where he cups and washes each breast with particular care.

In the back of my mind, I know I'm supposed to be actively mentally fighting against him. But I'll get back to that tomorrow. Just... need to close... eyes... for a second...

I wake briefly when I feel him rubbing frothy shampoo into my hair. He massages my scalp as I lean all my weight back against his chest. When he rinses, he holds my neck easily with one broad palm to tip my head backward while he pours water from a cup he fills from the bathtub faucet.

Then his hands move with the washcloth down my body, around my hips to my inner thighs.

He drains and refills the tub to get fresh water after his initial scrub down, keeping me against the heat of his body so I'm warm the whole while. Then he continues where he left off. He grabs the flesh of my inner thigh and kneads it with more strength instead of the gentle massage he did on my upper body.

I can't stop the groan at how good it feels. I spent the past few days crouched in such awkward positions. The first day I stood a lot, not wanting to sit on the smelly hay. I eventually gave in, but still. My body, however, is used to nice ergonomic furniture, not concrete floors and sitting on hay bales.

Even thinking about that should have me mad as hell again. But when Xavier flips my body around in the bath so he has better access to massage up and down each thigh with both of his strong hands, again I let myself put off other concerns for a later date.

Like tomorrow.

Or the day after.

You know... soonish... after my body recovers from the blissful pile of goo he's currently turning me into.

He continues working down to my calves and all the way to my toes where he proceeds to give a foot massage that—and I can't even believe I'm saying this—rivals his hand massage.

My head drops against the curved side of the tub with one of the jets at my back, further working any and all tension out of my body. I watch Xavier through half-lidded eyes. My eyes have fully adjusted to the dim light. His face looks almost fierce with concentration as he lifts my other foot into his lap, soaps it, and starts rubbing his thumb deep into my arches.

At my contented moan, his eyes flash up to mine. One edge of his mouth quirks upward but then his focus goes back to my foot. If he's self-conscious about his face, he doesn't show it. Maybe a little that first day when I initially reacted to it, but never since then. He always seems so assured of his mastery over me. *Master. Pet.* Ugh. I really will get back to being upset about that soon.

He squeezes the pad of my foot between his palms and my eyes drop shut again. I've all but drifted back off to sleep again when his hands shift me in the water.

"Hmm?" I ask drowsily.

"Wake up, little kitten." He sounds amused. I blink and look around. The jets are off and the water laps lazily around us.

"Lean your forearms on the lip of the tub, flank in the air." He indicates the wide surface at the edge of the tub opposite the faucet where a folded towel has been laid. Then he lifts me so that my elbows are braced on the soft towel. My knees on the bottom of the tub, ass just out of the water. Aimed right toward him.

My mouth drops open as soon as he's got me positioned just the way he wants. But then I close it.

All right. Here we go again. I really can't even fault him—okay yes, I can sure as *hell* fault him for the whole locking me up like an animal thing. But apart from *that*, from all I hear from my girlfriends, this whole bath time seduction scenario is far more than they usually get in the way of foreplay.

He rubs up and down my ass, or *flank* as he referred to it. The action feels like it's one he's performed a million times. I'm slippery from the water and he splashes more water up with every pass he takes, squeezing both my ass cheeks. He separates and kneads them in his large hands like he has every right to manhandle me so intimately without even knowing me a full week.

All the sleepiness flees under his touch. While before his caresses felt clearly meant to clean away the grime and relax me, now there's an intent to the way his fingers flex and stretch my flesh.

Still, I'm shocked when his palm lands on my ass. I yelp and swing my head around to look at him. His gaze is locked on my ass, which he's gone back to rubbing and kneading.

"Count," he says calmly, his thumbs circling closer toward... toward... *that place*, "and ask *Please, Sir, may I have another?*"

A rush of air expels from my lungs, all the relaxation from minutes ago officially *gone*. My stomach clenching in rebellion. I can't believe he's back to this BS. I gave into the food thing, can't he give it a break for a while?

He smacks my other ass cheek. "Count," he orders.

He spanks me again.

Then he massages the sting away. His thumbs have abandoned circling around my back passage, thank God, but his fingers now tease at my pussy amid the spanking. He lands another *smack*.

"One!" I finally shout, enraged. The single word echoes off the bathroom walls.

He spanks me yet again. "What else?" he immediately demands, sounding completely calm.

My whole body clenches up. Damn him. Goddamn him.

"You know what I want. Start over and do it like Master requires."

He smacks my already sore ass mercilessly. My body jerks with the blow and then his hand reaches between my spread legs. He teases my clit while inserting a long finger inside me.

My hands shake where I'm leaning over the edge of the tub.

Because I'm tired.

And angry.

Not because I'm turned on.

And certainly not because I'm thinking about giving into this bastard.

I've already given him too much today. I can't let him have more of me.

But wait, no. I blink and swallow against the liquid fire he's stoking low in my stomach. I can make all of this stop. *Remember— you're just letting him* think *you're going along with this*. What are a few little words? *Nothing*. Not in the long run.

I just have to do what I need to in order to get through today, and then tomorrow, and then this month and this year until I can get back to my real life.

I let out a huge blast of air right as another blow lands square in the middle of my ass cheek.

"One," I say through gritted teeth. "Please, Sir, may I have another?"

My toes curl in furious disgust at myself even as the words trip over my tongue.

But even though I'm not looking at him, I swear I can feel the surge of masculine energy take over the man behind me. His hand comes down even more stridently and I can't help the small *yip* that escapes my throat before managing, "Two," and then, "Please, Sir, may I have another."

If I thought he was teasing me before, it's nothing to what he starts now. Two fingers slip inside, and they stretch and flex like God created them specifically to drive a woman crazy. Not to mention his other hand that he curves over the top of my hip to rub at my clitoris. He pulls away only long enough to deliver another occasional *thwack* on alternating ass cheeks.

And goddamn him, but it feels... amazing. Sublime.

The forty-five-minute bath beforehand, all that time he spent acclimating my body to his touch, it was like a sneak attack. He's learned me somehow. He can read my body. It's not fair.

The spanking continues.

It's not fair... but oh *God*, I swear if he stops now, I will kill him, I don't care how much bigger than me he is.

"Eight! Please, Sir," I gasp for breath as he starts finger-fucking me even harder, "may I have another?" I lean back against his hands, back and forth, sloshing water all around. I don't care, oh God, as long as he just. Never. Stops.

He yanks me backward so I can feel his rock-hard length against my ass.

My body clenches hard around the fingers he has inside me.

Yes. Yes. *Fuck me.*

I ignore how traitorous the thought is as I rub my butt back and forth against him and buck on his fingers.

He lands another solid wallop on my ass before grabbing my hip for leverage and jamming his length up and down along the crack of my ass.

Nine and ten land in such quick succession I barely have time to count them before Xavier is lifting me up and turning me so that I'm sitting on the towel where my elbows were just braced, on the small flat surface between the tub and the wall. My bottom barely fits on the small ledge and I brace my feet in the water.

Xavier immediately pushes my legs open wider and then, *holy shit*, his head drops down and his mouth locks on my swollen bud. He sucks and licks and teases me until I'm insane with it.

I'm so primed it only takes half a minute before I'm screaming out my orgasm, hands gripping the edge of the tub because if I touch him, he might stop.

Ahhhhhh— oh God, *oh God!*

The high is so high it feels like the top of my head is going to pop off.

He just keeps sucking me through the whole thing.

It's— Oh, oh… So long, so bright, *oh—*

Until my legs quake with aftershocks.

Only then does he lift me by my waist back into the water.

I blink up at him as his huge body looms over me in the dimly lit bathroom, feeling absolutely dazed. I— *That was—*

I try to sort out what I'm feeling but it's like I can't connect one rational thought to another. He's literally fucked me stupid.

He leans me against the side of the tub but then gets a grip on the back of my hair like he likes to sometimes. He's on his knees in the tub and fists his nine-inch cock right in front of my face. With the hand on the back of my hair, he brings my face close to it and even in my brain-dead state, I get the picture. He wants me to suck it.

But he only brings me close enough so I get a full view of every inch of him. The hard, veiny length. The fat, bulbous head. The way it strains in his hand toward my lips. He jerks roughly down the shaft, then brings his hand back to the head, where he rolls and squeezes before tugging hard on the length again.

My eyes flicker up to see his face. His jaw is taut with what looks like a mix of pleasure and pain and satisfaction as his gaze moves between my face and what he's doing with his hand. Each time he jerks himself he brings me a tiny bit closer to the head of his cock, but never quite makes contact. My sex clenches and saliva rushes my mouth. I have the most ludicrous urge to stick my tongue out. To close that tiny distance between us and—

I squeeze my eyes shut against the ridiculous impulse.

"Watch," comes his quick rebuke.

My eyes snap open.

There he is again. All of him. There. Pleasuring himself right before my eyes.

Then he shifts forward suddenly so that the tip of him makes contact with my cheek. I gasp in surprise at the hot warmth of him. With his hand on the back of my head, he guides the front and then side of his cock all along my cheek and up into my hair. It's my first feel of him apart from when he was… inside me. The skin of it is so surprisingly *soft*. Like velvet.

He yanks my head back and slowly drags his cock across my nose and the top of my upper lip.

Like he wants me to get the smell of him. Right now since we've just bathed he mostly smells like soap, but there's just a hint of manly musk underneath.

My sex clenches again as he draws his cock over to my other cheek where he repeats pumping himself like he did on the first cheek, letting me feel all of his soft, smooth length. But so rock hard underneath the smooth.

He pulls back, but now when he jacks himself, every time his hand rolls across the tip, he rubs it against my face. Maybe on my cheek, maybe teasing my upper or lower lip. Maybe just underneath my chin. He never lingers or demands anything of me.

All I can hear is the increasing volume of his heaving breath and the slap of his skin on skin. He never lets up on his controlled grip on the back of my hair. With the way he has hold of me, I can't look up to see his face anymore.

Only his cock. It's too easy for the rest of the world to drop away and everything to narrow down to this—the water lapping around us, the steamy darkness, and his cock.

Where will he land it next? Will he finally push inside my mouth instead of just teasing at my lips? What would he taste like? These seem to be the only thoughts I'm capable of at the moment.

And then his forefinger taps at my lip. "Open."

Finally.

I open my mouth. He jerks himself twice as hard as he has the whole time. But still, he only lets the angry red tip barely make contact with my wet bottom lip.

"Good girl," he breathes out, sounding winded as he continues jacking off furiously. "Such a good fucking girl."

And then he ejaculates, white ropes of liquid spurting toward my mouth, down my chin and onto my breasts.

I gasp and my mouth closes as I swallow, getting my first taste of... *it*.

Salty and bitter but not altogether unpleasant.

"Open," he says again and I do. He rubs the tip of his cock over my lips, painting his seed on like lipstick. He squeezes himself and jerks his hand lazily up and down his length, continuing to rub just the tip of his head back and forth over me messily, up over to my cheek then back to my mouth again.

Finally he withdraws, but only to stick his thumb in my mouth.

"Suck," he commands.

I do, sucking his finger as well as all the... *cum*. My stomach flips at even thinking the word. I swallow down all the cum he got in my mouth.

"Good girl." The hand clenching the back of my head softens and he strokes his fingers through my hair instead. "That's my good girl."

And the praise makes my chest warm. I'm both horrified and fascinated by the feeling before I go sort of cotton-headed about it all and just enjoy the fuzzy, sleepy feeling.

After another few minutes, he takes the washcloth and cleans me up again. Then he pulls the plug on the tub and helps me step out. With several large fluffy towels, he dries me off like I'm a child.

I just stand there and allow him to do it. The whole blank-headed thing is still in full effect. It's far easier to just follow where he leads than try to sort any of this confusing shit out.

When he leads me to his bed and pulls me in beside him, then curls his warm body around mine, I don't so much as blink.

∽

IT'S ONLY the next morning when I wake up to an empty bed and sunlight pouring in the window that I wonder what in the *hell* I let myself become last night.

I shoot to a sitting position and pull my knees to my chest, looking around like I'm just waking from a trance. Which is when I realize I'm still naked.

My hands go to my head. I rub my eyes, then my temple.

What the fuck *was that* last night?

I had a freaking plan. I was just supposed to let him *think* I was going along with his shit.

Did he drug my food or something? Maybe he sprinkled some kind of compliance-inducing chemical on the eggs? Do those kinds of things exist outside of CIA laboratories?

I swing my legs over the side of the bed and stand up, trying to gauge if I feel drowsy or out of it in any way. I lift my arms and hop up and down. Which reminds me that I'm naked. I grab a pillow from the bed to cover myself.

But, all right. Everything feels ok. At least it does *now*. Maybe it was a drug that's quickly metabolized and wears off within twelve hours? Or however long I've been sleeping.

What time is it anyway?

I turn around and look over at Xavier's desk to try to find a clock. And see the two giant monitors.

He left me in here with all the electronics. Ignoring my nakedness, I run over to the computer and move the mouse. The monitor comes to life, but of course, duh, I'm met with a screen asking for a password.

"Damn it." I look around the desk for anything else that might be useful for communication. Doesn't the guy even have a landline somewhere? Does he actually get cell service out here in the boonies? But there's no phone to be found, and while there are three enticing drawers to the desk, they're all locked.

I jerk uselessly on one of the drawers yet again, frustration building, when I hear heavy footsteps on the stairs.

"Shit," I yip, then run back the few steps to the bed and jump in it, yanking the covers back up over myself right before Xavier pushes open the door.

I open my eyes and stretch like I'm just waking up but the amused look on his face tells me I'm not fooling anyone.

"Good morning, Pet."

I look up at him warily. His dark curls are matted down by the shape of his hat even though he doesn't have it on. He's carrying some clothes and... are those cowboy boots?

"Time to get dressed for the day."

He heads toward the bed and I can't help pulling the covers tighter to my body. He pauses at my action, a small frown creasing his brow.

"Gonna have to retread some ground," he murmurs under his breath, more to himself than me.

What? That doesn't sound like it bodes well for me.

He pulls the covers down as soon as he gets to the bed. There's a small tug of war before he pries my fingers off the cloth. Which makes me feel about five years old. But still, having no barriers between me and him, God, it just makes me feel far too... well, *naked.*

I squeeze my eyes shut. What now?

But all Xavier does is urge me to a sitting position where he puts on my bra, then lifts my arm, slides on one sleeve of a denim shirt, then the other. Then he crouches in front of me and buttons each button, slowly and methodically, not saying a single word the whole time.

Next he pulls me to a standing position, then taps one leg for me to lift and step into a pair of cotton panties, then jeans. They fit me comfortably. Everything does.

But still. Does he have to dress me like this? He even rolls on my socks. He pauses to rub my arches in deep massaging circles in a way reminiscent of last night before he finally urges each foot into one of the tall black cowboy boots.

The way he handles my body… I can't help gulping hard when he has his hands on my second foot, briefly massaging up to the calf before reaching for the boot. For a second, just a brief flash, I remember how I felt last night. And it's not just a memory—for that brief moment, I feel exactly the same way—like I could melt into his touch and willingly *want* to do whatever he asks. Not like I was drugged and doing things against my will.

"I got it." I pull the boot away from him and tug it on myself. It slides on with ease and when I stand up and walk around, purposefully *not* looking his direction, I'm surprised at how comfortable they are. You always see cowboy boots in the movies, or I mean, some of my friends have fashion label versions, but these are definitely the authentic thing. When did he get them? And how the hell did he know my size?

Not useful to think about right now, Mel. Just be glad it's not another goddamned dress.

Not that denim is any more my style. But at least there's sturdy cloth between me and Xavier now. Let's just take *not naked* as a win.

It doesn't stop Xavier from assuming he has full rights to my body, though. He closes the space between us and clamps his hand to the back of my neck with a firm but gentle pressure. Then he slides it slowly down the back of my shoulder, dips in toward my waist, and finishes with a light pat to my ass.

"Breakfast."

He heads out of the room with the confidence of a man who knows I'll follow.

And damn him, I do.

I'm hungry. Last night's meal was only enough to quench my initial hunger.

There are vegetable omelets waiting for us on covered plates when we get downstairs. I guess he cooked them before he came up to get me.

And there's the damned pillow by his chair.

At least he doesn't snap his fingers at me today. He just exerts a light pressure on my shoulder, urging me down when we reach the head of the table.

Path of least resistance. It's still my strategy even if there were disturbing results last night.

I go to my knees and he feeds me the omelet from his fingers. I can't help but be wary with every bite, waiting for whatever new bit of fuckery is coming next.

But breakfast goes off without a hitch. Normal as normal can be while, you know, crouched like a dog at my *Master's* feet.

"Up," he says after withdrawing the cup of orange juice from my lips. He rises and puts our dishes in the kitchen sink. "Full day of work ahead."

Okaaaaaaay. I get to my feet. I guess I'll finally see what he does outside all day. I'm not sure I like this new development. I was just A-Okay hanging out inside where there's air-conditioning, reading books all day.

If I'm going to be stuck here, at least let me be a properly *kept woman*. Especially if I have access to that awesome bathtub with the jets now.

But the way he's standing, eyes flicking expectantly between me and the back door tells me there's probably not going to be much lounging in my future. At least not today.

I don't suppose explaining that I was never much of an *outside girl* would help at this point? I spent my summers at debate camp and doing even the most menial internships I could find at small businesses in New York. Anything I thought might look good on a college application. The *outside* was a place you had to endure to get to and from the subway station when traffic was too bad to bother with an Uber or a taxi.

Xavier jerks his head toward the door as he picks up his wide-brimmed hat from a side table and I get the unspoken verbal cue—he's big on those—time to get moving.

I head out the door. From the clock in the kitchen I saw that it's eight in the morning. By the look of Xavier, he's already been up several hours. I think that the times I've seen him leaving in the mornings are actually when he's come back to the house after having been out already several hours, like today. As in, he gets up around four-thirty or something crazy like that, then comes back in for breakfast at seven or eight.

I've always been something of a night owl and while I worked my ass off and was never late, you never saw me at the office a minute before 8:55.

Morning people freak me out.

Shocker that Xavier loves waking up before the crack of dawn.

When I step outside, it smells like fresh grass and... is that cow manure? Awesome. Loving this already.

Not to mention the first sight that greets me is the pigpen that was my home for three days. For a second, my feet freeze. Is this all a ruse and he's just trying to get me out here so he can lock me back up in there again?

But no, his hand comes to the small of my back and he directs us away from the shed and around the far side of the house, toward the part of the property I haven't been able to see before. My room faces the front of the house and this area is what could be called the 'side yard,' even though it opens up to endless land.

Then we turn the corner and—holy shit!

There's one large barn or stable and then several smaller out buildings.

And horses.

A lot of horses.

Okay, so maybe only nine or ten, but to a person who's never seen a horse up close and in person, that's a ton of horses!

There are several large paddocks and pastures, some with several horses together, others with just a single horse. A couple are running with manes flying out gloriously in the morning sunlight.

I turn around to look at Xavier in surprise.

Right in time to see him twirling a lasso in the air.

"What are—?"

Which is when he lets it fly.

It lands over my head, right over my shoulders. He cinches it tight.

You heard me right.

The bastard just lassoed me like I'm a damn stock animal.

11

"Lesson one," Xavier says, calm as can be as he tugs me toward him by the rope around my upper arms. "Expect the unexpected when dealing with an animal that can weigh up to two thousand pounds and isn't afraid to let you know it."

He walks forward as he coils the rope and reels me in until we meet in the middle, his hand around the knot of the lasso that meets right in between my breasts. "Lesson two. Listen to everything I say today and not just because I'm Master. Every instruction I give you is for your safety. Do you understand?"

For just a second, he seems to drop the dominance act. When he searches my eyes, I feel like it's a plea that's made as if we're on equal footing, not something else he's trying to manipulate from me.

I nod. And then wait for him to remove the rope from around my body.

Silly me.

Xavier steps closer and while he does slide it down over my arms, he only cinches it tight again around my waist like a belt. He loops the lead rope in his hands and jerks it once to draw me forward.

"You've got to be kidding," I balk, stubbornly resisting his pull.

He looks back at me, eyes narrowing. In the bright morning

sunshine, the scarring on his face is clear, but it's not that I'm focusing on. I glare at him, then my eyes drop down to the rope tied firmly around my waist.

He walks the few feet back to where I'm standing and lifts the other end, positioning it right over my backside.

I look over my shoulder, mouth dropping open.

The bastard better not—

With a lift of his eyebrow, he uses the tail end of the rope to give me a solid smack on my ass. "Get moving."

I yelp and jump forward several steps.

That's all the start Xavier needs. He moves back in front of me and tugs on the rope again, pulling me forward. He's not even dragging me. It's just a steady pressure, taking for granted that I'll follow.

Path of least resistance. Path of least resistance.

I grit my teeth and trail behind him as far as the three-feet length of rope will allow.

"Just got a delivery this morning," Xavier offers as we get closer to the closest paddock where a huge brown horse—the only one in a big fenced-in circle that's separated from all the others by a long gated-off run—trots this way and that. He lets out a loud, angry-sounding squeal as we get closer. Xavier comes close to the wooden fence posts of the paddock but stops several feet away.

"I'm surprised he didn't wake you up. Samson was raising hell when they brought him in. He didn't like being trailered one bit." Xavier's focus is fully engaged by the horse now, his features a mix of concentration and admiration. I follow his gaze and watch as the great beast stomps back and forth. His eyes seem wild. His ears flick back and forth and he lets out occasional high-pitched snorts, nostrils flaring.

I initially came up to stand beside Xavier, but I quickly take a small step back. Up to two thousand pounds, he said. No, that thing does *not* look safe.

"Where did you get him from?" Even I can hear the quiver in my voice. Xavier doesn't expect me to like, ride that, does he?

"The BLM," he pauses when he looks over and notices my befuddled expression, "the Bureau of Land Management. They do roundups of wild horses sometimes so the mustangs don't overwhelm grazing resources and water. Then ranchers can adopt the horses so they don't spend their whole lives stuck in some BLM holding facility somewhere." His gaze goes back to the paddock. "Or be put down."

My breath catches as my eyes go back to the huge, snorting animal. "That's horrible."

Xavier shrugs and continues calmly, "No worse than hundreds of foals starving to death when there's not enough food to go 'round in winter because the population gets too big."

I jerk my head to look up at Xavier but he's still just staring out at the paddock, gaze intent on the horse there. I can't ever imagine understanding this man. He's entirely incomprehensible.

He taps the top slat of the paddock. "We'll be back, Samson," he calls out.

He starts walking, at first leaving slack on the rope, then tugging once when I don't move quickly enough for his liking. His back is still turned so I permit myself a good roll of the eyes. Then I jog to hurry up and follow at his heels like a good little *pet*. Ugh.

Next he gives me a tour of the stables and other paddocks. I get to meet the horses, all of whom are far gentler spirits than Samson.

Also, horses are way bigger in person than they look in the movies.

Like, *way* bigger.

And I'm pretty sure Xavier introduces me to the smallest one first.

"This is Lulu. Raised her up from a foal. She was born right here in this stable. Who's my good girl?"

Lulu all but breaks down the stall door of the stable in her excitement to get to Xavier. When he lifts up his hand to her, she nickers and nuzzles into him. He leans in close and she buries her muzzle in his neck.

And Xavier?

It's like a transformation comes over him.

Well, not completely. But his entire demeanor... I don't know exactly how to explain it. He... softens. The hard lines of his jaw loosen. His stern brow finally goes soft. His whole body relaxes. It's as if he's releasing all the tension he seems to perpetually carry around as he scratches at the mare's cheek and then strokes down her neck. Like I've been missing some key part of him until I saw him in this context with these animals.

"That's my good, good girl." Even the quality of his voice is different. It's pitched softer with a gentle croon to it.

Though I can't say I've never heard it like that before.

No, with a startled shock, I realize it's the same tone he's used with me after I've complied in the bedroom. Or... the bath.

That revelation's about as welcome as Lulu seems to find having another female around her favorite man.

When Xavier tries to introduce me to her, her ears constantly flick back and forth. She blows out a loud huff of air through her nostrils, pulling away and turning her head toward Xavier like, *who dis bitch?*

I yank my hand back since I'm not especially inclined to lose a finger before lunchtime. Or, you know, ever.

Xavier clicks his teeth at her and she ducks her nose, chastened. She butts her head into him again and he soothes her, then attempts the introduction again.

By the end of the introduction, Lulu reluctantly sniffs me, which earns her a carrot from Xavier's pocket. When did he get those? Looking down, though, I see his pockets are stuffed with them.

Guess he's anticipating I'm going to be a real hit with his fan club.

Because it's not just Lulu that he seems to have such a special bond with. He introduces me to a string of other animals, all of whom react almost the exact same way Lulu did. Ok, that's not fair. Even as a person who doesn't know a thing about horses, I can already begin to make out little personality differences. Though, by the time we get to the back pasture I'm not sure I'm getting all their names right.

There was Pioneer, Sundance Kid, Holy Hellfire—I remember him because he was one of the pasture horses who looked so old I was shocked he was still standing upright. Then there was Tornado,

Bob—that's right, just, Bob, and Paddyshack. Not Caddyshack, I double-checked. No, it's Paddyshack.

Xavier tells me the stories of some of them. Pioneer threw his owner so hard, he broke his leg. The owner was threatening to put the horse down, so Xavier took him in. Several others are retired racehorses past their prime.

"Is Holy Hellfire one of those?" I ask as we walk past another low building—another set of stables, I'm guessing. As grouchy as I still might be about being led around like a pack animal, I have to say this is all sort of interesting. And Xavier's spoken more this morning than during the entirety of my time with him so far. That seems like something to encourage.

He shakes his head at my inquiry, the right side of his mouth tilting. "No, he just spent his whole life being ornery."

That surprises a laugh out of me. "What do you mean?"

"Ever heard of a racehorse called Bierbaum?"

"If he didn't make Page 6 in the *Post*, it wasn't in my sphere."

He shakes his head at me. "Think Secretariat or Man o' War."

At my continued blank stare, he tosses his hand in the air. "Seabiscuit?"

"Oh," I perk up. "Wasn't that a movie?"

He draws in a long breath as if searching for patience.

"Okay, well just picture one of the greatest racehorses of the twentieth century. That was Bierbaum. And Holy Hellfire was one of his foals. Everyone in the racing world expected great things of him."

"And you..." I look out in the direction of the pasture where we met Holy Hellfire, "or your family, bought this foal? Or your parents owned the mare or whatever?"

Xavier shakes his head. "No, I didn't get him until much later. It was one of the wealthiest and most prominent racing families back east who bred him. They had all the best trainers work with him. But whenever they tried racing him... *nada*."

He shrugs, lifting his hands. "He just wouldn't run. He's a dreamer. Too interested in his own horse thoughts or staring at the clouds."

I pull back and look at him. "Really? Even with his dad being some super champion?"

Xavier keeps walking. "The mare had good racing bloodlines, too. No explanation for it. The family that invested so much in it tried everything from expensive trainers to medicine men. Finally sold him off to try to recoup some of their losses." Xavier's expression sours, the furrow between his brow deepening, which causes the burned half of his face to take on a menacing appearance. "That's when things got bad for my boy."

He comes to another paddock where two horses graze in the distance, a honey-colored one and another that's a darker brown. He leans his elbows on the fence so that he's in profile, the good side of his face toward me.

"His owners didn't pay close enough attention to who they sold him off to. The new owners were bastards who thought they knew better than all the professionals. They tried to force him to race by whipping and abusing him, shooting him full of illegal steroids. They got a few off-circuit races out of him, but he was uncontrollable and more hazard than he was worth. He was found crazed and half-starved when the DEA raided a stable yard in Arizona. They were about to put him down when I offered to pasture him here."

All of this has just come in a long stream while he stands, arms on the fence, looking out at the pasture and the grazing horses. He's just suddenly opened up like a font of information. I'm not sure if that's more shocking or the implications of all he's saying.

"So..." I put together the bits and pieces he's told me as I look over my shoulder and then scan the few outbuildings and paddocks all around us. Apart from the first separated paddock where Samson was isolated, they all create a loose hexagon shape. "You basically run this place to take care of old or abused horses. This is a horse rescue."

I have to blink a couple times as the concept sinks in.

He doesn't so much as twitch at my pronouncement. "Close your mouth," he finally murmurs. "You'll catch a fly."

Then he starts forward again, delivering one sharp jerk on the rope to signal me to follow, as always.

Like I could frigging forget.

Yeah, he's really got a heart of gold. The rescuer of all the poor, needy animals who also just happens to like keeping women tied on a leash like a dog. Right. Pardon while I go get a hanky for the touching scene.

I'm surprised when he actually opens the gate to the pasture. We haven't gone up close to any of the horses except those in the stable who were securely closed up behind stall doors. But he's just heading straight in, no buffer at all between us and the horses.

Um, hello? Doesn't he remember *lesson one*? Two thousand pounds and all that?

"These are two of my gentlest, both mares," he says, apparently not worried in the slightest. He explained earlier the difference between mares—females, geldings, and stallions. Geldings and stallions are males, but geldings have been castrated. I've been learning all kinds of fun facts like that all morning.

Xavier pauses to close the gate behind us. "Hot Lips is pregnant, though, so if she shies away from you, we won't press it. But Sugar is the gentlest on the ranch. Some more basics. Always approach a horse from the front left shoulder and make sure to let them get a look at you before coming close. Never come at a horse from behind or when he's agitated." This last part he says sharply, looking me in the eye.

I raise my hands. "Got it. Don't come up behind a horse."

"Which side do you approach from?" he quizzes.

"Left shoulder." Geez, he just told me two seconds ago.

"Good, and only after you're sure they've seen you. Above all, horses can sense your mood. If you're tense, they go tense. Breathe and be calm. The more you project calm and serene, the more the horse will respond to you."

With that, he turns on his heel and starts across the field. Not wanting him to tug on the damn rope, I hurry on his heels. He locks the gate behind us and then we're off across the uneven ground of the paddock. It's full of divots and—oh yep, that's a giant horse pie. I dodge out of the way and then jog to keep up before the line between us pulls taut.

He approaches the two mares with a carrot extended in each hand. We only go halfway through the paddock before the interested horses amble toward us.

These two aren't frenzied like Lulu, though they too nuzzle Xavier first thing. Their huge, sloppy muzzles come for his carrots, exposing large horsey teeth.

Holy crap those are big teeth.

I can't help taking a step back. Isn't he afraid he's going to lose a finger?

But no, he just keeps his hands out for them to nibble and lick at far after the carrots are gobbled up. A serene smile tugs at his lips. I take the opportunity to look the horses over. And wow, sure enough, the honey-colored one does look extra fat in the belly.

Pregnant.

Even as I think it, Xavier rubs down her left side and down to her belly, where he strokes her engorged stomach.

"How far along is she?" I ask, watching the gentle, almost reverent way his hand moves with the grain of her thick, coarse hair. Then I scrunch my eyebrows together. "Is it nine months for horses, too?"

"A normal, healthy equine pregnancy will be eleven months long. Hot Lips is six months in. And she's doing beautifully. Isn't that right, my lovely lady?" He scratches and rubs her some more, up and down her long body, from shoulder to flank. She turns into his touch, nuzzling her head into his shoulder. He bows his head and cradles her long neck so that for a moment, it looks like he's having some sort of spiritual communion or praying with the horse. I can just barely hear him muttering little noises of praise to her.

I can't help staring on in fascination. It's so bizarre to see this side of Xavier. I imagine him being as gentle with a little newborn colt.

Or holding his own baby in his arms.

The thought is a jarring one.

Because while I usually cringe at all things babies, the idea of Xavier holding a small baby is only... charming. Thinking of the giant man cradling a tiny baby? My heart goes all gooey in my chest at the thought.

I blink several times. I am *not* a woman who goes gooey over babies. Or men. So the combination should produce zero goo.

Luckily a huge snout headbutts the back of my hair, distracting the disturbing turn of thought. I turn to see Sugar has come up behind me. She nickers and snorts a big puff of air that blows my hair away from my face. I can't help laughing in surprise as she noses toward me again, bumping into my cheek.

Holy crap, this is a huge animal. She towers over me and my first instinct is to back away. But when her big, wet tongue slips out to lick my cheek, I'm startled into another laugh.

My hands rise and I'm not sure if I mean to ward her off or pet her. She's too busy nosing against the other side of my neck and making the decision for me. My fingers come into contact with her wet, snuffling nose. Then her tongue sneaks out again and licks my fingers. I squeal a little and laugh more.

I'm worried for a second that my shrill giggle will scare her off, but nope, she just keeps nosing at me, bumping me with her huge head, sniffing, and licking. I stumble a few times. She's so big and obviously has no sense of personal boundaries, but I'm finally brave enough to follow Xavier's example and gently scratch at the short, finer patch of fur between her nose and eyes and touch her mane. She seems to delight in the attention and bucks even more into my touch.

I don't know how long I've spent just getting acquainted with her before Xavier's pressing a carrot into my hands. Sugar immediately zeroes in on the carrot and there's no time to really second-guess it before she's chomping away at the vegetable. Within two bites, the huge teeth I was so freaked out by earlier tug the carrot out of my hand. Her wet horse lips slobber all over my fingers. I can't help grinning at the feel of it and I go back to scratching at her.

"You're a silly girl, aren't you?" I murmur affectionately. "Such a silly girl."

She finishes chomping the carrot and then goes back to headbutting me and generally trying to get my attention in any way possible

Careful to stand at her left shoulder, I finally loop an arm up as far as I can around her neck and hug her. She seems more than happy to welcome the affection. I marvel at the huge warm animal body tucked so close to mine. I press my ear against her shiny coat.

I had no idea... I mean, I was *never* one of those little girls who was horse crazy growing up. But I had no idea they were so... well, *amazing* is the only word I can think of to describe them.

I look to Xavier, only to find him standing with his arms crossed, watching me with an intensity that's discomfiting. Hot Lips has wandered off and is munching on grass near the fence.

I straighten up and let go of Sugar. Whoa. How did I just let myself get so totally absorbed in her? And how long has Xavier been staring at me like that?

I swallow and give Sugar one last pat. "She's amazing. A real sweetheart. What's her story?"

"She's a mustang like Samson. BLM rounded her up from the wild and I adopted her about a year and a half ago."

"What?" I exclaim as she lands an especially sloppy lick all the way up my cheek. She was a wild horse? As recently as a couple years ago? I wipe my cheek and look at Xavier to see if he's messing with me. But he looks completely serious as he steps up and pets her muzzle.

"Did they," I wave a hand, "tame her or something before you adopted her?"

He actually gives a half roll of his eyes—my statement is apparently that ludicrous. "I'm the only one I'd trust to train any horse on this property. Besides, that's not what the BLM does. No, she came here just as wild as Samson." He nods in the direction of the stable and the front pasture beyond it.

Then he looks back at her and his face softens like it did earlier when he was with Lulu. "She just needed someone to show her she didn't have to be afraid anymore. She was always a sweet girl underneath." He runs a hand up her long nose, his voice gentling. so that

I'm not sure if he's talking to me anymore, or the horse. "She had to learn how to trust. It took a while for me to break through, didn't it, girl? But we got there in the end."

He bows his forehead to her nose like he did with Lulu, doing that strange communing thing where both animal and man are still and quiet for a long moment.

When he speaks again, his voice is still just above a whisper. "But once I did, it was the most beautiful thing. You're my beautiful girl, aren't you, sweet Sugar?" Then his voice drops and he starts whispering things to her that I can't hear at all. She nuzzles into him and makes little delighted horsey noises.

I swallow hard, uncomfortable all of the sudden. Does he look at me the same way he did when he first got Sugar? As another animal he just has to train?

Finally, he steps back. "All right, now that you've met everybody, let's get started on the day's work. Lulu and Pioneer still need to be let out for the day. Then I want to get started with Samson."

Samson. The wild one. "You mean training him? So you just start straight off?"

He nods as we start walking back to the barn. I guess it's obvious, but I don't know. I thought maybe he'd leave the stallion alone for a day and let him just get used to the paddock.

You know, kind of how he did for me.

I cringe a little at the thought. God. I am *not* a freaking horse! Thankfully there's not much time to think about it anymore because we're soon back in the stable.

Xavier keeps encouraging me to interact with the animals. Pioneer allows me to approach him and touch his shoulder. Hesitantly, I rub down his left side to his flank. He steps and licks his lips and Xavier reminds me to breathe.

Yeah, I try that, but I'm relieved when Xavier takes the huge gelding's lead and guides him out into the center of three paddocks that branch off from the stable. Except for the fact that Xavier's also got *my* lead line in his hand, so, you know, again I get that feeling that I'm just another of the horses he's letting out of the stable for the day. Because that's not degrading or anything.

When he goes in to work with Samson, he ties me to a fence post.

"Stay," he says unnecessarily after looping the rope around the post. He ignores my furious huff and pulls a baseball cap out of his back pocket, which he settles on my head. I guess so I don't get too much sun? It's always such a weird mix of caretaking and humiliation with this guy, I don't know how to make heads or tails of him.

That goes double for the 'training' he spends the afternoon doing with Samson. I was expecting to at least get a little spectacle out of the whole thing. You know, like getting to see a real live cowboy *break* a horse. Isn't that what they call it? Sounds a bit barbaric, but hey, I didn't make up the term.

Instead, the afternoon just goes on and on and *on* endlessly. And all Xavier does is walk up to Samson. Samson starts stamping his feet and backing away and then Xavier walks back. Sometimes Xavier will snort and throw his head around like a horse. He walks back and forth in a manner a little reminiscent of Samson himself.

Is it odd to watch a grown man pretend to be a horse all afternoon? No more than anything else that's happened to me since I got here. I take it in stride fairly quickly.

What really surprises me is that Xavier doesn't even try to touch Samson or corral him with a rope or make him run in a circle—none of the stuff I feel like I've seen cowboys do in TV shows or movies.

He just spends ALL afternoon approaching and then stepping away from the horse. Oh, and I can't forget the really long stretches where he and the horse just stand still and stare at each other. Xavier's stance is never aggressive like I might expect—he just… stands there.

It's mind-numbing to watch. I sit in the grass and make daisy chains out of the long grass, think of all the thousands of things I could be busy doing if I were in New York right now, and dream of how I'll start my comeback once I'm done with this godforsaken place.

Maybe I'm already pregnant and we can get this show on the road.

My hand goes to my stomach and my heart jumps to my throat at the thought. Holy God, how could I even—no, just *no*. I can't even contemplate that whole thing until it's a reality. *If* it ever becomes a reality, considering he hasn't even slept with me aside from those first two times.

I look back at Xavier where he's locked in another stare down with the horse and shake my head. I can't make up my mind if I want to hurry up and get pregnant so this can all just be over or if... my mind flashes back to the pregnant mare. Growing a *life*... inside *my body*? For God's sake, that sounds more insane than anything that's happened yet, and being locked outside in a pigpen feels pretty damn crazy.

What's Xavier's deal anyway? He just up and decided he wanted a kid one day? So then he watches the news and saw my dad and figured I was an easy target, or what? From the little Mr. Owens told me, they'd obviously done their research into me and my family history. But why me out of everyone he could have chosen? Was there really no one who would have willingly had his child? How the hell did that whole thing play out? I haven't given it much thought because frankly, thinking about it all freaks me the hell out.

But the more I get to know him... it's impossible not to wonder *why*? Why does he want a child? For some horse farm legacy? Theoretically he's got a lot of money to be able to afford the big resort and do what he did for my dad, but the man is certainly not flaunting it if he's got it. And as far as I've seen today, these horses are the rejects, abused, and losers that no one else wanted. Not exactly a racing legacy to pass on.

Maybe he was just lonely out here all by himself with no one but the horses to keep him company? Or he has a terminal illness and he wants to pass on a family name before he dies?

My gaze shoots up to Xavier where he stands, tall, broad-chested, and confident in the bright light of the blazing sun. No, I can't imagine such a larger than life man ill. Not just that, but I can't see him as the kind of man who would bring a life into the world only to then abandon it. He's just too damn controlling for that.

I breathe out and close my eyes. I'm just the oven. Whatever he does with the bun is not really my concern. I mean, I would be worried if I thought he'd like, abuse it. I'm not a monster. But seeing how gentle he is with the horses and even with me sometimes... Anyway, I'm sure the kid will be fine.

And I can go back to living my own life. Right?

I just... this was all a lot easier when it was in the abstract.

I fiddle with the grass and try not to give in to my more anxious thoughts. And Xavier just keeps at his inanities with Samson. After at least four more *hours*, which I can only guess at because I start mapping the sun's progress across the sky since I don't have access to a phone with a clock, Xavier finally says something I can't hear to the horse. Then he backs up and eventually starts walking toward the gate where I'm tied up.

Right in time because I've got to pee like nobody's business.

Except that after a brief break for lunch—which yes, he feeds me —and the bathroom, thank God, he's dragging me back out for more work.

Turns out the afternoons are all about mucking out stalls. It takes fifteen minutes for Xavier to demonstrate.

I see how he keeps his giant, muscled physique in tip-top shape. He's using a heavy-looking pitchfork to sift the clean hay to the back of the stall and then drag all the messed hay—read, hay that's full of horse pee and poop—out of the stall to the middle of the stable. Then I get to shovel that into a wheelbarrow and haul it across the field to the compost bins.

I also now intimately understand what's meant by the term 'back-breaking work.' It takes me what feels like an hour to do a single stall. I almost immediately develop blisters from using the heavy pitchfork in spite of the thick work gloves Xavier gave me.

"How often do you do this?" I ask breathlessly after hauling the damn wheelbarrow back for the second time. "Once a week?"

His mouth twitches in amusement as he calmly sifts the hay in

Tornado's stall. "Every day. Twice if a horse is messy. Pioneer is especially bad about stepping in his own mess and getting it in all his bedding."

I just stare at him. "Twice a day..." He's got to be kidding me.

But the way he's standing, one arm propped on top of the pitchfork, implacable gaze fixed on me, it sure doesn't look like he's kidding. "This will now be your job. Once all the animals get used to you, you'll feed and turn them out each morning, then clean out their stalls."

I can't help the involuntary step forward I take in protest. Or the words that spring out of my mouth. "That's not what I'm here for."

The only response I get is the lift of that damn eyebrow. Oh, so now Mr. Loquacious is going to go back to clamming up.

I lift my gloved hands and gesture all around us at the stinking barn. "I did not sign on to be some freaking ranch hand!" I toss my pitchfork to the ground for emphasis.

"You keep bringing this up—" His voice is chilly as he takes a step toward me and places his foot on the pitchfork I just tossed to the barn floor in my little rant. "—What you *did* and *did not* agree to in coming here. It was my understanding that your father was in dire circumstances. I was the only one in the entire world offering to help him. One might think you'd show some gratitude to the man who saved your father's life. Your father," his eyes narrow and his jaw tenses, "who was, by the way, busy stealing the pensions of thousands of honest, hardworking people."

By the end of this small speech, I remember that oh shit, *right*, while I might have been lulled by the sight of the sweet horse whisperer I've been witnessing all day, this man can also go stone cold. And things don't always go pleasantly for me when that happens.

"Right," I grit my own teeth, looking at the floor and seeing bits of hay that I missed while sweeping. Oh my gosh, I've only been at this one day, and I already hate mucking out stalls with the fire of a thousand suns.

"Fine." I kick petulantly at the stupid hay, scattering it over the ground.

Almost immediately, Xavier's hand is underneath my chin, lifting my head so that I meet his gaze. "What I mean is that you need to abandon all your expectations. You are here now. For the time being, nothing else matters. It is you and me, and when the time is right," his hand drops low on my abdomen, "the child."

He says it all with such certainty. Like he has decided how everything will go in his universe and thus it will be so.

"Now, on your knees." He nods behind me. "Elbows on the bench."

I feel my eyes widen as I swing around to look at where he's indicating. There is indeed a bench along the back wall of the horse stalls, near the spigot and deep basin sink where we do washing and fill up the horse water buckets.

He's got to be... joking.

But with a sinking stomach, I know he's not. How many times have I had that thought since meeting this man? Never once has any of the outrageous requests he's made been a joke.

Just once it'd be really great if he could break that record. I turn back to him to check if maybe this time...?

Nope, the serious expression on his face tells me all I need to know.

Sighing, I turn around. Right before I can get to my knees on the hard concrete, Xavier tosses a horse blanket down.

Ever the gentleman. So I get to crouch on a horse blanket while he, what? Fucks me doggie style in a dirty barn?

Or would that be more accurately termed horsey style in this situation?

At least all the horses are out to pasture. I think it would be more humiliating if they were here to watch.

I get down on my knees on the blanket.

"Elbows on the bench."

I comply.

Behind me, out of sight, I hear the spigot turn on and the sound of splashing water. Is he getting a drink? Or washing up?

I swallow and shift where I sit on my knees. I glance around the empty stable. I've still had so few sexual experiences. Especially since it's Xavier, I have no idea what to expect. It's impossible not to tense up while waiting for him to do… whatever it is he's about to do.

But then, sooner than I expect him, his hands reach around the front of my jeans, unbutton them, and tug them roughly down around my knees. Next they go to my panties. He seems impatient.

Immediately his hands are on my ass, stroking the globes. He lets out a low hiss before grabbing them and giving a hard squeeze. I jump at the unexpected pressure.

He chuckles. "That's right, remember Master's touch." He squeezes and massages my cheeks in circles, pulling them apart and then smooshing them together. Then he leans over my back.

"And remember how much you like it." He pulls the cheeks apart again, squeezing extra hard. Then he lifts a hand in front of my face and shoves his thumb in my mouth. "Suck."

I breathe in sharply but do as he asks. I suck on his thumb. It's clean and has the sharp residual taste of hand soap.

"That's my good girl," he praises. Using the same language he did with the fucking horses.

That's screwed up in a big way. Right? It's not just me?

But then there's something brushing at my entrance. Not his fingers.

Startled, I look down.

It's a large, flat brush.

Is that a…?

A horse brush. He's teasing my clit with a fucking horse brush.

"Grooming is an important part of everyday life on the ranch," he murmurs. "A fine, gentle brush is a must on the most sensitive areas."

He pushes down the back collar of my shirt and his lips descend on my neck. His teeth immediately nip as well.

"Of course, you still have to apply pressure to make sure the job is done." He begins to move the brush in circles over my clitoris and I jolt forward. The bristles are still somewhat rough and I can't decide if it feels good or disturbing.

But the way he keeps nibbling on the back of my neck and whispering in my ear... and how his other hand has begun exploring at the lips of my pussy, a spasm rocks through my body.

"That's right," he whispers soothingly, his fingers teasing at my entrance, massaging and dipping just the littlest bit inside. "You'll notice the mare start to respond to your touch when you're grooming her just the way she likes." He presses the brush hard against my bud and wetness gushes over his fingers.

"Grooming can be a sweet time of connection between Master and mare," his teeth nip harder still, right at the skin behind my earlobe, which sends shivers up and down my entire body, "because she learns to trust that he knows just the way she likes to be stroked."

He dips one of his long, thick fingers inside me. "Grooming, just like all of horsemanship, if you're doing it right, should be about trust and pleasure, for both involved." He pulls back with the brush until he's applying the barest of touches and then he teases around and around my bud, then up and down, then around and around. I gasp and press forward for more pressure, but he pulls it away again, at the same time slipping another finger inside me.

And then both brush and his fingers disappear. My senses go on alert. I wait to hear the sound of his buckle and his pants being undone. Instead, I feel something at my entrance pressing in. I startle slightly and his hand comes to my back.

"Shh, girl, hold steady, you're all right."

What the hell? Did he undo his pants and I didn't notice?

But when I look down and crane my neck so I can see between my legs, I see that it's not any part of him sliding inside me. No, it's some kind of black pole...?

I jerk forward and it hits an awkward, uncomfortable angle.

"Steady," he warns, his hand firm on my back.

But when I look behind me and I see that holy shit—he's feeding the grip handle end of a leather horse crop inside me.

"What the fuck!"

"Language," he snaps, eyes coming up to mine, a scowl on his face. "Trust and pleasure."

"Well did you stick any riding implements up a fucking horse's cooch?"

I get the eyebrow lift for that one. "No, I am not into bestiality."

I breathe out heavily. That's a relief, at least.

"Bend over," he orders. "Eyes closed."

I lift my eyes to the ceiling. Am I really going to... I mean, holy crap, this is just beyond—

"Over. Now."

It's not a request.

I lean forward on the bench, propped on my elbows and squeeze my eyes shut.

"Good girl." He pats my ass and then slides the crop in even further.

My eyes flick nervously behind my eyelids. What he's doing, it's so — I mean, I've heard of people doing kinky things with riding crops, but I never thought— And he's— I mean, he's—

He's fucking you with it, Mel. That's what he's doing with it.

Oh my God. Will the insanity never stop or even slow down for a second with this man?

And the even crazier thing? When his other hand not manipulating the riding crop comes around to play with my clitoris already so sensitized by the grooming brush?

I clench around the pole.

I'm turned on. To my utter goddamned shame and humiliation, I'm getting off on this whole fucked up scene.

"Such a good girl. Look at you squirting your sweet juices for me," he murmurs in between suckling and nipping at my neck. "Your little cunt is so wet for anything and everything I could ever do. That's right, you're doing so well. That's *riiiiiiight*. It feels so good, doesn't it?"

His finger toying with my clit is as gentle as the crop inside me is relentless. He circles the bud this way and that, then presses before removing the pressure entirely and focusing on the crop. It's so lubricated with my juices that it slides in and out, the leather braided handle and rubber stopper at the end rub along my walls and drive me crazy with each pass.

"My precious little dirty girl. Look how sopping you are. I'm fucking you with a riding crop and you can't get enough of it. Your little cunt greedily sucks it back inside. That's right, clamp down on it. I know you wish it was my cock, but greedy little girls don't get Master's cock until they beg."

His fingers come back to my clit, rubbing and circling and *oh*, oh *God*—

"I can see how much you wish this was my cock. You wish it was Master, bending you over this bench and driving my huge cock inside you. Just like the day when I first took this tight little virgin hole."

His words, they're so filthy and wrong. And they're driving my orgasm closer and closer. I'm so close to the edge with how wrong and fucking hot every second of this is.

"Oh you loved that, didn't you? You lost your mind from my cock, juicing right up and getting so wet for me. Your sweet little body was so ready for me to come and take what was mine. Just like now. I'm so hard I'm about to bust the zipper on my goddamn pants you make me so fucking crazy—"

The rod lands deep inside me and his fingers on my clit press down and I scream out my orgasm.

I'm still shaking and blinking as I come down when Xavier withdraws the crop and tosses it to the side. Then there's the noise of his buckle coming undone.

Is he finally going to…?

But when I look over my shoulder, it's only to see him jerking on his cock roughly, up and down.

The next second, he shoves up my shirt and then comes on my back.

I can't look away from his face. His features are knit in the most beautiful expression of pleasure, pain, and relief. Then he slumps over on my back, his long, hard cock sandwiched between our bodies.

Why didn't he come inside me? It feels like rejection, as ridiculous as that is.

He uses the shirt he pulls off to clean up my back and then he pulls me into his lap a few moments later.

"Why?" I ask as he brushes my hair out of my face. "Why do it that way with the—" I gesture at the discarded riding crop. "I mean, okay, whatever, you've got your own way of doing things, but still—" He's got everything so jumbled in my head. "I don't get it. Isn't the point of this to get a baby?"

I hope he can see my confusion but not my hurt. God, I don't want to reveal that. And I need to understand.

I'm not sure what I expect his answer to be, but it's not for him to caress my cheek and then grip the hair at the base of my neck. He looks me in the eye, "Pet, my first priority is to have you out of your mind and desperate for my cock. You don't get me inside you again until you're begging for it, so the baby-making will just have to wait."

12

WHAT FOLLOWS ARE TWO AND A HALF WEEKS OF RELATIVE CALM.

Well, if you call hard ass work mucking out stalls and learning to groom and care for horses *calm*. Oh, and we can't forget the part where I'm getting screwed into oblivion every night or, you know, at random points throughout the day whenever Xavier gets a wild hair that it seems like a good time to give Mel an orgasm and or to fuck her with whatever implement he might happen to have on hand.

Of course, never with his almighty cock. No, because apparently, I'd have to *beg* for that.

Ha. As if. He's as crazy as he is inventive.

You see, he's a big fan of improvisation. He always gives whatever object he's decided to pleasure me with a good washing beforehand and he always sheaths it. He's even prepared ahead of time and bought several things new just for this reason—such as one riding crop that he's particularly fond of. He has a special leather bag in the stable full of his favorites. I have my own grooming brush, the crop, a bridle and bit he puts on me sometimes, and several other little toys.

At night inside the house is another story. There he has all different sizes and shapes of dildos he ordered for me. He gets an especially delighted grin every time he pulls a new one out of the box.

Sometimes he masturbates along with what he's doing to me. Other times he doesn't.

And even though I come every night, or hell, sometimes multiple times a day, I can't help the mounting frustration that's building. I don't know what he *wants* from me.

Or I guess, God, that's not true. He told me that first day out in the stables what he wants. For me to be out of my mind for him. And to freaking *beg* him?

I shake my head even as I scrape the pitchfork along the floor of the stall to separate Lulu's clean bedding from the dirty. Then separate out the soiled hay. Lulu's stall is one of the easiest. Maybe it's because she was raised from a foal, but she always poops in one part of the stall and pees on the hay in another without getting her bedding too messed. I always leave hers for last because it's a relative joy.

If only Lulu herself would warm up to me. But nope, while most of the other horses will let me approach them and I've even started grooming Pioneer, Bob, Paddyshack, and my favorite—Sugar—Lulu is still not a happy camper when I'm around.

She neighs and gets agitated, stepping back and forth, her eyes going crazy. Xavier says it's something we need to work on and that she's picking up on my anxiety, but I'm happy to just go groom one of the other nicer horses. Thankfully he hasn't pressed the point.

And he has his hands full with Samson and the other animals.

He always spends a portion of his morning and evening with Holy Hellfire. He must have a special affection or relationship with the old ornery racehorse. Or rather, the racehorse who refused to race, I guess I should say. He puts ice packs on the aging horse's hooves morning and night and feeds him a special grain. I'll see him out there some evenings just standing and brushing his comb down the horse's body long after the grooming should be done. If I wasn't bound and determined to see Xavier for the bastard he is, I might almost think it was sweet. But nope, I'm far too clear-eyed for that.

Even if he did stop with the lasso around my waist after a couple of days. I swear, it's like he's extra assholish on purpose so then I'm brainwashed into thinking he's being a good guy when he stops. Like how I felt all grateful after the shed. And now with letting me off the lasso. When he pulls back and gives me back a modicum of freedom, he's suddenly my knight in shining armor? Such BS.

The petty politics people used to play back in the corporate world have nothing on this guy. Though, I don't know, I go back and forth from being sure he's a master manipulator and then thinking he's just making up everything as he goes along, completely on the fly.

Because when he's working with the horses, he seems like the most natural and guileless person on the planet.

Now that I'm not forced to watch him training Samson, I find myself wandering out to the front paddock between my other chores.

The progression has been *sloooooooow*, but Xavier has made headway with the beast. At first it was a lot of standing around staring at each other. Samson would bolt every so often until Xavier walked close, hemming the horse in until he finally stood still again. Commence another stare-off.

After a couple days, Samson would stop long enough for Xavier to come near enough to touch his muzzle. By day three, Xavier was able to scratch up his long nose and touch his neck.

Then I swear he spends the rest of the week just doing that.

Just touching the horse.

Oh, and whispering to him. Can't forget that. The secret Xavier-horse language he's developed.

He *is* a horse whisperer. Like, a real one. He whispers to the animals and they respond with their horse noises. So much so that after three weeks, the jacked up, crazy-eyed Samson I met the first day doesn't look much like himself. I come out after cleaning Lulu's stall and put my arms on the fence to watch Xavier with him.

For the past two days, Xavier's been tossing a small blanket over Samson's back, then pulling it off again. Then tossing it on. Pulling it off.

I thought at this point Xavier could get away with anything, but at first, Samson seemed quite spooked at having something on his back.

Now as I watch, I see where Xavier is going with the whole exercise. Not only is the blanket on Samson's back, but now Xavier's hefting a whole saddle on as well.

Samson paws the ground nervously but Xavier gets it on. Then he pauses and goes to the front of the horse, whispering to him and cuddling him, forehead to nose. I can only shake my head in wonder.

Oh yeah, Samson's already under Xavier's spell big time. He might be putting up some last token resistance, but he's already a goner.

When Xavier pulls back, Samson stands perfectly still while Xavier buckles the saddle in place underneath his stomach. He's had a rope harness around Samson's head for about a week now, and he holds the reins loosely.

Then, straight away, Xavier lifts his foot into the stirrup and stands up, holding onto the sides of the saddle for balance. Samson shuffles forward, turning his head sharply to see what's going on. Xavier's forced to drop back to the ground.

I jolt forward, hands going to the fence as the horse turns around in a circle, neighing. Xavier starts talking to him, patting his long neck. Then he grabs the saddle, hikes his foot up into the stirrup and tries again.

My heart leaps into my throat as again Samson heads forward, dislodging Xavier. Xavier jumps back to the ground.

What the hell is he doing? Obviously the horse isn't ready for this step.

But Xavier just walks the short distance, grabs the saddle and yet again, hikes himself up.

With predictable results.

Damn him, why does he always have to push? It's a wild animal, for God's sake. Does Xavier just have some screwed up need to conquer everything in his path?

It's obvious the freaking horse doesn't want to be ridden. Of course he doesn't. He spent his entire life roaming free, allowed to make his *own* decisions about what he was going to do each day, where he was going to go next, what he was going to eat and how he was going to eat it, where he was going to sleep—

His body was his own.

Before.

But then along comes this man.

Every day putting his hands all over you, demanding you call him Master, treating you like he owns you, body and soul... Making you question everything you thought you knew. About the world. About *yourself.*

It's not fair.

I stare out at the mustang, willing him to hold true to his wild spirit. "Don't let him conquer you," I whisper under my breath.

Xavier hikes himself up into the stirrup again. Samson hesitates for just a moment before starting to shuffle forward.

It's enough for Xavier to take advantage of. He swings his leg over the saddle and when Samson finally takes off, Xavier has the reins. He encourages Samson to keep going, but when he tugs on the left rope, Samson goes left until they're riding in a brisk circle around the large paddock.

Xavier calls out loud praise to Samson as they go.

It's both beautiful and horrible. Their bodies seam together in what looks like an unbroken line. Horse and rider—master and steed—connected in a single purpose.

I quickly turn on my heel and start walking away as quickly as possible, a clenched fist held over my heart against brewing hurt and rage.

～

"I GOT MY PERIOD," I say, staring down listlessly at the turkey sandwiches I prepared for lunch when Xavier comes in half an hour later. "I need tampons."

That was a lovely discovery I made right after watching Xavier with Samson and went to the bathroom. Hello, Cousin Flo.

Goodbye hopes of this whole nightmare being over in nine months. And then I was flooded with relief, because, a *baby*? Like always, the thought of a screaming, squalling, shitting infant gets the same knee jerk reaction from me. Holy shit, just *no*.

Which was then followed by terror because what if Xavier was mad I wasn't pregnant? Which was then swiftly followed by fury, because if he wanted me to get pregnant, then he should damn well start doing something about it!

And that was all just way too many waves of emotion to process in a three-minute period, so I stuffed my panties with toilet paper and then came to the kitchen to make lunch.

Followed by sitting down and staring aimlessly at my turkey sandwich. Yeah, this is turning out to be a real winner of a day so far. Can I have a free pass and just go back to sleep? Maybe claiming cramps will get me out of all the bullshit? Does this work like P.E.?

"Come with me." Xavier takes my hand, drawing me out of my chair. Then he leads me up the stairs, all three flights.

"Lie on the bed," he orders.

What? "Look, if you can just give them to me, then I'll go downstairs, take care of it, and we can get back to lun—"

"On the bed." The furrow between his eyebrow appears at my equivocation.

I let out a huff of air and throw up my hands but do as he instructs.

"You're in a mood," he says as he comes back, tampon in hand.

I close my eyes and throw my hand over my face. Oh my God, is he going to do something kinky with a *tampon*?

He pulls off my boots, then draws down my pants. I'm surprised he hasn't responded to my dramatics with the arm over my face, but I don't move it.

Let him 'punish' me or do whatever the hell it is he's going to do. Not like I have a choice in it anyway.

I feel the bed shift when he gets up and then he returns a few moments later. Then he pulls down my panties and his hands are at my most delicate place, removing the no doubt bloody toilet paper from between my legs. I'm glad my arm is over my face because I have no doubt I'm going beet red.

Oh my gosh, some things were meant to be left *private*.

But no, there he is, just barging in. I try to squeeze my knees together. Naturally, he just spreads them right back apart. Then I feel him running a warm wash cloth methodically all around.

I have to bite my lip against tears at how gentle he's being.

Why?

Why is he doing this to me? And what the hell is *this* anyway? He seems to want something more than a baby. Or maybe it's that he just wants to have me completely under his thumb before I'm allowed the *honor* of carrying his seed?

Goddammit, going in circles trying to figure him out will make me crazy.

I squeeze my eyes shut and bite down on my bottom lip even harder. It's just hormones. PMS stuff. And being locked up in this place with nobody but him to talk to for three weeks. Him and the damn horses. I'm bound to go a little nuts.

Still, I can't help the strange flutter that goes through my stomach when I feel the gentle probe of the tampon as he slides it carefully into my channel.

There's nothing inherently sexual about the act.

And when he leans over and I feel the press of his lips right over the hood of my clitoris, I feel more like he's giving me some sort of blessing or it's something spiritual for him rather than trying to excite me, for once.

Which makes my emotions go haywire all over again. I lift my arm from over my eyes and peek down at him, dark head bowed right over my womb.

Is he sad I'm not pregnant? Or is this something else? How can I live day in, day out with this man, sleep by his side every night and yet know so little about him?

"Thanks," I say, squirming away from him and his bowed head. "We should get back out there. It's time for the afternoon feeding."

I swing my legs over the side of the bed and slide my underwear and jeans back up my legs. I'm just pulling on my first boot when his voice rings out firmly.

"No."

I pause, mid-boot, and look over at him warily. "No?"

He shakes his head decisively, leaning against the backboard of the bed and observing me. "Since you aren't with child, it's time to get you up on a horse."

My foot slides into the boot at the same time my stomach drops through the floor. "Oh, that's not necessary." I wave my hands. "They're perfectly happy as they are. They don't need me bumbling my way—"

"Part of getting to know a horse is riding them. That's where relationships are truly forged. You've been teaching the horses to trust you by feeding and grooming them. Now it's your turn to prove that you trust *them*."

I can only stare at him open-mouthed for a long moment.

Trust *a horse*? With my life?

Does he hear himself?

"But they're two thousand pounds!" I protest.

"Sugar's only about fifteen hundred," he says mildly, a twitch at one side of his lips like he's amused by me.

My stomach calms down a little at hearing that it's Sugar he's thinking of trying out this insane idea on, but still!

Then I remember, "She's a mustang."

"And?" Eyebrow lift.

"And what if, I don't know," I throw up my hands, "she suddenly remembers what it was like to be a wild horse and gets it in her mind to go tearing off. With me on her back!"

He gives me a level stare. "Have you known Sugar to be anything but calm and sweet natured?"

"That's not the point," I scoff. "You said she was as wild as Samson."

He props his elbow on his knee, then his chin on his fist. "Oh please, do tell me more about the disposition of my horses, since you have so much experience in this area. Not to mention that your discriminatory attitude against mustangs is *fascinating* to behold."

I let out an outraged huff. "Discrimin— How dare you accuse me — I was just—"

"Fine," he stands up, holding out a hand toward the bedroom door. "No Sugar, though she's the sweetest mare you'd ever sit saddle on. Pioneer is almost as sweetly dispositioned and he seems taken with you. We'll gear him up and have you riding circles before sundown."

"Pioneer is the one who threw his owner!"

"His former owner was an abusive bastard."

"Exactly." I raise my hands. He's making my point for me. "All the animals you've taken in are rescues. The same thing I was saying about Sugar could apply to any of them if they suddenly think of their former owners or situations and—"

"Enough." Xavier's voice crackles in the suddenly silent room and his dark eyes are enough to communicate that I've worn through his patience even if his tone didn't.

He comes up to me, immediately invading my personal space. He lifts my chin and tilts my head so I'm looking up into his eyes. His other hand rises and he places his palm directly over my chest.

Can he feel how hard my heart is beating?

Just because of my fear about this preposterous idea of riding a horse. It has nothing to do with his physical proximity. Nothing at all.

"Fear has no place here." His voice is softer now. "I would never endanger you." His thumb caresses up and runs over where my heartbeat is a flutter at my throat. His eyes avert to stare at his hand as, for just a moment, his fingers close lightly around my throat.

"Trust," his gaze comes back up to meet mine, "is the most precious gift you can give to any being."

With that, he lets go of my throat and steps out the door, heading down the stairs.

I swallow hard, my own hand lifting to my neck where his was only moments before.

And then I follow.

13

I stand fidgeting near the fence while I watch Xavier take Pioneer out and start to saddle him. Yes, I groom these guys every day, but that doesn't stop them from being so freaking *large*.

They tower over me. Pioneer is something like twelve to fifteen times the size of little old me. I have to get up on a two-step stepladder to groom Paddyshack, one of the ex-racehorses, he's so tall.

Pioneer is calm as can be as Xavier tosses the saddle on his back.

Meanwhile, Sugar comes over to me and bumps into my shoulder.

Which makes me feel like crap for dissing her earlier.

"Not now." I take a few steps away.

She just follows, her big head nuzzling at the back of my neck.

Then comes the licking. I swear she's as bad as her owner about personal space.

"Sugar, not—" I gently push her away and take another few steps forward, but she also shares Xavier's stubbornness. She just keeps following me and gently butting her head into my neck and shoulders until I turn around and give her the attention I usually do.

With a sigh, I give in and start scratching at her muzzle, then up her long nose and around to her flowing dark brown mane.

"Are you trying to turn me into a softie? I'm supposed to be a mean New York bitch." She noses against my hands and makes a blowing, chuffing noise that I know means she's happy and even excited.

I roll my eyes and then lean my forehead against her nose. "Oh my God, I can't believe I'm about to do this."

She keeps rolling her head back and forth against mine.

I turn around and look at Xavier. He's paused, his hand on Pioneer's bridal, just watching me with Sugar. Smug bastard probably already knows what I'm going to say. I roll my eyes again as I gesture toward Sugar.

"I'll ride her."

At least he doesn't make a big deal out of it. He simply leads Pioneer close and ties his lead to the fence, then returns to the barn for another tack and saddle. Within ten minutes, he's led both horses into a smaller paddock, got Sugar saddled, and set what he calls a *mounting block* on the ground beside her.

Holy crap, holy crap, holy crap, am I really going to do this?

Sugar might be a sweetie, but she's so damn *big*.

I look around anxiously at the fence posts of the paddock. Okay, so they look sturdy enough, but are they really enough to stop a fifteen-hundred-pound horse if she gets it in her head that she longs for the wilds out yonder again?

Sugar turns her head toward me as if to say, what's the matter here?

"She can sense your unease."

I look to Xavier sharply. "Will that make her bolt? If I'm nervous?"

He smiles at me and pats Sugar's neck. "Nope, not our girl. I lent her out to a horse therapy program for a couple months earlier this year. She's always calm as can be. I told you, it's her nature. Once I realized that about her, I started training her with therapeutic work in mind."

I pause, my own hand lifting to Sugar's flank, and stare at him, my gaze flicking for the briefest second to the maimed half of his face.

For the most part I rarely notice it anymore. Which is strange because at first it seemed so monstrous. It's not like I don't see it when I look at him or even that my eyes skirt past it. It's just... part of him. And it's really only the upper portion of the left side of his face. I'm far more captivated by the rest of him, even his face if I'm being honest.

Ugh, I hate that I'm captivated by him, but there it is. The naked, bared truth. And my damn curiosity about him refuses to be slaked.

Were there therapy horses where he was when he was recovering from... whatever the hell it was that happened to him? Is that why he started this horse farm out in the middle of nowhere? Why is he the way he is?

"I can stand here all day," Xavier says, leaning a hip against the paddock post. "You're not getting out of saddling up on that horse."

My eyes jump to his face as I'm jolted back into the moment. Right. The horse. My first riding lesson. The stubborn-ass man in front of me.

But as I switch my gaze to the saddle and Sugar's broad body fills my field of vision in both directions, suddenly I want to do this for *me*, not him.

I'm not some shrinking violet. I was the youngest account manager at New World Media and Design. I dealt with multi-million-dollar accounts and hobnobbed with New York's snobbiest and most elite. I will *not* be bested by a gentle horse who has a penchant for apples and sugar cubes.

I step up on the mounting block, grab the saddle where Xavier showed me, and put my foot in the stirrup, then hike myself upwards.

For a second, I'm terrified that she's going to stamp forward like Samson did and I'll fall off straightaway.

But Sugar stands perfectly and placidly still.

Meanwhile I'm frozen, one foot in the stirrup, standing on one side of the horse and realizing just how *very* high up off the ground I suddenly am.

"Breathe," comes Xavier's calm voice. "You're doing wonderful. Just breathe and shift your weight forward. Grab the saddlehorn with both hands and swing your leg over the saddle."

That seems like way too many instructions at once. I look down at him, panicked.

He puts a steadying hand on the calf of my leg that's in the stirrup and repeats himself. Eventually, I do what he says.

And then, holy shit! I'm riding a horse!

Okay, I'm sitting on a horse, but then the next thing I know, Xavier has handed me the reins and Sugar is moving and I *am* actually riding a horse.

"Oh my God, I'm doing it!" I squeal excitedly.

"You're doing beautifully."

I have a death grip on both the reins and the saddlehorn. When I dare a glance away from Sugar's mane to look in Xavier's direction, he's beaming one of those rare, full-toothed grins at me. It's enough to take my breath away.

Well, that and the fact that Sugar picks up her pace and really starts to walk forward like she's decided she's got some place to go.

"Oh my God, oh my God, what do I do?" I ask in a panic, my grip on the saddlehorn going white-knuckled.

Xavier chuckles. "You're fine. Just pull back *gently* on the reins if you want her to slow down."

Naturally I yank too hard. Sugar comes to a sudden stop. She turns her head around to look at me like, *who is this noob riding me who has no idea what she's doing?*

"Sorry, sweetie," I apologize, daring to reach forward and pat her.

In a swift motion, Xavier is up on Pioneer's back and riding up beside me. The full grin has faded, but there's still the clear air of pride and satisfaction shining in his eyes when he looks over at me.

"Let's take a walk. Hold her reins loosely."

I take a deep breath then hold the reins like he demonstrates on Pioneer. With his patient instruction, he leads me through my first horse ride. Initially we just go in circles around the paddock. Then he teaches me how to make turns and finally he sets up cones and I try to lead Sugar through the obstacle course—with middling to fair levels of success. On our last pass, we manage to only knock over one out of seven cones.

And I can't help the ridiculous grin from splitting my face by the time the sun is setting. Xavier tells me it's time to get off but I beg for another half hour.

Which, yeah, I'm regretting by the time he helps me back off the mounting block and I realize just how sore my inner thighs are. Turns out I'm not used to being spread-eagled riding a large beast for a whole afternoon.

Haha, insert that's-what-she-said joke here, I know. I'll definitely be sore tomorrow. And even still, I kind of immediately want to say screw it, I'll just take a hot bath and do some stretches and then let me back up there because that was the most awesome thing *ever*!

Xavier's still holding my forearms from helping me down when I look up at him expectantly. "I can ride again tomorrow, right?"

"Looks like someone's caught the fever," he chuckles. "We'll see. It depends on how sore you are."

"I'll stretch." I bend over and start stretching my inner thigh muscles and hamstrings.

"Don't forget your gluteus," comes Xavier's voice from behind me. Then his hands are on my ass, giving me a deep massage. "Horse riding can be punishing on the derrière."

I jolt upright and twirl around, face heating. "Yes, I'll take that into consideration."

He seems amused at my red cheeks. And seriously, I ought to be used to his audacity by this point, but we're here out in the open. Usually he grabs me when we're in the barn or the house. I tense slightly, sure he's about to throw me down right here in the open paddock with the horses looking on, but instead he just makes a clicking noise toward the horses and nods toward the stable. "Let's groom these guys and get the rest of the crew into stable for an early night."

I look him up and down but he's already turned his back to me, leading Pioneer toward the stable.

An early night?

Oh dear, that can only mean he's got something insane in store for me. What's it going to be? Introducing anal? I keep waiting for that one. I'm sure it's in his bag of tricks since he likes shoving every other object possible in my body. He's teased a few times at my anus but never gone whole hog back there, thank God.

But since I'm on my period, maybe now he'll think it's the perfect time for experimentation?

I'm tempted to hurry through grooming but after the special experience Sugar gave me, I want to spend a long time with her, even running detangler through her tail and brushing it out until it's glossy and shining. Then I run through the basic grooming regimen on all the other horses that I'm assigned to while Xavier takes the other half.

I can't imagine how he did all of this alone before I came here. Each grooming session, even if you rush, takes around twenty minutes. First there's the curry comb, then the hard and soft brushes, then brushing out the mane and tail (occasionally having to use detangler on the tail), and finally picking out their hooves. It's insane the amount of work that goes into taking care of a single horse, much less ten of them. It's endless and unrelenting. You don't get a single day off.

And Xavier's been doing it alone for who knows how long. Along with taking in mustangs like Samson and other problem horses along the way?

Every day I spend here, the more curious I get about his background. Who the hell *is* he? Then again, there are far more pressing questions of what the enigmatic man is going to do to me tonight.

As I finish hanging up Bob's brushes by his stall—each horse gets their own individual grooming gear to keep from spreading infection, see what a knowledgeable horsewoman I'm becoming?—I look across the stable that's dappled with long shadows in the early evening sunlight. Xavier's bent over, cleaning out a bucket by the spigot near the wall, his powerful back muscles flexing as he flips it over and spills soapy water into the wide basin to drain. He's pushed up the sleeves of his shirt and his thick forearms glisten with water droplets as he finishes washing the soap off the bucket and sets it upside down to dry. Then he glances over his shoulder and catches me watching him.

I quickly avert my gaze and look out the barn door at the pink sky where the sun is slowly dropping toward the horizon. "Should I go in and see if the roast is ready?"

"Give me a second, I'm just finishing up here. I'll go with you."

I swallow and nod, feeling incredibly stupid and awkward all of the sudden. Like I'm back in junior high staring at the boy I have a crush on.

Which is just... *what*?

Xavier turns off the spigot and grabs a towel to dry his hands on, then I feel him by my side. It's a hot day. We're both sweaty and stink of horses I'm sure—you sort of become desensitized to the smell when you're surrounded by it all day, but still I feel self-conscious when he wraps his arm around my waist and starts walking with me back to the house like that.

It's a position that seems like it would be awkward—and it has been when the few boyfriends I've had in the past have attempted anything like it. Hell, even holding hands with other guys has been uncomfortable. But somehow Xavier just fits my body into his and, in spite of our height differences, he makes it work. He takes command of my stride and just seems to, I don't know, absorb me into him. Take me into his sphere so that I'm stepping when he steps and if there are any fumbles, his strong arm around my waist is always there to smoothly guide me over them.

Before I know it, we're at the back door.

And like normal, he leads me to the sink to wash my hands. I extend them just like always and let him squirt the soap into them. Then I wait while his large, calloused fingers move over my hands, which are beginning to slowly develop callouses of their own.

Life with Xavier has become a series of rituals.

His fingers intertwine briefly with mine as the soap turns foamy.

His hands are so much larger than mine. They overwhelm my small ones. Just like everything about him. He overwhelms me.

I'm glad when he urges our conjoined hands under the running water to clean away the soap. I'm not sure why today things feel different. So much more... I don't know—intense? Or... *vibrant*, maybe, if that's the right word.

Like I said, my life with Xavier has become one of rituals and routines. That's been something of a safe haven for me. When there's routine, you can try to lose yourself in the monotony of it. Granted, I'm never truly able to do that with Xavier because he's always changing things up, surprising me at all times of day with his strange desires and ways of pleasuring me. But still, there was a basic assumption to the way the day would go.

But now... It's stupid. I just rode a horse. And got my period.

Nothing has changed.

I'm making something out of nothing.

Except that after dinner, after Xavier exchanges my tampon—which yes, he insists on doing *himself* again—we take a shower instead of a bath.

Xavier is no less attentive during the shower. And he's extra gentle.

"Such a good girl," he whispers, massaging my scalp as he washes my hair with a honeysuckle scented shampoo. "You handled Sugar so beautifully today. I felt honored to witness the trust you showed her."

He pulls me against his warm chest, his hands still in my hair as the shower sprays my lower back.

I scoff, my neck feeling warm from his praise. "I didn't really do anything. It was just Sugar. It was natural."

His hands drop from my hair suddenly and he wraps his arms around me, pulling me into him. Like... hugging me. Is Xavier actually hugging me right now?

"Exactly," he breathes out, his chin notched on my head. For another long moment, he just holds me there. And then, like the moment never happened, he retreats and goes back to shampooing my hair.

The rest of the shower continues. He washes my shoulders, my back, my rump. He lifts my arm and soaps my armpit and shaves me as carefully as always. But when he moves around to my breasts, he doesn't massage or squeeze them. He merely washes them with brisk efficiency.

Usually this is the point when our bathing time starts to get erotic.

I think surely when he pumps soap into his hands and taps my legs for me to spread them that things will start getting intimate.

Nope.

He just shaves my legs and then... well, you know.

Then he quickly soaps himself down and washes his hair.

Then.

He.

Turns.

The.

Water.

Off.

When he pulls the curtain aside and grabs a towel, I'm left standing there like, wait, *what*?

There is a routine to things and he just broke the rules.

I do backbreaking work every day and then I, you know, get a reward.

I blink. Like a hard blink. And realize how fucked up all the thoughts I just had were. What, suddenly I'm expecting to get paid for farm work in orgasms? And since when did I start looking forward to— I mean, isn't that just something I endure— I'm not supposed to want— GAH!

Xavier seems completely unperturbed by anything. He whips open the towel and starts drying me, calm as can be.

Oh my God, sometimes he's so placid I could just scream! Is he not... you know, interested, because I'm on my period?

My mouth drops open to ask but then I clamp it shut. What am I really going to say? He's the enemy, remember?

Holy crap, it's already happening. I'm getting brainwashed. I was just about to whine to the man basically holding me captive because he's not keeping up his campaign of sexual manipulation.

I squeeze my eyes shut as he runs the fluffy towel between my legs, spending what seems like an inordinate amount of time making sure I'm dry there.

And the unwanted thought pops in: *but seriously though, is he like grossed out because of my period?*

Ugh, shut *up* brain!

Because if he is, then he totally shouldn't be all up in there volunteering for tampon duty.

"I'm really tired," I announce, stepping forward and taking the towel out of Xavier's hands to wrap around myself. "Can we go to bed now?"

He looks briefly startled at my quick motion but the next second seems amused by me.

God, I hate it when he's like that. When he gives off this aura that he knows exactly what's going on in my head and he's laughing at me.

I turn on my heel and stomp toward the bedroom. I swear I hear him chuckle behind me which makes me even more infuriated.

I know he likes me to leave my wet towel on a peg near the head of the bed, but instead I drop it on the floor and slide underneath the covers. Then I cringe and pull the sheet tight around myself. God, Mel, are you *trying* to get him to react? What the fuck is wrong with you?

I jump out of bed and hang the towel up.

Which Xavier naturally observes from the bathroom door. I pretend I don't see him as I get back into bed. Covers pulled high, I turn on my side. Facing the half of the room *away* from his side of the bed.

Oh my God, we have *sides* of the bed. Like an old married couple. No, *not* like that. *Nothing* like that. At all.

In fact, I'll just scoot to the middle of the bed. There. See? No sides. Ha.

But... maybe he'll think I'm trying to initiate something with him. Which I am *not*.

I wiggle back over to my side.

I scrupulously do not look over at him to see what he might think of all these odd acrobatics.

I settle in and freeze in place. Nothing to see here. I've fallen asleep. Just like that. I've suddenly mastered the art of falling asleep in zero point two seconds. I try to regulate my breaths.

Totally convincing.

The light flips off.

Ha. Completely pulled it off.

The bed dips with Xavier's weight.

I hold my breath. No, damn it, don't hold your breath. Regular—in, out, in, out.

A big, muscled arm snakes around me and he pulls me so that I'm sandwiched against his body. "You sure are damn cute, precious."

Precious.

Not *pet*.

My eyes are already shut but I squeeze them tight at the swell of emotion his simple words elicit.

He's hard against my backside.

I wait for him to start touching me.

I wait for *something*.

Precious.

His chest moves up and down behind me and within several minutes, there's only the light sound of his quiet snores filling the room.

But for me, sleep is a long time in coming.

14

I continue my riding lessons.

And Xavier continues *not* touching me at night.

Well, of course, he's Xavier, so a day doesn't pass without him having his hands all over me.

But no intimate touches.

No more orgasms.

It's because of the period. It's got to be. He has some weird hang up about it. And I'm too chicken shit to ask him to explain. And anyway, I'm *happy* about the new order of things. I never wanted him touching me. This is all a good thing, dammit.

It's just the not knowing that's driving me crazy, that's all. That's the only reason I'm glad when my period peters off.

Right?

Right, Mel, you just keep telling yourself that.

Okay, so let's just ignore that snarky bitch who runs around inside my head sometimes trying to tell me inconvenient truths. She doesn't know what the hell she's talking about.

Anyway, Xavier's more than aware when I'm all done with the crimson tide. To my eternal mortification, he hasn't let one opportunity pass to change out my tampons—seriously, wtf? But whatever, it just means he's perfectly informed when I'm back in ship-shape order.

That night, baths resume instead of the shower.

He goes back to a more extensive massage, welcome after my week of more and more strenuous outings on Sugar, and then Pioneer. Xavier likes to take Samson out for our daily ride and it's safer for me to be riding Pioneer since he's a gelding.

Xavier says that he'll geld Samson soon but that he didn't want to add stress to the stallion upon his arrival. The way his eyes flick to me when he says this, I wonder if he also simply didn't want anyone else out on the ranch when I was first here.

Anyway, the bath tonight is extra hot and my entire body relaxes into the water as Xavier massages up my thigh.

Then finally, oh God, *finally,* his hand dips between my legs.

My back arches in anticipation.

My sex clenches up and my stomach swoops, going liquid.

But after a brief, efficient rub over my pussy lips, his hand moves on.

I just stare at him.

Because again, wtf?

If he feels my stare, he doesn't react. Not even to return my gaze. He just continues on washing me like everything's right as rain. The rest of the bath continues. And then ends. Nothing.

Nada.

The water's draining and my libido is left fully on edge.

I splash the little bit of water left in the bath in frustration. "What?" I look up at him. "What am I doing wrong?"

Eyebrow lift.

I huff out a loud breath and lift my hands in the air. "I don't get it. What do you want from me?"

"I told you clearly what I want."

He steps out of the bath, his glorious ass flexing right in my face. I have the urge to take a bite out of it. Teach *him* what it feels like to be teased and forever on edge without relief.

Then his words register. He's told me what he wants.

Son of a bitch.

He wants me to beg for his cock.

No way. Absolutely *not*. Keep dreaming, mister.

I stand up and stubbornly hold my face away from him as he dries my body with the same meticulous attention that he does every night.

Then it's off to bed where he spoons me tight, slinging his thigh over mine, arm cinched tightly underneath my breast.

"I'm hot," I say and try to wriggle out from under his hold.

His only response is to throw the covers off and then draw me close again.

Well dammit, now I'm chilly. I roll my eyes. I know I won't be for long, though, because I usually have the covers tossed off by morning anyway since he's like a giant damn heater behind me.

I let out a huff of frustration.

The bastard behind me has the audacity to give me one of his low, throaty chuckles. His hand skirts down my abdomen and whispers across my sex before retracting again. His hips press forward and I can feel him rock hard against my ass. My sex clenches reflexively.

"All you have to do is say the word." His breath is warm on the back of my ear.

I turn my face into the pillow and I grit my teeth.

God, does he think I'm some desperate tramp? I'm not going to be begging him for sex. I never wanted any of this in the first place! He's just freaking insane. Absolutely out of his gourd.

So why the hell is your body so damn keyed up if he's the crazy one?

Shut up!

I plump my pillow, punching it into shape, and then pull it close and try to fall asleep.

Annoyingly, like happens so often lately, sleep is a long time coming.

WE'RE in bed a few nights later, still at the same impasse, when yet again, I'm having difficulty sleeping. I fell asleep for a while, but then some noise must have woken me, and now I can't get back to sleep.

My stupid brain won't shut up.

I think because when I woke up, I was turned around, my body chest to chest with Xavier, my head nestled into the crook of his neck.

Unconsciously, that's the position I sought in sleep. I couldn't have placed myself more vulnerably.

Does it mean something? That even though I'm fighting him so hard when I'm awake, subconsciously I've already given up?

Or is 'given up' the wrong phrase? Somehow, down deep, do I, like the horses, ultimately find Xavier trustworthy?

Don't they say that animals have an innate sense about these things? Like, the fact that the horses take so well to him might indicate he actually is a good person? Or am I just making that up and an evil person can trick horses just as well if he's a master of manipulation?

God, I'm *so* confused. I look toward the ceiling in the dark room. What time is it anyway? Two a.m.? Three? Just a few hours before Xavier will be dragging us out of bed for the morning.

I shut my eyes again, determined to get back to sleep. The days are long and punishing on my body. I'll be regretting it tomorrow if I don't get all the rest I can tonight. I pull the covers up tight.

I'm cold without the contact of Xavier's body but I couldn't bring myself to snuggle back up against him after finding myself in that position on waking.

I settle into my pillow again.

"Stop!" Xavier suddenly cries out. "Don't open the gate!"

Then he swings out, narrowly missing me as I pull back out of the way of his massive arm. He writhes in bed and in the dim light of the full moon streaming in our window, I can see that his face is a scrunched as if he's in terrible pain.

"Xavier," I call his name, alarmed.

He continues thrashing in the bed sheets.

"Xavier," I try again.

"No!" he shouts, so loud it almost hurts my ears.

I reach forward and grab his shoulders.

Wrong move.

Immediately he's on top of me, body-slamming me into the bed.

"Xavier!" I cry. "Stop, it's me!" I claw at his arms holding me down. "It's Pet!"

His eyes have been open yet distant, like he's watching some other movie playing out in front of him. But suddenly he blinks and he jumps back from me, looking down at his hands in horror, then at me.

"What—" he starts, then stops. He looks confused and bewildered like he's a small child who's woken up somewhere he's never been before. It's heartbreaking to see in a man usually so absolutely in control.

I crawl across the bed to his side.

"Shh, you're okay. You just had a nightmare. You're okay now." I draw him into my arms, pressing his head to my chest. He wraps his arms around my waist and clutches me close like I'm the only solid thing in his world.

I lay my cheek on his head, inhaling the scent of his simple, clean-smelling shampoo and enjoying the texture of his springing curly hair. I run my fingers through his hair and for once, he actually lets me. I revel in the feel of him.

"What was the nightmare about?" I ask after several minutes. "Sometimes it helps to talk it through?"

And God, I only realize after I ask how much I want him to tell me, to trust me enough to start sharing his secrets with me.

Instead he pulls away. "It was nothing. Let's get back to sleep. Just a couple hours before we have to be up."

He tugs me back to lie down with him.

In control again.

I can't help my frown.

For a few minutes, I was seeing beneath that damn shield he keeps up around himself at all times.

He's so big on trust, but he's never willing to give me anything of himself in return. How is that fair?

And you? What have you been giving him lately?

I scoff back at my stupid internal voice. I've given him *so* much. I eat from his damn hand. I do all the stupid farm chores he asks of me. I don't complain when he tells me to do this or do that.

But, what about you? *Have you really given him* you, *your real, true self?*

Well hell no, I haven't. That was the whole point. I was always going to keep the core of me to myself. He was never supposed to be able to touch it.

So I guess I shouldn't balk when he's not willing to reciprocate or do so in return.

Then why is there this stinging ache in my chest at the space between us that feels more and more like an empty chasm?

I barely sleep a wink and am tired all the next day.

But after seeing Xavier so vulnerable the night before, I can't help looking at him in a different light.

There are demons in this man's past, I'm sure of it. And if I just knew what they were, I bet I could understand him, and even what he wants of me, so much more clearly.

Now—how to find them out. That's the real question.

One that I'm no closer to figuring out by the end of the week.

Any question I ask only gets deflected with more instructions for riding lessons. And I swear he's intentionally trying to drive me crazy by dressing more provocatively every day.

Like, by midday, he always takes off his denim button up so that he's left with nothing but his white tank top underneath. Which reveals acres and acres of his bronzed, muscled skin. And really, are all those muscles necessary?

I mean, yes, he's hauling around fifty-pound bags of feed and giant water buckets, but when he gets sweaty, which is inevitable on the hot summer days, the tank top just gets soaked through and I can see the definition of every single one of his abs.

It's just not fair on a girl's libido.

Which God, seems overcharged all the sudden.

I swear, I don't know what the *hell* is going on, but all I can seem to think about, 24/7, is jumping him. When he mounts Samson in the mid-afternoon, my thoughts are all—*damn, I wish he would just fucking mount* me *already.*

When he's grooming Tornado at night, I'm like, *uh huh, honey, that's right, why don't you turn a brush on me and rub me down sooooooooo good because I've been a dirty girl.*

Real helpful thoughts like that.

He does nothing to make the situation better. Always being so goddamn handsy. Whenever he passes by me in the stable, he never forgoes an opportunity to grab my ass. When reaching for a brush, if there's a chance to brush my boob, he takes it.

Throughout the day, I'll feel his heated stare and glance up to see him checking out my assets. Yeah, Xavier's not big on subtlety.

I'd at least get off on the fact that I'm torturing him as much as me but while every day I feel more and more like a cat in heat, he seems to grow calmer and more serene. I'd think he's sneaking away to jerk off, but we're around each other all day long and I'd know. How can a man have that much discipline?!

It's enough to drive a girl batshit.

Two weeks into this interminable dance, I feel hornier than ever, which is making me snippy as hell.

"Make sure to give Sugar extra water when we get back," Xavier reminds me for the umpteenth time as he helps me down from Sugar. She and Pioneer drop their noses and start to munch on the tall grass underneath a tree that shades us from the punishing summer heat. We rode these two today because he taught Samson a new skill this morning and felt it was enough for the stallion to take in in a single day. So he took Pioneer for our daily ride. We've been exploring farther and farther out on his property each day.

Today our halfway point is a small ridge where there's some tree cover to drink water and let the horses graze before turning back.

The horses are good and sweaty from the ride in the heat.

"I got it," I snap, covering my eyes with my hand as I step out from under the shade to look out at the endless acres of land beyond the ridge. "I got it the first twelve times you told me," I mutter under my breath. It really is beautiful out here. Nothing but more and more land as far as the eye can see. Frankly, it's a little overwhelming sometimes for a city girl like me.

Xavier lifts his eyebrows as he stares at me from underneath the shade of the tree. I've come to know this can mean many things. It can be the eyebrow-lift of amusement. Or surprise. But this one is in warning because of my snippy tone.

I don't fucking care.

I'm hot and horny and he's the bastard not taking care of my needs.

I lift my eyebrow exaggeratedly as I rejoin him in the shade and take a long swallow of water from one of the bottles. "What?" I ask. "Yeah, see, I can waggle my eyebrow, too. And you don't have to tell me to do every single thing a million times. I'm a smart girl. I hear you the first time."

His jaw sets and he takes a step toward me.

"Oh no," I mock in a high-pitched voice, dropping the bottle to the ground behind me. "Is Master going to spank me?" I lift my hands up in pretend fright. "Have I been a bad pet?"

His eyes narrow and I feel a thrill shoot up my spine.

I'm poking the beast. It's reckless and I know it. But the past couple weeks of inactivity have made me thoughtlessly desperate for something—anything—to start moving this whole thing along again.

Xavier steps forward and grasps me, locking my arms against my body. "Careful, Pet."

"Or what?" I breathe out, my heart thumping furiously, my eyes searching his face. I don't know what I'm looking for—affection? lust? something... more?—but I hunt for it all the same.

He jerks my head forward and whispers low in my ear. "Or the Big Bad Wolf just might eat you up."

I laugh a shaky laugh. "He doesn't seem so big or bad to me lately."

He yanks my head back and I can see that was the wrong thing to say. Or maybe it was the right thing to say, considering what he does next.

Because he drags me over a few steps, then he sweeps my legs out from under me. Next thing I know, I'm landing on the soft grass.

Then he's yanking my boots off and my jeans are around my ankles.

And then finally, oh God, *finally*, that delicious, heavenly, perfect mouth is back where God always intended it to be—licking and tonguing all around my clitoris.

After almost three weeks without any action down there, it feels like all my nerve endings come alight at once. I gasp out a high-pitched squeal of pleasure and my hips buck up against his mouth.

Which has his hands coming to firmly grip my hips, holding me in place exactly where he wants me. All those muscles I was so admiring earlier sure are a damn nuisance now when all I want is to ground up and into him.

"More!" I beg, writhing underneath his hold. "Xavier." His name is a gasp. "More!"

His tongue licks long and deep all the way up my slit at my plea and I quake down to my bones in response.

Oh my God, no one will ever know my body as well as Xavier. Ever. I'm doomed forever because of this man.

But then rational thoughts get dim because he tongues around and around and one of his hand leaves my hips to start exploring my lips. One finger slips inside. Then a second. They press furtively at first, just a little bit of explorative pressure.

Little whining noises escape my throat, especially when his elbows force my legs wide open. His tongue withdraws from my clit and he pulls his fingers out of my pussy. But only long enough for him to make his tongue hard and long so he can plunge it in and out of my entrance in imitation of... of...

Oh God. My sex tries to clench around him but he's already gone, licking back up to my clitoris.

But he's not suckling me or even leaning in with any kind of satisfying pressure. I wriggle underneath him, looking up at the swaying branches overhead.

Please. *Oh God*, it feels so good, but I need *more*. The fire he's stoking—*oh Jesus it's*— I can't even— I had no idea how much I'd been missing it. But I'm liquid fire. The need is all consuming. His touch. His tongue. His heat.

I've never needed anything more in my life.

And.

Then.

He.

Stops.

As in, completely stops.

He pulls away from me, stands up, and starts walking away toward his horse like he's ready to mount up and head back home.

Just leaving me there, spread-eagled and half naked on the grass underneath the fucking tree in the middle of nowhere.

"Wha—" I scramble to a sitting position, shooting daggers that would kill a lesser man. "Get the hell back here!"

He turns to me.

And dares to give me the goddamned eyebrow lift.

"Is there something you wanted?" he asks innocently.

Son of a mother-fucking bastard piece of—

But then my inner tirade stops.

Because it hits me.

There never was any other choice.

We were always going to end up here.

And right now, tortured and on the edge of the sweetest release, with him so mouthwatering, even if part of me does still want to strangle him, I'm all right with that fact.

It seems stupid that I fought it so long.

Still, I can't help adding a bit of sass as I kick off my jeans and drop my legs open even wider.

"Fuck me, Xavier, please, I'm *begging* you." I blink my eyes prettily and put my hands underneath my chin like I'm praying. "Oh please won't you put that glorious cock inside me and fuck me because I simply cannot live another moment without it?"

His eyes narrow, but he reaches behind him and in one swift motion, jerks his tank top over his head.

My eyes widen at seeing his huge, sweat-slicked chest on display. I know I see him mostly naked every night during our baths—he's taken to wearing boxers in the tub, like even *seeing* all of him is a privilege I have to earn—but the sheer size of him never ceases to amaze me. Where the hell do they grow men like him? Did he accidentally swallow some Miracle-Gro as a child or something?

His pants come off next. And boxers.

Oh, wow. He's fully hard. Like, *fully*. I really haven't seen... that part of him since... well, for a long while now. And in the full bright late afternoon sun, just, holy baby *Jesus*.

It's long and pulsing and pointed straight at me.

Xavier stalks my direction, gaze dark, his mouth a hard line.

Suddenly all my bravado from moments ago dissipates like a popped bubble.

Um, can I retract my former request and forget I said anything? We'll just go back to the whole grooming and dinner routine like nothing ever happened? How about that? That's sounding swell right about now.

Xavier drops on top of me like I imagine a lion might descend on a kill—swift and with dark intent.

"Why don't we take it slow since—"

His cock is at my entrance and pressing in before I can get another word out.

Oh. Or well, you know, we could just get right down to it and—

"Oh!" I exclaim when he shoves right in, grabbing my ass for better leverage as he drags his cock in and out several times. A low growl rumbles throughout his chest as he hovers over me, holding himself up by one arm propped on the ground.

All my breath is expelled from my lungs at the sudden fullness of his cock. The feeling of him—oh God, he's *inside me*—is both completely foreign and in the back of my mind rings a note of familiarity. He's the only one who's ever been in this position, but God, so much has happened since he first...

He drags back out in a slow stroke and then with aching attention pushes in. The grass under my back is scratchy, but all I can focus on is him. He, too, seems to be concentrating all his attention on the feel of the head of his cock as it presses in and out of my entrance. And the look on his face—it's not one of conquering like I might have expected after all this time, him finally getting his way.

Damn him, his features are open and awed. Like he's regarding the whole experience with reverence.

When he opens his eyes and our gazes lock, my sex clenches around him. His cock jumps inside me in response.

No, this is nothing like the first time.

With the hand not propping himself up, he continues to clutch and massage my hip. He only lets go briefly so he can grab my thigh to urge my leg up and around him. I lift it happily, eager to lock my body around his and ground myself in any way possible.

The feelings he elicits from me. Oh *God,* it's insane.

Every stroke seems to take me higher. He swivels and grinds his pelvis against my clit, but more than that, especially when he grabs my leg again and lifts it up to his shoulder, he drives in at an angle that has me gasping and my eyes popping open in shock.

That—holy shit—what *is* that? I've never—

He hits the same spot with his next in stroke and I swear, my eyes roll back in my head.

"Don't— stop," I whimper. "Never— fucking— stop!"

Whereas before his thrusts had been slow and somewhat measured, now he starts fucking me with abandon. Every time, hitting that spot so deep, deep inside me. Along with the friction at my clit, oh God, I can't, I can't—

My fingers claw at the grass. It's so—

A high-pitched keening noise starts in my throat.

"Xavier, Xavier!" I call out, almost scared by the intensity of everything I'm feeling. It's too much. All too much. But oh, don't stop. Never stop. Never, ever, *ever* stop.

"Eyes," Xavier calls out. "On me."

My eyes have been flicking around wildly but I finally focus up on him. The wind whips up, whistling across the ridge. His nostrils flare and his stern face is drawn with strain as he thrusts and thrusts and thrusts.

"Precious," is all he says and then he leans down, drawing me close to him with his hands slipping underneath my armpits and wrapping around my shoulders from behind. He begins to fuck me like a man possessed.

My orgasm hits on a wild high and continues while he thrusts in and out and in and out. He pushes in and holds it for one long moment while I'm still at the height of my high.

He's coming. Inside me. We're coming at the same time. I cry out and tears leak down my cheeks.

I abandon the saddle blanket and wrap my arms around him, clutching him instead.

Never stop. Never let go. Ever.

He pumps inside me several more times.

By the time he pulls away, the devastation at his loss goes so much deeper than the physical separation as he pulls out of me.

Because I know there's no way out of it now.

I'm going to be absolutely wrecked by this man.

15

I stop fighting.

I give myself up to it.

To him.

For two weeks, it's nothing but eating and fucking and taking care of the horses. And then more fucking. Always the fucking. It's like once we've gotten a taste of each other, we can't stop. When we wake up in bed, in the middle of the night, mid-morning when our initial chores are done.

Anytime, anywhere.

He plays my body like a finely tuned instrument and only he knows the melody.

One morning, when he makes French toast out of thick slices of bread, I'm salivating and attentive at his feet. I lick the syrup off his fingers after he feeds me a bite, tongue teasing as I blink up at him seductively.

He manages to last for a whole half a piece of French toast before hauling me onto the table and fucking my brains out, breakfast forgotten. I mewl like a cat as my orgasm hits, scrabbling at the table for purchase.

He thrusts even more vigorously, riding me through the first and right into a second. Turns out, he has even more energy in the mornings than at the end of the day.

I'm sweaty, satisfied, and breathless when he pulls my jeans back up and returns me to my cushion at his feet. I lay my head on his thigh, still recovering, and he strokes my hair back from my face.

Back in the city I always got it cut promptly each month to keep the bob fresh, but in the month and a half I've been here, it's started growing out. I'm constantly pushing it behind my ears to keep it out of my face.

Xavier hasn't said anything about it, but I think he'd prefer it longer.

And suddenly I'm very keen to conform to whatever Xavier might like best.

Even a few weeks ago the thought would have disturbed me. Outright disgusted me. But as I nestle my cheek against him and let out a contented sigh, now I wonder, just, why? Why was I pushing so hard against him?

I can't remember the last time I felt this happy or content. This free.

And yes, I'm clear-headed enough to realize how ridiculously contradictory that sounds.

But it's true all the same.

I feel liberated.

Like I have no worries in the world. I don't have to worry about anything. Xavier's taken it all for me.

I laugh at the realization, feeling a strange giddiness and press my face into his thigh. My whole life has been a mad-dog fight. For grades. Then for the best internships. Then to be better than all my male colleagues to get ahead at work. And for what? What did all that get me? I was never really *happy*. It was all about just waking up again the next day and striving more for the next hurdle to overcome.

But now?

I think this feeling flooding me is genuine *happiness*.

Here of all places.

With Xavier.

Because of Xavier.

I raise my head and grin up at him. He pauses stroking my hair, his expression wary and a little befuddled.

I laugh and stand up, then climb up into his lap face to face, straddling him on the chair. I take his face in my hands. The burned part feels smooth and cool to the touch. My finger traces down between the raised ridges of one of the spider lines that runs across his cheek and he reaches up to grab my wrist. He shakes his head back and forth.

I purse my lips but then say what I haven't been able to stop thinking about all morning, double now after our breakfast table quickie. I can't help the grin from taking over as I lean my face into his, searching his eyes.

"We might have just made a baby," I whisper. For the first time in my life, the concept doesn't immediately send me into a crazed panic either.

I'm not sure why exactly, except that I know it's because of Xavier. Everything's changed because of this giant who just barged in and inserted himself in the center of my life. Or rather, he stole me away to his world and like a sun, my life now revolves around him. There's a voice shouting in the back of my head, *unhealthy! Unhealthy!*

But when his eyes flare at my words and his hands drop to my waist, I don't care.

Especially when next, a goddamned miracle happens.

He kisses me.

And not on my ear or my neck or one of the other hundred places his mouth has explored before.

No, I mean he kisses me on the lips.

It's not just some gentle peck either.

He kisses me on the lips and immediately goes for the kill, pushing through the seam of my lips with his thrusting tongue.

I can't help clamping my legs tighter around him and kissing him back.

I've been kissed before. A fair amount even. I was a virgin but still curious. There were a few boyfriends that I kissed a *lot* before I broke up with because I didn't want them getting ideas that all the kissing meant I was willing to go further.

But no kiss in my life has come close to anything like this one.

As with everything else, Xavier immediately takes command of the kiss. And it doesn't just involve his tongue and lips. No, his whole body is tense and alive underneath mine. His hands grip and knead my waist with a desperate intensity. He kisses me with the ferocity of a man bent on devouring his prey.

And me? I might be happier than I ever imagined, being under this man's power, but that does not mean I'm about to become some meek little delicate flower.

Hell no.

I give back as good as I get.

My tongue tangles with his and I thrust back into his mouth, as eager to taste and explore him as he is me.

I'm no longer satisfied with the façade he's been willing to show me thus far. Dammit, I want it all. I want to know the name of the first horse he ever owned and what his goddamned favorite color is. I want to know what haunts his sleep and what makes him happy and sad and everything in between.

So I kiss him back like my life depends on it. Because maybe if I'm lucky, this is the first chink in his armor and I'm paving my first inroad to getting to know this eccentric and, sure, a bit fucked-up man.

But maybe he's *my* eccentric, fucked-up man? Or he could be?

Xavier's hands travel up my body, pausing to squeeze my breasts before coming to hold the sides of my face again.

And God, him cupping my face while kissing me with those soul-deep kisses? It's enough to have my stomach dropping out beneath the floor.

I can't help the low moan that rumbles out of my throat. I know I just came twice but I'm already primed and ready again.

"The animals will be fine for one day, surely. How about we take the day off?" I look up at him hopefully.

But Xavier pulls away, shaking his head in amusement, eyes still centered on my lips.

I try to lean forward to recapture his lips with mine. "Then how about just for the morning. They'll be okay for *one* little morning. Think of it as letting them sleep in."

He laughs full out, halting my progression by grabbing my upper arms. "Horses barely sleep. I never break routine. And," his eyes flick up to the clock on the wall behind me, "we're already late as it is."

Then he's standing up, hauling me with him as he goes.

He ignores my pouting lip. "Would it make a difference if I begged?" I try.

I get one of his rare grins at that. Along with a smack on my ass. "By all means, go ahead and find out."

I put on my prettiest pleading face. "Please, Xavier, can we postpone chores so that I can feel your delicious cock filling me up *so* good?"

His jaw tenses and eyes darken at my words but then he smiles and smacks my ass again. "No."

And with that single word of dismissal, he turns and heads for the door.

My mouth drops open. "No? What do you mean, no?" I demand, stalking after him.

He holds out an arm, gesturing for me to go out the door ahead of him. As if he's some gentleman.

I cross my arms and glare at him.

"Pet, don't test me. Remember who's the Master here. Nothing's changed. I make the rules and you obey them."

I expel a huge breath of air. Nothing's changed? Nothing's *changed*?

Okay, good to know that even in my new state of relative bliss, he can still piss me off like no one else ever before in my whole life.

"But you said all I had to do was beg," I remind him, both genuinely confused and barely suppressing the urge to flip him off. "I'm following *your* rule."

"That was a one-time offer. You don't get to simply snap your fingers and I drop my pants at your beck and call." He says it so calmly.

"Oh, but *you* can snap your fingers and *I* do?"

His eyes don't even flicker once. "Now you're getting it."

I scoff in outrage, throw my hands up in the air, and then stalk off in the direction of the stables. It's barely sunrise, light just filtering over the horizon, dew wet on the ground.

I walk as quickly as I can, but annoyingly, Xavier is at my side within two strides, easily keeping stride. Stupid man with his stupid long legs.

But then he reaches down, takes my hand, and intertwines our fingers.

And a dumb, girlish part inside me squees, *zomg, he's holding my hand!*

"We couldn't waste any more time inside," Xavier finally explains, leading us around the stable, "because we have to bring Hellfire in from the pasture and get him ready for the farrier."

I look over at him. Why couldn't he have just said that from the start? Frustrating man. I decide to let it go. At least he's explaining now. "What's that?"

"A farrier?" He glances down at me, then shakes his head. "It's easy to forget how green you are sometimes." My teeth start to grit, but then he finishes his thought, "—you're getting so good with the horses."

Oh. Well. That sorta makes me glow inside.

"A farrier specializes in taking care of horse hooves," he continues, "trimming them and putting shoes on if they need them. Hellfire's got chronic laminitis and it flares every summer. The farrier trims his hooves and I've been packing his ankles with ice packs to try to make him more comfortable."

I nod. I've seen Xavier attending to the horse morning and night.

We round the stable and head toward the back pasture.

"Is it serious?"

The grim look on Xavier's face tells me all I need to know. "We've been keeping it under control for several years now."

We crest a small hill and the back pasture comes into view. Paddyshack is standing near the back fence.

Xavier drops my hand and starts running before I realize anything's wrong.

I head after him. "What? What is it?" But then I get it. I don't see Holy Hellfire anywhere in the pasture.

At first I think it means that he got out somehow. That he broke through the fence.

Xavier's long-legged stride has him all the way across the field by the time I'm only halfway and when I see him drop to his knees in the tall grass, it dawns on me.

No, Hellfire didn't go anywhere at all.

I pump my arms, determined to get to them. Xavier's hands are raised to his head as he bends over the horse, who I can now see is laying down.

Maybe he's okay? Just resting? I rarely see the horses down like that, but from what Xavier was saying, Hellfire's feet were hurting so maybe he just—

When I finally get up to them, I breathe out a huge breath of relief.

Hellfire is *alive*.

His eyes are wide open and his nostrils flare out with each breath. Definitely one hundred percent alive!

I look over to Xavier, excited, but he still looks absolutely devastated.

My head snaps back to look at the horse.

"What?" I ask Xavier. "Is he sick? But you said the foot specialist is coming today. Is it something else? Can you call a regular vet to come, too?"

Xavier shakes his head, his gaze locked on Holy Hellfire, eyebrows dropped low in sorrow. "It's the laminitis." He reaches out and gently runs his hand down the horse's mane like he's bestowing a benediction. "He's in too much pain. It's finally time."

"Time?" My eyes flick back and forth between Xavier and the horse. "Time for what?"

Xavier closes his eyes and bows his head. "Time to put him down."

"What!" I take a stumbling step backward. How can Xavier even tell he's in pain?

Though looking closer, even I can see that Holy Hellfire's eyes are glazed and searching wildly. He only calms momentarily when Xavier's hand strokes down his mane again. Still, it's obvious he's in some sort of distress.

I haven't spent much time with the elderly horse, preferring instead to dote on Sugar and the others on my grooming roster, but I know that other than Samson, Hellfire is the one Xavier spends most of his day with.

I thought he was just spoiling the horse because he was a favorite.

But was it because he knew this day was coming?

"Go to the bedroom and call the vet from the phone inside my desk, top left-hand drawer. Here's the key." He reaches inside his pocket and draws out his keyring. He unclips a carabiner with the single key and hands it to me. "Speed dial one. Just push star, 1. That'll get you the vet. Tell him Xavier Kent needs him right now for Holy Hellfire. He'll know what it means. Then feed and water the other horses."

He lets go of the key the second our fingers make contact. Like he can't stand to touch me right now. He turns his head away, his focus going completely back to Hellfire.

I stand there a moment, imagining this glorious horse in his prime, refusing to budge when the top trainers tried to make him race, a regal legacy flowing through his blood and sinew—because he had a willfulness and stubbornness to match.

"Go!" Xavier snaps, all but roaring at me.

Both Hellfire and I startle at his abrupt tone and Xavier immediately starts murmuring how sorry he is for yelling.

To the horse.

Not to me.

Considering the circumstances, I let it pass. I turn and hurry across the field, trying not to focus on my smarting feelings. Xavier's hurting. It seems impossible anything could rattle the man who always has it all under control.

But every day I'm learning more about him, aren't I?

First thing I do is run up to the house and then to the third floor, key clutched in my hand. I open the desk where he indicated and there, lying inside the otherwise empty drawer, is a phone. It's an older model, though it is detachable. It sits in its charging cradle. I pull out the receiver, staring at it with an awed kind of reverence.

Technology. A communication device.

I look over my shoulder like this has all been some elaborate test to see what I'll do once given my first chance at contacting the outside world.

But no, of course there's no one there.

Then I remember the cameras he had watching me the first days I was here. Has he set up cameras in here? Are they recording me even as I hesitate holding the receiver, looking around like an idiot?

While Holy Hellfire suffers out in the pasture.

My hand immediately lunches for the number keypad. Still, I stop where my finger hovers over the star button.

This could be your chance. Xavier is distracted by the horse. You could call someone. Tell them about what's happened.

But who would I call?

Most of my friends back in New York were more of acquaintances than close friends. And even if I could call someone, the thought of going back to that life...

I frown. Wasn't it just this morning that I was thinking how much more fulfilled and happy I am here with Xavier than I was back in New York?

But God, maybe that's just Stockholm Syndrome talking. That's a real thing. I read a whole *New Yorker* article about it once.

I look back down at the phone.

The only person I would have called would be my dad.

Dad.

I blink. God, what am I even thinking? Xavier shows me a picture of him with a paper every week, looking hale and hearty, but Xavier's unspoken threat to him still stands. If I try to get away, then Xavier will... Xavier will *what*? Let Dad be *killed*?

God, would Xavier really do that? Is he capable of...?

No, I shake my head. He kept his promise. He's been sending pictures of me to Dad, too. I never know when he'll snap them. Sometimes I catch him with his camera phone out, other times I'm completely unaware until I ask to see what he sent Dad that day. In every picture I look happy, carefree even. Riding Sugar, a wide smile on my face. My brow knit in concentration as I stand over the stove, trying out a new recipe. Glancing up at Xavier.

In response, Dad looks less stressed out in the pictures I get in return. I know he must be confused and worried still but at least he knows I'm healthy and not being abused. That I'm even... happy?

I've just let myself get so caught up in all of— I press my hand to my forehead. How can I even *start* to justify any of this? Is it a betrayal of Dad to actually be happy? To forget what brought me here?

But then my stomach squeezes. Because the image of Xavier's devastated face as he crouched over Holy Hellfire flashes in front of my eyes.

And damn it all to hell, I press the number for the vet.

∽

DOING the rounds with all the horses takes about an hour on my own. My arms are killing me from hauling the feed around by myself.

I hurry back to the house and only have about five minutes to spare before I see the truck kicking up dust as it drives up the dirt road toward the ranch.

I jog outside. The sun is fully up now, but it's still insanely early. I can't believe how people out here—wherever *here* is, all keep such insane hours. When the vet answered my call earlier, he sounded bright eyed and bushy tailed and not as if I was waking him from a dead sleep. Even though it was only 5:45 in the morning.

As the truck pulls to a stop, a large blue 4x4 that's maybe a decade or so old, I glance down at the license plates.

Well, look at that. Unless the doc is randomly sporting out-of-state plates, I've been holed up in the state of Wyoming for the past almost two months.

I think I expected him to be an old country doctor, maybe pushing sixty or something. Anything but the tall, blond, mid-to-late-thirties man who steps down from the cab of the truck with a large medical bag in tow, eyes interested as he looks me up and down.

"Howdy," he says. "I'm Hunter. Hunter Dawkins. You the one who called about Hellfire?"

I nod, not knowing how to take in this outsider to the odd bubble that Xavier's built around me. Seeing another person feels, I don't know… forbidden.

He strides toward me and extends one of his large, tanned hands in my direction.

I shake it, trying to force my lips up in a semblance of a smile. *God, act human, Mel. Have you really forgotten what civilized person etiquette is in such a short time?*

Maybe I have. The thing is, I just can't stop thinking every second —how would Xavier want me to behave around this guy?

Which is disturbing all on its own.

I drop his hand and turn to walk around the house to the pastures. "This way."

He follows me but like Xavier, his long legs quickly have him at my side. He also seems to know his way around the ranch and doesn't seem to need my guidance.

"Haven't seen you around here before."

I don't look over at him even though I can feel his curious gaze on me.

"Nope," I answer without elaboration.

We walk in silence for a few moments, then he's pressing again. "So, you know Xavier long?"

"A little while. You?" I look over at him. His eyes are very blue. With those eyes, his blond hair, and the whole rugged cowboy thing he's got going on, I imagine he does well with the ladies out here in the middle of nowhere. Clean him up and put him in a suit and tie and he's the kind of handsome I would have gone for once upon a time.

But now? I give him the cursory once over like he did me when he first stepped out of the truck. Wide chest, slim hips, lean thighs that are snugly hugged by well-fitting Levis... but nada, I got nothing. Not even an ounce of attraction.

"I've known Xavier for maybe five years now. Ever since he retired from active duty."

Active... like the military? I look up in surprise but don't know how to get more answers without revealing my ignorance about all things Xavier. Even as I'm dying to pump Hunter for info.

But then I remember Holy Hellfire lying out in the pasture in pain. And Xavier, clutching his head. His face knotted in devastation.

God, my brain is such a fucking jumble. I can't make heads or tails of things. Of what I want.

We pass the stable and I point on ahead. "You can get there faster than me if you hurry. Xavier was really upset. He thought the horse was in a lot of pain."

Hunter nods but doesn't move. He stares at me hard. "You got a name?"

When I smile this time, it's genuine but measured because I can't get my mind off Xavier. "Sure do." I nod out toward the pasture. "Hurry up."

Hunter tips a non-existent hat toward me. "Ma'am."

By the time I catch up, Hunter is examining the bottom of Holy Hellfire's back leg. Xavier's still at his head, all but hugging the horse as he whispers to him and strokes his mane.

"How is he?" My hands knot into fists in fear of the answer.

Seeing Xavier like this, on his knees and so obviously in pain for his horse is almost impossible to stomach. I want to drop to the ground and hold *him* in my arms, but I don't know if he would welcome the gesture or brush me off.

Neither of them answers me.

Hunter's evaluation takes about another five minutes. Apparently it's a fairly open and shut case. When he looks over Xavier's way, there's an apologetic sorrow in his face.

No. Oh no.

I glare at the vet, willing him to have another answer for us.

Hunter's eyes flick briefly toward me, then focus back on Xavier. "I'm sorry. You did everything right. He's just been fighting this too long. With his age, it was bound to—"

"Don't give me your bullshit spiel." Xavier interrupts. "Just do it." His jaw is rigid, and he stares at the ground as he says it.

"Do you want some time to—?"

"Do it," Xavier says sharply. "I don't want him suffering any longer than he has to."

Hunter nods solemnly and opens his black bag.

I turn my face away. I can't watch.

A few minutes later, I hear Hunter say, "All right, it should be less than a minute now."

I force myself to turn back around. Hunter's putting a large syringe back in his bag.

Xavier has laid down beside Hellfire, his long arms wrapped completely around the horse's neck. Hellfire takes one last breath... and then... he's still.

Xavier freezes as well.

Then he presses his forehead to Hellfire's. For a moment, everything's quiet. Is Xavier praying? Communing with Hellfire's spirit as it leaves his body? Or just quietly mourning? Xavier's face is blank, giving nothing away.

And then he lets go of the horse and gets calmly to his feet. He ignores the wet grass stains all over his light-colored work shirt and blue jeans.

"Arrange for the disposal of the carcass, Hunter. Charge my account. Call Kimball and cancel him coming out this morning. I'd appreciate it." Next he looks my direction but not directly at me. Somewhere over the top of my left shoulder. "See to the chores today. No riding, though. That's an order."

Any other day, I might have balked at being ordered around like an errant puppy in front of a stranger, but today all I can do is worry about how weird and detached he's being.

"Xavier," I try, taking a step toward him with my hand out, but he's turned on his heel before I can even get close, striding in the direction of the house.

"Don't take it personally," Hunter says, coming to stand beside me as Xavier stalks off across the field. "Like I said, I've known him for five years. I've tried inviting him out for beers more times than I can count, but he always turns me down. At first I thought it was because he might not like to go out in public because of, ya know." He gestures vaguely toward his face. "So I invited him over for a barbeque at my house, just me and him. We sort of bonded when he took in a stray dog a little while ago. He tried keeping him on the property, but the dog just kept going nuts around the horses. Eventually I adopted the little guy. Thought Xavier might want to come over and visit him. But still nothing. I guess he's just not a people person."

Why the hell is this guy telling me all this? Is he really just trying to make me feel better or is this some sad attempt at flirting?

As if he can read my thoughts, he continues quickly. "My wife would love to have you over. She's always dying for female friends. We met in the city and I dragged her out here to the middle of nowhere because this is where I grew up and always envisioned myself living." He smiles sheepishly. "Turns out the life of a small-town vet in Wyoming isn't quite the sensational adventure I might have made it out to be."

I snort. I can imagine. "I used to live in New York," I offer.

He brightens. "Now you've got to meet her. She's a Boston girl but she's constantly complaining that no one around here has any sophistication."

I offer him a smile even as I look worriedly in the distance at Xavier's retreating back. "I'd like that," I say. Not that I know if Xavier would be up for letting me go out for a social call. Which is bullshit. I frown. Some things need to change around here and some hard conversations need to be had. But not today with everything so screwed up.

I offer an awkward wave. "Look, there's a lot to get done and I'm getting a late start."

"Sure, sure," Hunter says, shifting his medical bag from one hand to the other. He looks back at Hellfire's body. Paddyshack is nosing at the still form and my throat gets tight.

Carcass.

How could Xavier speak so coldly of the horse he was cradling in his arms just moments before? Was it a defense mechanism or can he really just turn off his feelings like a flip of the switch?

"How soon will you be able to..."

Hunter follows my line of sight.

"I'll have someone come remove him later today."

I nod. "Thank you."

"I'll let Janine know to expect your call."

"Oh," my eyes flash up to him in alarm. "I don't know. We're really busy here and I'm not sure when..." My voice drops off. "I'll talk to Xavier about it. But now's just not the time." I look back in the direction Xavier left but he's gone now. "I'd really like to meet her someday, though," I finish lamely.

Hunter looks at me a little curiously but nods. "Okay, then. It's nice to have met you."

"Mel," I say quickly. "My name is Mel."

He gives me a genuine smile at this, then tempers it slightly when he looks behind me, no doubt at Hellfire's prone body. "I'm sorry about the circumstances, but it's a pleasure to have met you, *Mel*."

∽

THE DAY IS HELLISHLY hot and all the horses are uneasy. I'm trying to be as calm around them as possible but it's like they can all sense that's something's off.

And my back aches like a son of a bitch and it's only midday. It turns out doing all the work of a horse farm on your own is incredibly difficult. Ever tried hauling a fifty-pound bag of feed when you yourself weigh less than three times that? I reminded myself to *lift with my legs* too late and hence, my back is killing me.

The horses are restless and not keen to have me being the one releasing them to pasture for the day instead of their beloved Xavier.

I finally go armed with carrots to the last three stalls of the horses that I don't normally groom. Bob gets feisty and kicks the back of his stall, which naturally scares the crap out of me. Makes me appreciate Xavier's number one rule—never approach a horse from behind or when they're pissed off. Pretty sure I'll respect that one for all time after seeing Bob's powerful hind legs give the wood at the back of his stall a pounding so hard the whole stall rattles.

Finally, *finally*, all the horses are fed, watered, and out for the day, which means I can at last go in for lunch and to check on Xavier.

I jog in eagerly toward the house.

Only to find it empty. At least the first floor. I don't know what I expected.

Okay, that's not true. I expected him to be waiting with lunch, ordering me to the floor like a good little pet.

He must be upstairs in his room. I can't exactly imagine Xavier taking the day off. The horses are out so there are stalls to be mucked out now.

Besides, what would he do with a day off? Lie in bed all day? That just doesn't seem to compute. Surf the internet for porn? Ugh, that's plainly a little offensive when I'm right here. Why go to all the trouble of acquiring me if that's what he's into?

Or maybe he left.

He does drive off once every couple weeks on Sundays for several hours to get groceries. But would he really just leave without saying anything?

I jog up the stairs to the third floor. One thing I have to say for all this grueling farm work, it's getting me in insane shape. I've never been so muscular or felt so physically strong in my life.

When I reach the top of the stairs, I see that the door to Xavier's room is shut. These days, he usually only shuts it when we're inside. I try the knob. It's locked.

I knock tentatively.

"Xavier?" I call. "It's me."

Duh. Because there are so many other people out here who would be in his house knocking at his bedroom door.

No answer.

I knock harder. "Xavier, open up. Let's eat lunch."

I wait for several long seconds.

Still nothing.

I knock again, even harder.

"Leave me alone!"

I step back from the door at his roar.

Okay. I swallow hard. So he's home. Good to know.

Then I turn around and run back down the stairs.

16

Xavier stays locked up in his room for four whole days.

Leaving me to do *all* the work of keeping up a horse farm on my own. I drop into bed each night exhausted and heartsick. Sleeping in a bed without his big body beside me feels *wrong* now. Which makes me furious. Come to think of it, pretty much everything makes me furious these days.

Like the motherfucking too-dry tasteless scrambled eggs I shove into my mouth on the morning of the fifth day. I was spacing out while I cooked them, wondering about a certain asshole who's decided he just gets to check out while I'm left here as his *slave* doing all the work of two or three people. He's insane trying to run this place by himself. The horses need exercise and him telling me not to ride them is bullshit.

Well, screw him. If he wants me to obey him, he can goddamned well get his ass out here and tell me himself.

Because I'm out here feeding his goddamned horses all on my own.

Before sunrise, with a flashlight.

I push into the stable and yank on the cord that turns on a couple of lights.

"Good morning. Yep, still just me," I announce. "Your Dad is still being a piss-ant and leaving everything to Auntie Mel. I know, I know, I'm not nearly as entertaining as Mr. Frowny-pants, but you'll survive."

Then I begin the arduous task of feeding and watering everyone.

I approach Lulu's stall. "Don't even give me your attitude this morning, Miss Thang. I promise you I will out-bitch you today."

For once, she just steps back like a good little pony and lets me give her fresh feed and water.

"That's right, you respect your elders."

I'm just standing back up and stepping out of her stall when I feel it.

A cramp.

I cringe and grab my abdomen.

Shit.

I close my eyes and hang my head.

And then all my bravado sweeps out in one swift wave. I slump down on the stable floor and start to cry.

If I'm cramping that means I'm getting my period.

And if I'm getting my period that means I'm not pregnant.

The tears turn to sobs.

Above me, Lulu noses at the top of her stall, making a repeated bump, bump noise. I look up through my tear-heavy lashes and smile at her.

She's picking up on my mood and seems anxious. I pull myself up off the ground. "Thanks, hon. We ladies gotta stick together, huh?" I give her nose an affectionate rub. She leans into me.

She was the last I had to feed, so I decide to head back to the house to rest for a bit before turning them out for the day.

About halfway there, my anger lights back up.

Because screw Xavier.

I do *not* feel like mucking out the damn stalls today. It's back-breaking work and my back always aches already when I'm on the rag. I've been absolutely exhausted the past four nights. I refuse to do all this work by myself for another day.

Yes, Holy Hellfire dying was sad. Devastating even.

But there are nine horses that are still alive who need him.

Not to mention one measly little human woman.

I never asked to be here. He's the one who basically kidnapped me. So he's stuck with me. He wanted to be my goddamned *Master*? Well, he can't just bugger off from the role whenever he feels like it.

I stomp up the stairs. Another brief little cramp hits and I grab my abdomen as I go. Ugh, I don't even want to think about the fact that I'm probably bleeding all over my underwear.

He's got the damn tampons. Another reason to break his stupid door down if I have to. I don't exactly know how I'll accomplish that... but never underestimate the power of a pissed off woman!

I pound on his door repeatedly with a closed fist.

"Open up, goddamn you," I yell. "I've got cramps which means I'm getting my period, and if you don't open this door, so help me God, I'll—"

The door swings open before I can complete my threat. A good thing because I don't know exactly how I was going to finish that sentence.

Xavier looks like shit.

Pale, gaunt, and unshaven. His hair is unwashed and wild and is that... whisky? He stinks like some sort of strong alcohol. His eyes are bloodshot with it.

He immediately reaches for me, dragging me inside the room.

"Wait, I—"

He lays me down on the bed and draws down my jeans. Then, to my utter embarrassment, he examines my underwear. It's one of those situations where I want to cover my face, but I'm curious, so I look down. There are just a couple spots of red on my panties.

His face comes up, strained and alarmed.

"I'm probably just starting," I explain, feeling my face heat. "It's light at the beginning."

He turns away and goes to his desk. He wakes up his laptop and then quickly types in his password. I pull my underwear back up and then sit on the bed, looking over his shoulder. He's pulled up a calendar. From the bed, I can see the title of the large calendar reads, *Melanie's Cycle*.

My mouth drops open. Holy crap, he's charting my... That's just—

"Your period should have started three days ago." He turns back to look at me. "You've always been very regular. Your records said so."

Oh my God, there's just so much to unpack there. He's said from the start that he had access to my records, but I guess it was never confirmed before now that he actually somehow hacked or got access to my freaking medical records. How the hell did he—

And then there's the part about how my period was supposed to have started several days ago. Because he's right. I'm one of those rare women who's like clockwork. Every 28 days. You can set your calendar by it.

If I'm late, then that means...

I blink, looking down at my abdomen.

Xavier's light-years ahead of me, because he's already on the phone, barking out orders. "Drop everything and get out here as soon as possible. No, I don't want to hear excuses. I pay so I can be your first priority. I expect you here within 45 minutes. Take the goddamned chopper if you have to!" He slams the phone down.

Then he's rushing back over to me. "I'm so sorry. Lie down. God, lie down."

He urges me onto my back on the bed, then he lifts shaking hands toward my belly. He stops just before making contact, though.

"Fuck," he whispers under his breath and runs his hand through his hair instead. For a brief second, tortured eyes come up to meet mine, full of regret and self-recrimination. Then he gets up and turns away. He stalks off toward the bathroom, shutting the door behind him. He doesn't slam it at least. Moments later, I hear the spray of the shower.

I drop my head back to the bed, my mind swirling a hundred miles an hour.

Could I really be *pregnant*?

Even thinking the word freaks me the hell out. Maybe I'm late because of all the extra farm work I've been doing. Don't like, athletes miss their period sometimes because of all the strain on their bodies?

Except that even when I did crew in college and worked out for four hours a day on the weekends, I was still regular as clockwork.

I glance down at my flat stomach before quickly looking away again. Still, I can't help my hand from creeping to touch low on my abdomen.

What if I am?

What does the cramping mean?

Oh God, what if I lose the baby before I even realized I had it?

I lose my breath at the thought.

Baby.

My baby. *Our baby.*

Can't breathe, can't breathe—

I stagger to my feet.

Sudden images flash before me: Me, my stomach heavy and round. Xavier holding a tiny baby, the grin that so rarely appears cracking his face as he looks down in wonder at the bundle in his arms. Tiny fingers grasping mine.

Oh God, what if— what if— I stumble to the bathroom.

When I try the doorknob, I almost weep with relief to find it unlocked.

Xavier's in the shower. I only kick off my boots before stepping inside and collapsing into him. He catches me in his arms and holds me as the tears start up again.

The spray hits my back as I cling to him. "What if something's wrong with the baby?" I cry into his chest. "I can't— The baby—" I claw at his back, desperate for something solid. "What if I— I've been doing all this hard work all week and what if—"

He pulls me against him tighter, pressing my cheek to his chest. "Shhhh. It's going to be all right. Dr. Winthrop is the finest obstetrician in Cheyenne. She'll be here soon and she'll have answers. I won't let anything happen to you, Precious. I swear." He kisses the top of my head and then repeats in a rough, low voice, "I swear it."

I nod against his chest, the terror that briefly cinched my lungs slowly releasing. Still, I can't let go of him.

This is the Xavier I know and I need him right now more than ever. In command and control. When he says everything's going to be okay in that tone of voice, it's impossible not to believe him.

"Let's get you out of these soaking clothes," he murmurs.

I stand mutely while he peels off my shirt and tugs down my jeans. Soon the clothes are a soggy pile in the corner and we're flesh to flesh. His cock is rock hard but he ignores it, twisting his hips to the side so that part of him doesn't make contact as he briefly pulls me close again.

It feels like maybe he needs to hold me after going so long without contact. Or maybe I'm reading into it, because God knows that's how I feel. I need to feel him real underneath my arms. Real and solid. I can't handle him disappearing on me again. Especially now. But he doesn't seem inclined to.

He pulls away briefly to pour shampoo into his hands but he tugs me close again as his fingers delve into my short hair. I close my eyes against the familiar sensation.

"I want the baby," I whisper, trying the words out loud for the first time as he massages my scalp. "I actually want the baby."

"Of course you do," he murmurs. "And you'll be the perfect mother."

I melt against him. He really thinks that? Even though every time the topic of babies has ever been brought up all I can talk about is how much I don't like them and how terrible I think they are?

He detaches the shower sprayer to get the shampoo out and then he's on to the body wash. I can't imagine ever being separated from him and going without this. The past four days have been terrible. Right now, his hands on me feel as necessary as breathing.

He washes my pussy with special care, his face reverent. He doesn't tease or try to arouse me. His big fingers just separate my lips gently and then he turns the showerhead to a gentle mist as he cleanses me down there.

Then he reattaches the showerhead to the wall, fills his hand with his own body wash and starts to wash himself. His movements are rough, almost punishing.

"Let me." I try to take the bottle he just put down but he stays me with a hand on my wrist. I want to give him some of the comfort he's just given me. But with a gentle shake of his head and an expression I can't read, he pulls my hand back.

"Just stand under the spray," he says.

He goes back to his quick, rough strokes. He usually washes himself briskly, but this seems more curt than usual.

What was he doing locked up in here for the past four days? Obviously drinking himself into oblivion. But just over Holy Hellfire? Yes, he had affection for the horse. He loved him even. And maybe his bond with the horses goes deeper than I understand but locking himself up like that is not a normal reaction. It's got to be about something deeper. Maybe connected to the demons that wake him up yelling in the middle of the night. How? I have no clue.

Because he doesn't talk to me.

And he won't let you touch him.

I wrap my arms over my abdomen, feeling cold in spite of the warmth of the shower spray. I might be having a child with this man, but how well do I really know him? So much has changed since I've come here—*I've* changed so much. And I like the person I'm becoming even if I don't fully understand all the ramifications of who that person is yet. I feel as strong as ever, yet not as *hard*, if that makes sense.

But can this really work for the long term if he won't fully share himself?

"Are you all right?" Xavier's brows knit in concern and he steps closer, covered in suds from his intensive wash-down. He reaches out a hand to my upper arm. His touch is warm and I can't help but lean into it.

Because as screwed up and emotionally unavailable as he might be, it's too late.

I've fallen for him.

Hard.

"I'm okay. Here," I step out of the spray to make way for him. "Wash off."

He stares at me uncertainly for another moment, scrutinizing my face, but then acquiesces and begins to wash off the suds. He washed his hair before I came in, so it's just a matter of quickly rinsing off and then we're out of the shower and he's toweling us down.

Once he's got me dressed in a thick terrycloth robe, he lies on the bed beside me, brushing my hair back from my face.

He said I should take one of the pharmacy pregnancy tests he's apparently stocked up on. In spite of all his assurances of their accuracy, though, I'd rather just wait for the doctor. If they say negative or positive, I'll still be freaking out that I'm miscarrying based on the results. I can't handle that shit right now.

So instead we're just lying in bed with each other as we wait for the obstetrician. Xavier didn't bother shaving and I have to say, I sort of like the five days' scruff that's almost a full beard on him. Makes him look dark and dangerous. Though it also highlights the burned streaks on the left side of his cheek where the hair won't grow in. I imagine if the beard had more time to fill out, it might eventually hide them.

We've spent the last few minutes not talking. He's just been lying there, staring at me. With anyone else, I imagine such a silence would feel supremely uncomfortable. With him, though, I just feel comforted and... *not alone*. He doesn't shy away from me looking at him and I rarely get a chance to examine him up close like this.

His face is wide and broad like a boxer's, but his wide mouth that stretches his whole face and deep brow balance it out. When he smiles, it's dazzling and when he's pensive, like now, you still can't help but stare at his lips.

But I chance looking into his blue, crystalline eyes.

"Will you tell me what happened?"

He immediately glances away.

"Please? Don't I have a right to know?"

His mouth tenses into a line and maybe that was a low blow but at the same time, I feel like it's true. I do have a goddamned right. I might be the mother of his freaking child. He just put me through hell for the past four days. And I *need* for him to start opening up to me.

He's quiet for so long I think he's not going to answer me.

But then, finally, with a hard swallow that makes his Adam's apple bob up and down, he starts speaking. "I was in the Army. A lieutenant stationed at a detention facility at Bagram Air base."

I'm only partially surprised he's not bringing up Hellfire. Deep down, I knew this was about so much more than a favored horse.

He stares at the ceiling while he talks and each word seems like a struggle to get out. He has to take a deep breath before finishing. "Men under my command made a mistake that cost a lot of people their lives. It was something I could have prevented if I'd prepared them better."

What he doesn't say is clear on his face. He blames himself for the deaths of those people, whoever they were. I hesitate before asking my next question but I don't know when he'll be willing to talk so openly again.

"Is that when…?" I reach toward his face but withdraw my hand before he can push it away. "Is that when you got hurt?"

He nods.

I wait for him to give me anything more.

He takes another deep breath and opens his mouth, but just then, the doorbell rings.

He jumps to his feet like his ass is spring loaded.

"That'll be the doctor." He's out the door before I can so much as blink.

Dammit. I sigh, sitting up. Well, I mean, I'm relieved the doctor is here, but God knows how long he'll clam up now.

It's only a minute later before Xavier is back, literally dragging the poor doctor into the room by her wrist.

It's the same woman as before.

She looks both harassed and scared, eyes locked on Xavier's hulking frame.

"Xavier," I snap at him.

He looks down at me. In his other hand, he's carrying a heavy, black, hard-covered suitcase that I imagine is some sort of equipment the doctor brought with her. He sets it down but still has hold of the doc.

"Let her go. You're freaking her out. She's here to help us and it'd be nice if she's not peeing her pants."

Xavier lets go of her and the doctor looks at me, eyes wide with surprise. As tense as I am about my situation, I can't help but be amused by the way she's looking between me and Xavier.

"Yeah." I shrug. "Things have changed a little since you last saw me. Let's get this show on the road. Do I need to pee in a cup or something?"

She nods, swinging a black bag off her shoulder. Her hands are shaking. I glare at Xavier but he looks unrepentant.

"Can I set this up?" he asks, fidgeting with the latches on the hard suitcase.

"Don't touch that," the doctor says, then her eyes widen and she quickly adds, "Please."

I roll my eyes.

"Xavier, if you can't stop scaring the nice lady, I'm going to send you to the other room."

He levels me with a stare. "Try."

I smile sweetly at him.

The doctor glances back and forth between us, then shoves a little plastic pee cup in my hand. "If you can just deposit your specimen into this, please, we can get some initial information. I brought the transvaginal ultrasound, but we'll only do that if there seem to be any problems."

"Oh goody," I deadpan.

I take the pee cup and head to the bathroom. "Come with me, sweetie pie," I call to Xavier. "Let's let the nice doctor set up her machine without you freaking her the hell out and making her accidentally break something important."

Xavier glares at her. "She better not."

"Oh my God." I get off the bed and grab his bulky upper arm, dragging him to the bathroom with me.

I drank two glasses of water after the shower in anticipation.

"Turn around," I say to Xavier once he shuts the door.

He stares at me with an intensity that seems unwarranted for being about to pee into a cup. "You're so goddamned feisty. If I weren't so worried about you, I'd be fucking you into next week."

I grin at him. I can't believe he can still make my stomach flip even right now. I twirl my finger at him, mock glaring.

He gives me another hard stare but finally turns to face the door.

After a few tries, I manage to pee into the cup.

Xavier is immediately there with a towel to take it from me and hurry it out to the doctor while I wash my hands. After I do, I splash some water on my face.

Holy shit. How long does it take before we have a positive or negative? Will the doctor have to send it off to a lab?

I walk back out to the other room.

I'm surprised when I see my cup sitting on the nightstand with two little plastic sticks that look very similar to the ones from the store sitting beside the cup.

The doctor has gloves on and she's looking at her phone. Xavier's head is also bent, looking at the phone.

"What is it?" I come closer and see that it's a timer. So it really is just like the at home tests. I'll be damned. I stare at the timer with the same silent intensity.

Two minutes and twelve-seconds left. Eleven. Ten.

Commence with the slowest two minutes *of my life*.

At the end of which, the doctor checks the sticks only to look up at us and announce, "Congratulations, you're going to be parents."

17

It's another three weeks before we can hear the heartbeat.

Xavier's called Dr. Winthrop about fifty times in the interim with all sorts of ridiculous questions. Should I be eating a special diet? How limited should my activities be? Should I, in fact, be on bed rest? That question came after a knock-down drag out fight between us when he tried to keep me in bed for two days straight after she left the first time.

Xavier had shown her the little bit of blood on my underwear and she'd calmly explained that light spotting happened in twenty to forty percent of first-trimester pregnancies and that, with such a small amount, it was nothing to be worried about. It most likely meant the fertilized egg was implanting in the uterine wall.

Xavier wasn't impressed with *most likely*. He wanted her to do the ultrasound but she stood her ground and said she could, but it wouldn't show much at this early stage and the wand might irritate the cervix and cause more bleeding.

That shut him up.

Instead, she just did a physical exam with her hands and determined that everything looked perfectly normal.

That didn't stop Xavier from going crazy commando about my

health right after she left and all but chaining me to the bed. When he found me wandering the resort looking for good books, he ordered me straight back to bed.

The first day I didn't mind. I'd been working my ass off for a week. A day of R&R being pampered, resting in bed, and reading? Sign me up.

But it turns out that over the past two months I've gotten accustomed to being active. I only lasted half a day before I suited up and joined Xavier out in the stables.

Or rather, I *tried* to join Xavier.

He scooped me up and trotted me right back to bed.

Annoying, stubborn, mule of a man.

He turned the goddamned cameras back on me and threw a shit-fit if I got out of bed for more than a five-minute bathroom session.

Yeah, that lasted a whole half-day more before I'd wait until he got back out to the stable before getting up to go downstairs. He'd see me on the camera and come to drag me upstairs. Then he'd go out to the horses again... and repeat. Until finally a nice shouting match ensued and I finally got him to call the doctor and ask her opinion.

And ha! She said that regular activity was important at this stage in my pregnancy. As long as it wasn't too strenuous. So no more lifting huge feed bags. Naturally Xavier wasn't going to let me even carry water buckets. Or muck stalls.

Basically I was relegated to grooming duties.

Okay, so I couldn't say I minded about not having to muck the stalls anymore.

Plus, Xavier suddenly thought I needed all the sleep I could get.

So now I get to sleep in *past* sunrise. Miracle of miracles.

I feel lazy watching him doing all the hard work while I just basically hang out with Sugar and Hot Lips in the pasture or spend long hours watching him continue his training with Samson—which no longer seems boring.

I know, it shocked the hell out of me, too. But I keep wandering over to the front training paddock. The transformation of Samson is truly an amazing thing to behold. Over the past few days, Xavier has taken to tying a dark handkerchief over Samson's eyes. His *eyes*. The horse is blinded by the handkerchief but he still confidently follows Xavier's lead. Even when Xavier leads him out of the paddock and out into the unfamiliar field beyond.

Naturally, Xavier makes me go back to the stable and watch from afar for this part, but still, even as I squint, I can see that the horse never makes a misstep or falters under Xavier's confident leadership.

Which makes me wonder more and more about the small tidbit of information he gave me the day we found out about the pregnancy.

Men under my command made a mistake that cost a lot of people their lives.

I've been dying to ask him more about it.

But with as tense as he's been about the pregnancy, I can never seem to find a good time to bring it up. The only time he relaxes is with the horses. Even at night with his arm wrapped protectively around my stomach, he seems to radiate tension.

Twice I've had to wake him from nightmares. Both times I asked him if he wanted to talk about it. He simply grabbed me close and closed his eyes again, murmuring about me needing sleep.

The truth is, we're both trying to act like everything's all right, but I know we're each nervous about the doctor's visit. Sometimes over the past few weeks, I've caught Xavier pensive, face dark as he stares out across the pastures. It scares me how far away he seems, lost in some dark place. Whenever I call his name or get his attention, he pretends like everything's fine and he wasn't just a million miles away.

I'm glad when Dr. Winthrop arrives an hour earlier than expected, right after I manage to get down a few bites of toast—a feat for me. Morning sickness has just started being a bitch the last week. One morning I sat up in bed and immediately had to run to the toilet.

Apparently, it's better if you eat a couple saltines before you even sit up. We've been trying that. I still feel like throwing up whatever I ate the night before, but sometimes I can manage to keep it down.

And calling it *morning* sickness is a total joke.

It's *all day* sickness. I feel awful all the time.

I guess it does ease up a little bit at night. Which means Xavier tries to stuff me full of all the food he can manage to get down my gullet because he's constantly worried about me and the baby not getting enough nutrition. Explaining to him that the baby is the size of a pea doesn't seem to matter.

Xavier sets down the piece of toast he's feeding me when the doorbell rings. He's taken to feeding me my breakfast in bed each morning. He figures if a few crackers can help settle my stomach, why not just keep me in bed for the whole meal? And glaring at me when I only manage the few bites I can choke down.

His constant refrain is, "Just *one* bite of the eggs? Not even for our son or daughter?"

Guilt trips are his new favorite manipulation tactic and he uses them relentlessly to get his way. If I thought being pregnant would earn me some leniency from his controlling tendencies, ha! No, it's just won me Xavier 2.0.

He loves barking orders at me and while I still get the nice long showers at night, there are no longer any of the perks. Just a quick wash and off to bed now. It's starting to get insufferable.

Sometimes I wonder if I matter to him at all anymore or if I was always just a vehicle to get him what he really wanted—a kid to carry on his name and his genes.

Part of me thinks: *duh, that's obviously all he wants, it's the whole reason he brought you here.*

But another, maybe deluded, part objects: *no! We've built something. There really is an* us. *He constantly refers to the baby as* our *son or daughter. Not just* the baby. Surely that means he envisions me in the picture. Right?

Right???

Because even though I swore I never wanted to be a mother, now that it's a reality, I can't imagine anything different.

Me. Xavier. This baby. *Our* baby and the little family I keep envisioning every time I close my eyes. But what if I'm deluding myself? Fear about it all is almost enough to keep me up at night—except I'm constantly exhausted so I always drop off as soon as my head hits the pillow.

Dr. Winthrop knocks briefly on the door and then steps through. She has the large, hard-backed, black suitcase with her again, and today she immediately sets it on the bed and opens it.

Oh. The whole thing is a machine—a portable ultrasound machine, I imagine. The top half of the case holds a monitor and the bottom a keyboard and what I assume is the rest of the machine. Along with a wand attached by a long wire that the doctor begins to uncoil.

She looks up at Xavier as she pulls out a cord from the other side. "Do you have somewhere I might plug in?"

Xavier hurries to drag the cord to a plug near the bed and soon the machine is beeping to life and the doc is sticking what looks like a condom over the wand and then up my hoo haa it goes.

She pokes it this way.

Then that way.

Then, holy shit— Is that—

A swift, steady *wheeoo-wheeoo-wheeoo* sound fills the bedroom.

My hand shoots out to the side where Xavier's sturdy fingers grasp mine.

Wheeoo-wheeoo-wheeoo-wheeoo-wheeoo-wheeoo.

"That's a strong, steady heartbeat," Dr. Winthrop announces, smiling as she looks between me and Xavier.

I expel a relieved breath and then look up at Xavier. His eyes are glued to the screen where the doctor goes on to point out a small circle she says is a gestational sac and a little dot that's apparently our baby.

"Since you're so regular," she smiles at me like it's a personal accomplishment, "we can confidently say you're seven weeks along."

Seven weeks. Holy shit. Holy shit. *Holy shit!*

Xavier's hand squeezes around mine and I wonder if he's having the same internal reaction. Like, yeah, I've been thinking—okay, obsessing—about the fact that we're having a freaking *baby*. But it's still been a kind of esoteric idea.

All of the sudden it feels *real*. Like, holy shit, this is actually happening. To me. I'm going to be a mom and Xavier a dad and holy *shit*!

I look at Xavier again with what probably looks like an insane Joker's grin from the mix of excitement and terror running through my veins.

He's looking at me this time and I have to swallow hard at what I see.

There's a sheen over his eyes that he doesn't bother blinking away. Instead he pulls me close and crushes me to his chest. He kisses the top of my head. "Precious," he whispers barely loud enough for me to hear.

Oh my God. We're having a *baby*. I've never wanted anything more in my entire life.

Which means I'm *not* like my mother after all. I do have the capacity to love this baby. I can do everything differently.

Except…

I have no idea what the hell I'm doing.

I pull out of Xavier's grasp and turn to Dr. Winthrop. "Ok, so tell me everything I need to know. What are the dos and don'ts? What do I need to do so I don't fuck up this kid while he or she is still inside me?"

If she hears the sudden panic in my voice, she doesn't let on. She just ticks things off in a calm voice. "No highly strenuous physical activities. No running or jogging unless that's already a part of your normal routine," she pauses and I nod along.

"No high impact aerobics," Xavier takes up where the doctor left off, listing them off on his fingers. He's obviously already memorized this stuff. "No saunas or hot tubs—anything above 102 degrees can be unsafe." No wonder he's switched us to showers lately. God, he could have just *told* me.

But still, the fact that he's already studied up on all this stuff kind of makes me want to jump him right here. Speaking of…

I look back to the doctor. "What about sex?"

She pauses in discarding the wand condom and looks up at me, mouth dropping open slightly before she closes it and resumes her professional manner. "Um. What about it?"

"When can I have it again?"

"Oh." She looks surprised. "There's no reason for you to have stopped, um…" her gaze shoots briefly back and forth between Xavier and me, "relations. Your cervix might be a little tender during your first trimester and there might be light spotting, but you're perfectly healthy. It won't cause any risk to the baby."

My mouth drops open and I swing my head around to look accusingly at Xavier. "I thought she said we couldn't—"

His mouth is a flat line. "I never said that. I just didn't think it was a good idea considering—"

"I'll be heading out now," Dr. Winthrop says, probably wisely as she sees the daggers I'm shooting Xavier's way. She wants to get out before the hormonal pregnant woman loses it on the baby daddy. "*What to Expect When You're Expecting* or other books like it are a good resource to answer your questions and of course my line is always open to you."

She closes up her machine, then takes it and her bag and makes a quick exit.

I'm left glaring at Xavier.

"You've been denying me for no reason at all? Not even any orgasms? I thought she'd told you the muscle spasms would be bad for the baby or something!" Maybe it sounds dumb now that I say it out loud—but I haven't had access to Google.

I chuck a pillow at his head and he deftly dodges out of the way. Ugh! Annoying quick-reflexed bastard!

I throw another one but I'm quickly out of ammo.

"The doctor says you shouldn't engage in strenuous activity," he has the gall to respond.

"You heard her, she said aerobics and hard-core jogging. She probably meant weight-lifting and stuff like that. Besides, she specifically just said sex was safe."

He heaves out a heavy breath. "Well, there are other things that aren't."

I throw up my hands. "Like?"

He steps forward until he leans over me where I sit in the middle of the bed. "No contact sports and no horse riding."

I'm about to object to the last one when he silences me. "Even the most experienced rider can take a tumble. I will *not* take the risk with you and our child."

Well, that shuts me up. *Me* and our child.

So... am I *not* the only one picturing Daddy and baby and me makes three?

It's been a big enough hurdle getting accustomed to the idea that I actually want to be a mother. I haven't wavered since the initial realization. That's not how I work. I'm not sure if it's a strength or a weakness—but once I commit to a course of action, I'm *in it*, come hell or high water.

So, me and this motherhood thing? I might have never changed a single diaper in my life or have any clue what the hell I'm doing, but this kid is *mine*.

Thing is, that wasn't part of the contract.

Neither was falling for Xavier.

I want them both.

Life has proven a tricky bitch when it comes to giving me what I want, though.

"What happens after the baby is born?" I ask, moving to the edge of the bed. I need my feet on solid ground for this. My need to know suddenly outweighs my fear of his answer. "Are you still planning to ship me back to New York and keep our baby for yourself?"

My arms cross over my stomach protectively and I lift my chin. "Because you can go to hell if that's what you think. I don't care about the stupid contract I signed."

There it is. My line in the sand. I'm not sure if I'm saying that when push comes to shove, I choose our baby over him, but I do know there's no goddamned way he's pushing me out of this child's life.

Xavier's face goes hard and his blue eyes icy as he stands above me beside the bed. "I will chase you and our child to the ends of the earth if you ever try to leave me."

"What? That wasn't even—"

He lifts me by the armpits onto the bed and then drops on top of me, covering my body with his own. His eyes are still dangerous. He hovers several inches over me but it's no less intimidating. "If you ever so much as *think* of leaving me, I'll tie you to this bed. You'll think those few days in the shed were a walk in the park compared to the chains I'll lock on you while your belly gets fat with my son or daughter."

"Just while I'm pregnant? Can't bear to let your precious cargo out of your sight, huh?" I struggle underneath the slight pressure of his weight that he uses to hold me down with and he grabs my wrists, pinning them to either side of my head. I scream in frustration, then spit out, "Was I ever anything more to you than a goddamned walking incubator?"

I squeeze my eyes shut and turn my head away after my outburst, knowing I've revealed too much. Exposed my raw insides.

When I feel his large fingers underneath my chin, I resist his pulling my head back toward him. Naturally, I lose the struggle and finally give in.

"Look at me," he orders.

I keep my eyes stubbornly shut.

"Look at me." He gives my chin a firm shake.

Goddamn him, I know he won't give up until I do as 'Master' commands, so I open my eyes, flashing them furiously. Anger is my best shield at the moment.

I expect to see him looking just as hard and angry.

What I'm *not* prepared for is the softness that takes over his features. Or the way his eyes flick back and forth between mine like he's searching for something.

"I never saw you like that." He speaks the words softly. "I've been training you because I wanted you to stay. For you to choose to stay." The blue of his irises has never seemed more vibrant. "So I could keep you."

I— Does that mean—

I blink. I'm not sure if he means 'training me' like training me to *work with* horses or training me *like* he trains the horses.

So I could keep you.

In the end, it doesn't matter which way he meant it. I'm in far too deep.

"I love you," I blurt.

His eyes widen and then he crushes his lips down on mine.

I feel like I could fly.

I feel like—

He rolls us on the bed so that I'm on top of him. His hands roam down my body.

I feel like—

"Gotta throw up!" I yelp and shove away from him.

"Shit," he mutters but immediately moves into action, jumping off the bed and helping me to the toilet.

After he's held my hair back and I've lost the little bit of toast from earlier, I'm laughing and crying as I hunch over the freshly flushed toilet bowl. "Consider this no reflection on my feelings. I really do love you."

He wraps one arm around my waist and drops his forehead to the small of my back, hugging me tightly. His deep chuckle echoes around the bathroom.

18

"And now to complete the tour, here's the stable," I say into the camera phone, on Skype with my dad. I'm careful to keep the camera trained on my face rather than putting it somewhere stationary. Halfway through the second trimester, I'm clearly showing. I don't think Dad's quite ready for that bombshell yet.

Dad looks skeptical on the other end. This is only the second call we've done like this and no matter how many times I assure him that I'm well, healthy and happy, I know he's worried that Xavier's right off camera, like, pointing a gun at me to get me to say these things. I think only time will convince him I actually mean what I'm saying.

The stable is much darker than the bright summer day outside but the camera adjusts and I take Dad around the stable. I introduce him to the horses and stop in front of Hot Lips's stall.

"Now I'm going to groom Hot Lips. She's pregnant and about to pop. We keep her in here where it's cool and she's got plenty of access to food and water."

"Enough about the horses," Dad says shortly. He leans forward into the screen and whispers, "Is he around?"

I rub a hand down Hot Lips's mane and sigh.

"No, Daddy, he's not, but it wouldn't make a difference even if he was. I told you, I'm not a captive here. It's not like that. I'm perfectly safe. I can come and go as I please." I'm not exactly sure if that's true, but I think it is. It brings up a good point, though. I should ask Xavier for the car so I can go and visit Hunter's wife. I think we've reached that stage of trust and if we haven't, well, that's a big problem I'd rather face now rather than later.

"Dad, I'm happy. Really happy." I grin, thinking of the string of wonderful days Xavier and I have been sharing lately.

By the middle of the second trimester, the nausea is much better, thank *God*. Dealing with the urge to throw up was bad enough, but Xavier's constant paranoia about me not gaining enough weight and obsessing about every morsel of food that did or did not go into my mouth? Yeah, that might have driven me right to the very edge of insanity.

And it's hard to have much of a libido when you feel like hurling every other second.

But the blessed second trimester!

Something no one ever told me about pregnancy? Well, it's not like I ever had any pregnant friends or anything, working my way up the corporate ladder in a mostly man's world—but anyway.

It makes you horny as *hell*. I'm not even kidding. It hits somewhere around the second month of the second trimester. The morning/all day sickness is finally mostly gone and then *boom*. All I can think about all the time is getting Xavier naked.

"Oh my God," Dad whispers. "You're in love with him."

I jerk my attention back to the small screen in my palm. He looks stunned and worried but I don't look away. I just meet his gaze and nod. "I am, Dad, and he's worth it. I wish you could meet him. He's a good, honorable man."

Dad swallows and rakes a hand through his hair that's graying just at the edges. He's gotten very tan over the past months and he looks more fit as well. Earlier he told me he does a lot of swimming and his diet consists of fish, much of which he catches himself, and lots of fresh vegetables. "I don't know what to think, baby. I mean, there's this man. And... horses?"

I feel my expression soften and I laugh. "I know. None of this is what I could have ever expected for myself either. But I'm happy. Please be happy for me, too, Dad."

He hesitates, eyes still wary, but finally he nods.

My phone beeps and I see the battery sign flashing in the corner. "I'm about to run out of battery, Dad. Love you and talk to you soon."

"You better," he warns. "Love you, honey."

"Love you, too." I blow him a kiss and then hang up, slipping the phone back in my pocket.

God, I love that Dad and I are back in contact again and I know he's not as worried about me anymore. Just another of the compromises Xavier's been willing to make lately in order to see to my happiness.

I give a good, long stretch, loosening my lower back muscles, then get to grooming Hot Lips. It's early evening and I like to give her a lot of attention these days. I feel bonded with her since she's so big with her foal. I can only imagine how hot and uncomfortable she's got to be, just a few weeks away from giving birth. She's comfortable with me and I like to take her out to the side paddock to walk her in circles so she can get some low-impact exercise each day. Well, so both of us can. One of my compromises? I do very little strenuous work around here now.

"That feels good, doesn't it, girl?" I ask after finishing with the curry comb. I'm about to reach for her hard brush when I see Xavier walk into the stable.

My mouth immediately goes dry. At the same time, my sex starts pulsing so hard between my legs I have to twist them together.

I mentioned the horny as *hell* thing, right?

He's sweaty and he pulls his button up work-shirt off, revealing a sweat-drenched tank top underneath.

I remember the day he teased my clitoris with a soft grooming brush and all but moan where I stand.

We've had sex since the doctor told us it was safe. But with my wicked morning sickness that seemed to last *forever*, the occasions have still been too few and far between for my liking.

That's it.

No more.

He's sweaty, I'm wet, and like the horses, this is a lady who's ready to be ridden *hard*.

I swing Hot Lips's stall door closed, hang up her brush, and then stalk toward Xavier, unbuttoning my own shirt and flinging it to the ground in a move that's probably over the top. By the widening of his eyes, though, I'd say I'm getting my point across.

I'm wearing a camisole underneath and I don't hesitate in whipping it over my head as well. In almost the same motion, I unsnap my bra and then I'm standing before him in nothing but my Wranglers and boots.

My nipples quickly pebble to hard points under his gaze.

It's when his gaze drops lower to my rounded stomach that his eyes really flare, though.

That's a development as of a couple weeks ago. I was embarrassed at first but then kind of struck with awe. The peanut's big enough that he's starting to make my belly stick out. Okay, according to the baby site Xavier and I now check religiously each week, at five months, he or she is now the size of an eggplant. His or her brain function and hearing are developing this week, so the kiddo can start recognizing the sound of our voices.

Cue Xavier talking and singing non-stop to my stomach.

Which, yes, is freaking adorable. He has a really good singing voice, too. The things I'm learning about this man.

On my first day here, could I have ever imagined the scary hulk on his knees cradling my stomach to his lips and crooning Hozier and Decemberist lyrics to my belly? Uh... no.

Except right now, I'm hoping he's not thinking about our sweet little eggplant.

When his hand reaches out, it's not my stomach he touches.

But he doesn't go for my breasts either.

No, he grabs my hips. Just long enough to twirl me toward the wall.

"Over," his rough voice demands, pushing my back down.

I bend over and grab onto the edge of the sink basin for balance. Xavier rips my jeans down my legs.

"Are you wet?" he growls out.

"Yes," I rasp.

There's no foreplay or preamble.

His cock shoves right in.

"Oh God, yes!" I scream, pounding a hand on the sink. I don't care if I scare the horses. This is what I've been needing. He's been so goddamned careful with me the times we have had sex and goddamn it, I've just needed him to—

"Fuck me," I yell at him. "I just need you to ram me so fucking hard. If you hold back, I swear I'll—"

"Like this?" he roars back, pumping his hips furiously. His cock feels so goddamned amazing every time he bottoms out, his balls slapping my ass. The sound is so profane and fucking *hot* and just, *God*.

"A pet should let her Master know when she needs taking care of." He reaches around and palms my breast, first squeezing the whole thing in his hand, then plucking the nipple with his fingers as he continues his merciless drive in and out of my pussy. "You've been a bad girl, not communicating your needs."

He squeezes my nipple so hard I cry out at the exquisite torture of it and then he smacks my ass.

"Oh fuck, yes, I'm a bad, bad fucking girl," I pant, grabbing on to the sink and meeting him thrust for thrust, writhing and grinding my ass against his pelvis. His hands go to my hips and I hear him swear. He clutches me with what feels like a white-knuckled grip as he drives in even harder still.

Finally he's hitting that perfect spot so deep inside me.

"Oh God, yes. There. Right there!" I've never been so vocal during sex but, God, I need it, never needed it so much, so hard, just—

"Ohhhhhhhhhhhhhh—" I screech and he rams and rams me again in the perfect spot and stars burst.

I squeeze the fuck out of his dick as the climax hits me so goddamn hard. Oh God, it's so sweet. So hard. So *goooooooood*.

But still, not enough.

I want more.

I want it all.

"More," I gasp when I can breathe again. "Give it to me again."

"Greedy," he says, one hand clutching my hip even tighter while the other plucks at my peaked nipple. Then his glorious cock is slipping out of me. I whine in frustration but he's chuckling and drawing me with him to the stable floor where he's thrown down a saddle blanket. He lays both of us down and drags off my boots and jeans so I'm entirely naked in the center of the stable. I couldn't care less. I can't take my eyes off his thick, pulsing cock.

Then finally, finally, he pulls me down on top of him so I'm straddling him.

Again, with no preamble, he grabs himself and within seconds, he's directing his monster cock back inside me.

I groan and my eyelids flutter at how right it feels having him there.

"I know you've missed riding. So let me give you what you've been missing, Precious."

He lays back, propping his hands behind his head as he looks at me straddling him, that mischievous grin on his face. "Here's your chance. But you better grip my cock as tight as you can. It takes a lot to satisfy me. You've gotta grip me hard with that luscious cunt if you want to get the job done."

My inner muscles respond to his crude words. I'll show him. I'll give him the fucking ride of his life.

This is a new position for us but it works well with my expanding stomach. I shift my hips experimentally and Xavier's entire body flexes in response.

I grin, wondering exactly how much self-discipline it's taking for him to keep his hands behind his head instead of grabbing me, flipping me over, and controlling the situation like I know he loves to.

But hell no, I'm not giving up this power.

I shift my hips again, a rolling motion, grinding down and against his pelvis. My eyes pop open because, holy God, that hits the spot.

Xavier's grin settles into a smirk as he watches me. I narrow my eyes at him. Oh, I'm going to drive him just as insane as he always makes me, just you wait.

"Good Masters deserve rewards, too," I say, intentionally making my voice somewhat breathless. I start rolling my hips, drawing up and then down on his cock, each time grinding my clit against the base of him.

I don't have to fake my breathy moans as I draw my hands down my neck. I grasp my breasts and arch my back.

"Oh God," I gasp. "I can feel your cock so... *deep*. Fucking me. It's *so good*." Yeah. Not an act. Goddamn him, but he really drives me this insane. And actually letting it out—just saying out loud all the things that are always going through my head? It feels so dirty and ramps everything I'm feeling up even higher. Especially when I see Xavier's responses. The way his jaw is getting so tight and how his nostrils flare every time I pinch my nipples.

I cinch them between my thumb and forefinger until they're hard little points, my high-pitched pants ramping up higher and higher as my pleasure heightens. Xavier swallows hard as his blue eyes darken. "Fuck. You make it so fucking good. Every... oh God, every time." I close my eyes and throw my head back, clawing at my own breasts.

Then I drop a finger down and run it through my own juices at my clitoris and my lips where Xavier's giant cock rises to meet my every downward hip roll.

I tilt my head back to stare at him right as I suck the forefinger soaked in my juices into my mouth.

Apparently that's all it takes to break through his iron-willed control because with an animal growl, he finally gives up on the whole observation-only approach. His hands move from behind his head to seize my hips.

Then he takes control of everything. He holds my hips in place as he pumps into me from below, thrusts that are so intense and deep they take my breath away. His sweat-drenched abs flex with every lunge.

"That's right. Take what I give you. Take it and fucking love it." His eyes move between an intense focus on his cock dominating my pussy and locking with my gaze as he drives me closer and closer to the peak.

"Oh God, oh God, oh *God*!" I cry as he drags me back and forth over the base of his cock with each up-thrust. My hands fall to his rock-hard chest. We're both wet from sweat and my pussy squelches on his cock I'm so fucking wet for him.

When he does an ab curl and his lips begin devouring mine, I'm done for.

I cry my climax into his mouth. It's so strong and high and long I clutch him, feeling the entire foundation of my world rocked. "I love you," I gasp right on the tail end of the comet.

"Fuck. *Precious*," he whispers with a hoarse gasp and then follows me right over the cliff, pushing so deep and stilling there.

We lie there gasping in each other's arms. I'm hot and sweaty and the air is scented with sex and a moment has never been more perfect.

At least until I feel the baby start to move.

"Xavier!" I gasp. I grab his hand and put it on my belly. "Do you feel it?" I ask excitedly.

Feeling the baby move has been one of the freakiest and most amazing things of my life. But every time I try to share the experience with Xavier, the kiddo gets all zen and goes back to sleep. Without fail, whenever I grab Xavier's hand so he can feel, movement goes from super active to *nada*.

When I look up into Xavier's face, I can see the same hopeful expectation. Followed moments later when nothing happens by resignation.

"Not today," he says with a small disappointed smile, moving to withdraw his hand.

Which is when the kiddo starts doing freaking acrobatics.

"Shit. Holy shit!" Xavier says, moving so he can press both hands to my stomach even though it means upending me off his chest.

I laugh though because I can see the wonder on his face as he finally feels the miracle that's been amazing me for several weeks.

His eyes shoot up to meet mine, a childlike sort of astonishment written all over his face, before he goes back to intensely staring at his hands on my belly like he can see through it to his son or daughter beyond.

And I don't know if the kid got woken up by all the activity of moments before or if it was the salsa I had with my eggs this morning, but he or she is doing friggin' somersaults in there.

Xavier keeps his hands on my stomach for a good ten minutes, his face a picture of devoted concentration and awe.

"You're going to be an amazing father," I say when Jr. finally settles back down and stops moving.

Xavier looks at me. For a second I can't make out the expression on his face. His eyebrows are drawn together, his mouth open like he's at a loss. Finally, he whispers, "I don't know how to be this happy." He shakes his head. "A man like me doesn't deserve it."

I scrunch my face. "What are you talking about? Of course you deserve—"

But Xavier's suddenly in motion. He's up, grabbing my underwear and jeans. Naturally he doesn't hand them to me like a normal person would. He starts to dress me.

I throw a hand over my face. "I don't want to move."

He chuckles. "Somehow I bet you'll think different when the mosquitos start coming out. It's almost sundown and you know they'll be out in droves."

I groan but when he holds down a hand to help me up, I grudgingly let him pull me to my feet. I step back into my boots even though my legs feel like total jelly. I stumble a little while pulling my shirt back on over my head. He holds me steady at the last second.

"Whoa there." He can't keep the smirk off his face. "Have a bit of a rough ride, did ya?"

My eyes are at half-mast. I know it's the guys who are supposed to get sleepy after sex, but I'm always taking naps these days. According to the websites, I'm supposed to get a second wind of energy somewhere here in the second trimester but that has yet to hit. I'm still Ms. Nappy McNappy Pants.

His eyes soften and he reaches forward to push a stray piece of hair behind my ear. "Let's get you to the house for a before-dinner nap, how about that?"

I use my last ounces of strength to lift up on tiptoe and kiss his lips. "You really can be a sweetheart." Then I pull back. "When you're not being a pain in my ass."

I get a swat on my backside for that one.

I laugh and jump ahead a few steps. He naturally chases me. I'm still giggling when I get out of the stables and freeze at seeing a serious-looking man in a business suit frowning at us.

I back up a few steps and run into Xavier, who's arm immediately snakes around my stomach protectively.

Standing as close as we are, I feel the sudden tension that makes Xavier's muscles go rigid. I look up and his face is hard, his jaw stiff.

"Father," he bites out. "What are you doing here?"

19

"There's not much time left to live up to your end of the bargain. I've come to check on your progress."

Xavier's silent while the man—Xavier's *father*—looks me up and down.

Out of old habit, I can't help looking at his suit. The cut is excellent. And the fabric. Top of the line tailoring. Tortoise shell buttons. Hand stitching.

And his shoes. He's standing out here in a horse paddock full of cow pies in a pair of goddamned Stefano Bemer's, if I haven't lost my old touch. Not a household name, but those shoes can retail at three to four *thousand dollars* a pair. We're talking stupid money.

"But I see you've made a start of it." The corners of Xavier's father's mouth turn down. "I can't imagine where you found her. *Farmer's Monthly?*"

Xavier steps in front of me, blocking me from his dad's sight.

"Get the hell off my property."

His father sighs even as I strain to look over Xavier's shoulder. I can't help but want to get a peek at the man who sired my surly, mountainous lover. He looks a little familiar. Maybe I'm just seeing Xavier's features in him?

"Look, I'm sorry," his dad says, holding out a hand. He's a tall man but not nearly as broad-shouldered as his son.

Maybe his mom was a female heavyweight champ or did Olympic shot put?

"We've gotten off on the wrong foot again," his dad continues, sighing heavily. "I just want to talk. Maybe we could go inside and..." He lifts his leg and tries to shake some caked up mud off his fancy shoe—at least hopefully it's mud.

He looks beseechingly at Xavier.

Xavier stands unmoved with his beefy arms crossed over his chest.

Awkward silence doesn't even begin to describe the quiet that falls over the three of us. Xavier might be cool with that and even his dad bears it out bravely, but I'm a wimp and my Chatty Cathy instincts bust to the fore.

"We haven't been introduced." I step around Xavier before he can stop me. "I'm Melanie Va—" I catch myself just in time. It's been half a year but I doubt the world has forgotten so quickly about my father's scandal even though out here, it feels a million miles away and about three centuries ago. "I'm Melanie," I finish a little lamely but smile as I hold out my hand.

Xavier's dad seems glad for the reprieve and he takes my hand and shakes it warmly. "Lovely to meet you, Melanie. I'm Pritchard." There's a bit of silence, then he looks between Xavier and me. "So, how long have you known my son?"

"Wow, Dad, that took you a whole three seconds after introductions," Xavier says scathingly.

I glance back to Xavier, then swallow, and, on what is probably the wrong impulse—decide to tell the truth. "We met about six months ago when we agreed to this mutual experiment," I rub my baby bump. Then I wince at my wording. "I mean, you know, this amazing adventure," I rush on in a gushing voice. "Nothing more amazing than bringing a child into this world!"

I lean in chummily to Pritchard. "Except giving one a good kick in the pants when they deserve it," I point a thumb back at Xavier and then force a chuckle of camaraderie. "Am I right?"

Oh God, oh God, someone shut me up. Am I really trying to bond with the enemy? The way Xavier was acting, it sure seemed like his dad was an enemy. But, holy information Batman. This is my baby's *grandfather*. And there's so much I don't know about Xavier. Surely this is the man who can give me the motherload—or rather, fatherload—of info I'm so hungry for. And what did he mean *bargain*? Like the baby was some sort of bet or something between them.

Pritchard chuckles along with me. "You have no idea. He's been a constant pain in my ass since he was about eighteen months old and mastered the word *no*."

I keep a pleasant smile on my face in spite of my roiling thoughts. "Come on, join us for dinner. We've got a shepherd's pie warming in the oven."

Both men look at me in surprise. I'm not sure who looks more so.

"That sounds... delightful..." Pritchard says with a broad smile that belies the reluctance of his words.

Xavier scoffs. "I don't know, Dad. Do you think your highly developed palate can handle something as common place as shepherd's pie?"

Pritchard ignores his son and looks at me. "As I said, it sounds delightful. If you might show me where I can clean up for our meal?"

I struggle not to react to his overly formal speech and mannerisms. I glance back at Xavier one more time and he makes an overexaggerated gesture for me to lead on.

I start back toward the house and am surprised when not only Pritchard but Xavier himself follow me. Once the house is in view, I gesture on ahead.

"You can let yourself in through the kitchen, the bathroom is down the hall and to the left. You can clean up there."

Pritchard pauses, his gaze briefly locking with his son's before he heads up toward the house.

I immediately swing around to Xavier.

"Holy shit!" I smack him on the chest. "You never told me your father was Mr. Moneybags. I mean, I guessed you were rich because of the whole get-my-Dad-out-of-the-country thing." I pace in front of him. "But you don't wear it like *that*." I pause and look at him again. "So, what is it? Are you guys old money? Did you strike it rich back in the day like the Rockefellers? Or do you run guns?" I start nodding. "I thought mafia from the beginning."

Xavier just stares at me, totally deadpan. "Worse than all of those."

My mouth drops open and I stop pacing right in front of him. "What? What is it?"

"My family are career politicians."

I pause and frown. "What's your last name again?" I heard it once briefly the day Holy Hellfire died but everything was happening too fast for me to really catch it.

His jaw goes taut. "Kent. My dad is Pritchard Kent."

"Shit." I can feel my face draining of color.

"Language." The chastisement barely has any energy to it, though.

"He's the Speaker of the House," I whisper.

Xavier nods, apparently completely unimpressed by this fact.

"Oh God, did he invest with my dad?" I put a hand to my forehead.

"No, but your father was already on my radar," Xavier watches me gravely.

I stumble back from him. He denied it in the beginning but what if he was lying? "Oh God, please tell me—" Dad said he'd borrowed from bad, powerful men. "Were you out for my Dad all along?"

Xavier shakes his head, vehemently. "No." He takes a step forward, closing the gap between us. "But I know who is and, yes, it's someone else in my father's world. Years ago when they lent your father money and went into business with him, I knew about it because Dad and I talked about everything back then. We had a brief period of getting along." His mouth tightens. Obviously that didn't last too long. "He was trying to groom me to walk in his footsteps and he didn't want me heading into the family business naïve or blind to how things actually work in Washington. When I saw in the news about your father's indictment, I knew you were both in danger. I figured you and I could come to a mutually beneficial arrangement. Help each other out."

I lean over and put my hands on my knees. "Your dad said something about a bargain, I don't get it. What was he talking about?"

Xavier rubs my back and I'm not sure if I want to pull away from his touch or lean into it.

"My grandfather was a very rich man." Xavier's voice is short and to the point. "There's an inheritance. I live on a yearly stipend until then. But the inheritance is enough to let me continue and even expand the rescue comfortably for the rest of my life. I could have accessed the money earlier, when I was twenty-five, as long as I sought public office. Continued the family tradition."

His voice drops off and when I turn my head, though his hand still moves methodically over my back, he's staring off into the distance.

"That didn't work out," he finally says. It's obvious there's more to the story he's glossing over, but he moves on. "I got back from the army and opened this place up. I thought I got the money when I turned thirty. But no, it turns out there's a provision that I have to have a natural-born child by the time of my next birthday in order to inherit the money."

"So me and the baby." I take a sharp breath in. I guess when I thought about it I assumed family was just something that was very important to Xavier. I never guessed it was about… that it was all part of some… "You just need us to get the money?" I can't help the accusation in my voice.

"Don't twist my words." He grabs both of my hands when I try to turn away from him. "You." He pulls me close and drops a hand to my stomach between us, his blue eyes burning into mine. "This child." His head starts to shake back and forth. "You're nothing I ever thought I would—" He swallows and looks down. It's unlike him to be at a loss for words and I can't help pressing.

"What?" He can't close up on me now. After learning what I just did, I can't deal with vague half-truths.

His eyes come back to me. "You're a dream, all right? Something I'm afraid I'll wake up from and you'll be gone. I don't deserve this. I don't deserve you." It's the second time he's said that in the space of half an hour. What the hell is that all about? But he keeps talking so there's no more time to unpack it. "I thought with the inheritance that maybe I could do something good. I could live out my life in peace without hurting anyone, maybe help some old horses. Then I found out about the heir clause." His nostrils flare. "And then there was you."

The intensity of his gaze is making my stomach curl, with warmth and love and the lingering embers of the orgasms he gave me not fifteen minutes ago. But there are still so many questions.

"So what does all this have to do with your father? Does he get the money if you don't?"

Xavier's mouth tightens. A sure sign I'm hitting a nerve.

"If I don't have a child, my father can direct the money toward the political super PACs and political charities of his choosing. So while he doesn't get the money per se, he's still invested in the outcome of where it goes."

"But I guess," he kicks at the grass, another very out of place gesture for my usually so in control man, "he still thinks he might be able to spend that money on my candidacy."

My eyes pop open at that. Xavier's... *what*?

"My father was never happy with the career path I've chosen. He was very invested in me joining the family business. And I was a rank and file soldier who went along," he tilts his head back and forth, "if a bit grudgingly at times. He's still got it in his head that all of this is a phase." He nods out at the land then back at the stable. "Not to mention this is not the face of a politician. You can't exactly kiss babies when one look at you makes them scream."

Now I'm the one scoffing. "It's not that at all. It's just that I can't even imagine you in a suit." I try to circle one of his muscular biceps using both of my hands and they still don't touch. "Do they even make suits in your size?" I shake my head. "God, I just can't picture you anywhere but out here in the open air. You have such a sense with the horses. You're so natural with them." I can't stop shaking my head, it's too strange an image to even *try* to compute.

"I've told him enough times that this is my future. My *only* future. When I had my lawyer look into the inheritance issue right after I turned twenty-nine last year, I was shocked to find out about the stipulation that I had to have a child for the inheritance to pass to me."

His voice takes on a lower, growling quality. "Dad knew the whole time. He kept it from me because he was trying to force me back into politics. So I'd effectively have to depend on him for my livelihood through his influence and financing of my campaigns. He said we could play off my deformity for votes because in Afghanistan I was an *American hero*." He spits the last words like they're filthy curse words.

His hand is fisted and when I look closer, I see that his whole arm is shaking.

What the hell happened to him over there?

"Xavier—" I reach out to him but he turns his broad back to me.

"No."

I can't help flinching. It hurts. God, it hurts that he won't open up to me.

"I just can't, Precious." His voice sounds ragged. Raw. "Please don't ask me."

I sigh deeply, feeling overwhelmed by this entire conversation.

"All right. I guess we should go in." Then I look over my shoulder toward the pastures behind us. "I haven't brought in Sugar yet or brushed her down."

"She's fine." Xavier's voice still sounds off, but it gains strength as he talks about the more mundane topic of his horses. "I leave her out to pasture for whole weeks sometimes in the summer. Let's just go try to survive this dinner."

We take a few steps before something else occurs to me and I stop again.

"Wait, so when do you turn thirty?"

He's still faced away from me when he answers. "December 23rd."

I gape. That means...

If I hadn't gotten pregnant when I did... that would have been *it*. Inheritance lost. He only ever had two months to get me pregnant.

And apart from a couple tries, he basically wasted the whole first month I was here! Wtf?! I assumed it was because he had all the time in the world, but he only had two months and he—

"Why?" I tug on his arm. There's no way my tiny pull would move him, but he turns back at the pressure.

His eyes meet mine and he obviously reads the meaning of my question in my face. "I needed to know you would be safe. Before we really tried."

That I would be *safe*? What does that—? My first impulse is to be insulted.

He needed to know he could *control me* is what he really means. He needed me to be a dog begging at his feet for scraps.

But— No, that doesn't feel exactly right.

He never gave me just scraps. He fed me richly. He's taken care of my every need. Sumptuously.

His nightly massages in the bath. Touching me whenever we're near. Holding me so close after his nightmares. He's needed me too.

Suddenly a barrage of things he's told me over the months come flooding back like one of those cheesy montages in a movie.

I've been training you because I wanted you to stay. So I could keep you.

When he talked about Sugar that time: *She was always a sweet girl underneath. She just had to learn how to trust. It took a while for me to break through with her.*

And:

Trust is the most precious gift you can give to any being.

After those first couple of attempts, he realized he wasn't willing to have a baby with me until he could trust me.

And that whole begging for his cock thing?

Well, there was no better way to prove that I trusted him than allowing him to be intimate with me.

But... he had so much to lose.

Turns out, everything was on the line.

"It mattered that much to you?" I ask him. I can still barely wrap my head around the idea that he gambled so much on me. "That I trust you first?"

"There was no point otherwise."

My mouth drops open. "That's insane. What if I hadn't come around in time?"

The right side of his mouth hitches up. "No chance. You were panting every time I came into the room. You licked your lips when I took off my shirt and you couldn't keep your eyes off my ass."

I make an outraged noise and the smile teasing at his lips turns into a full-out grin. He wraps his arms low around my waist and then yanks me up and against him.

I gasp in a deep breath and lift my hands to his shoulders.

"Yep," he says, leaning in, his breath warm on my ear. "A little like how you're panting right now."

He's joking and playing it off, but still. He had so little chance to start with. Only two months. Two opportunities to get me pregnant, two of my eggs. If he was only concerned about the money and securing the inheritance, then the smartest move would have been for him to screw anything with a viable uterus and spread his seed far and wide. Or even to have gone the scientific route and fertilized a bunch of eggs in a lab for surrogacy.

But no. Not my Xavier.

He hikes me up just enough so that his rapidly growing hard on digs into the perfect spot between my legs. He drops his head to kiss me and I lick my lips to moisten them in anticipation.

He grins in the way that takes my breath away.

"Just proving my point, Precious."

I startle, then realize I just licked my lips. Annoyed, I start to push him away, but he just chuckles and lands the most loin-tingling, soul-searing kiss.

I'm half crawling up him by the time he pulls away, still chuckling but also with lust darkening his blue eyes.

"If my father weren't waiting and no doubt spying on us out the kitchen windows, I would drag you to the ground right here."

I groan as he sets me back on my feet and starts leading me toward the house.

∼

Dinner is as awkward an affair as I might have imagined. I fill in with mindless chitchat about life on the farm. Xavier's father tries to look interested but I can tell it's a strain to keep his attention focused on our equine feeding schedules or even how Xavier is training Samson.

"It's really incredible," I continue gushing. "He was completely wild only a few months ago and now he's gentle as a kitten when Xavier's got his hands on him."

Xavier scoffs. "I don't know about that. He's still got some snap in him. He about took my finger off when I approached him from the right flank the other day."

I raise my eyebrows in surprise and Pritchard drinks some of his ice water, clearly biting back some comment.

"You haven't worked on that side as much, I guess." I look to his dad. "I didn't know this before I came here, but apparently ideas and things they learn don't automatically transfer between both spheres of their brains like they do for humans. So if you teach a horse a skill from the left side, you have to teach him the same skill starting from scratch on the right side. Totally crazy, I had no idea."

Xavier nods. "Ranchers joke it's like getting two horses every time."

I shake my head. I can't believe I never knew that. It just seems like one of those fun facts people would talk about all the time. Xavier jokingly talks about Samson as Lefty and Righty. As in, *oh, I spent the day with Lefty today.*

"Guess you need to focus on spending some time with Righty, then," I smile at him.

Xavier inclines his head before shoveling in a huge bite of shepherd's pie. I'm really happy with how it came out today. Since I've gotten pregnant and don't have to work so hard out on the ranch, I've taken to experimenting in the kitchen.

Well, at least the past couple weeks once the first trimester was over and the smell of meat didn't send me running for the nearest bathroom. This is one of my favorite recipes because it's hard to screw up. It's the third time we've had it in the last two and a half weeks.

What? So I'm *slowly* expanding my menu of things I can cook. I grew up a New York where take-out was a major food group.

It's also a bit odd to be using a fork and feeding myself. God, it's the first time in months and it feels a bit... well, unsettling and lonely being so separate from Xavier all the way over there at the head of the table with his father sitting across from me. I can't believe him feeding me has become such a source of comfort and connection after how much I fought it in the beginning.

The few times I catch Xavier looking at me, his eyes focused on my fork disappearing between my lips, I wonder if he isn't thinking something similar.

"So, son," Pritchard says after Xavier's midway through his second helping, "what will it take to get you to come home?"

Xavier's fork only pauses briefly on its way to his mouth. Behind him, I notice it start to rain outside.

He continues to take his bite, chews normally, and washes it down with his water. He has beer in the fridge, and I'm surprised he didn't want to take the slightest edge off for this meal with his father. I take a sip of water as I look back and forth between the two men like I'm at a tennis match. Oh dear. Is this where the yelling starts?

But Xavier only says with an easy smile, "I am home, Dad."

Pritchard gives a half-roll of his eyes and puts his napkin down on the table after wiping his mouth. "Be serious. Your mother and I indulged you long enough with this horse farm fantasy, but it's time to grow up. Especially now that you'll be starting a family—" He gestures in my direction.

"Leave Melanie out of this," Xavier says. It's shocking to hear him use my name. I think that's the first time I've ever heard him even say it out loud.

"I won't change my mind on this, Dad. You need to let it go. I left that path a long time ago."

Pritchard exhales loudly and sits back in his chair. "Why? That's what I don't understand. Sure, what happened over there was unfortunate but it wasn't your fault—"

"Stop." Xavier's voice is cold.

"No, I won't stop," his father continues earnestly. "I've talked to some doctors and they say you have all the classic symptoms of PTSD and survivor's guilt. But it wasn't your fault all those people died. You weren't even directly involved in the Quran burnings. You just happened to be in command of those men."

"Stop." Xavier's jaw is working and I can tell he's barely managing his usually easy control.

His father just continues on, though, oblivious or too desperate to press the subject, I can't tell. "Then with the insanity of the riot— I understand. Really, I do. I know you find it difficult to believe, but in Vietnam I—"

"You were a REMF in 'Nam, Dad," Xavier explodes, standing up and pushing his chair back. I startle and grab the table's edge. I've never seen him so worked up apart from the moments right after one of his nightmares.

"Just like you tried to make me in Afghanistan. Station the boy in the center of a green zone at a big air base so he can get some *military experience*," Xavier spits out the words mockingly. "Looks great for the future political career but keep him safe from any of the actual shit of war. Well, guess what, Dad? My fancy Ivy League education didn't help me when the protestors were at the gate throwing acid at anyone wearing a military uniform. And I was one of the fucking lucky ones. I came home with a fucking heartbeat."

Oh my God!

"Xavier," I cry, stepping forward.

The rain has been picking up and thunder rumbles so loud, it seems to shake the house. Or maybe that's just everything that's been revealed in the last few minutes.

Xavier yanks back from me. "I've gotta go check on the horses. Stay here."

He turns and stomps out the door, grabbing his coat and hat before slamming it behind him.

Xavier's father sits down heavily in his chair at the table and sinks his head in his hands. I wonder just how old he is and if Xavier isn't wrong about his motivations for coming here. Sure, he might still have political aspirations for his son—you don't get to his position in American politics without being an extremely motivated man... but maybe he just wants his son back, too.

Men. I sigh, thinking of how my own father spent his life trying to protect me because he loved me but ended up screwing things up so royally.

Why couldn't he have just said the words?

I love you.

Three simple words that seem so impossible for these emotionally stunted men.

The words Xavier has yet to say to me.

I walk toward the door, looking at Xavier's retreating shape through the heavy sheets of rain. I press my hand to the glass. More than anything, I want to run after him but I have the feeling he needs to be alone.

I turn back and look at his dad. "So what exactly happened? There were protests at the airbase? And," I gulp down tears, "someone threw acid at him?"

Pritchard looks up at me, bags that I didn't notice before heavy underneath his eyes. "He's right. I did send him there because I thought it would look good for his career. But if I'd had any idea." His face crumbles and he looks away from me. "If I'd known it would have lost me my son..." His voice trails off.

After a few long seconds, he finally continues, still facing away from me. "He went to Afghanistan as a commissioned officer, a lieutenant. He was a good officer. He was always a natural leader. Probably why we got into as many scuffles as we did during his growing up."

He shakes his head. "He was only there two months when it happened. Barely enough time to get his feet wet and no chance at all to really get a feel for the place. No one blamed him."

"What happened?" I press.

"He was stationed at the detention center at the base. Not a top position but he had responsibility enough. He was smart and he discovered that Taliban prisoners were using their religious text as a means of communicating with each other. They were writing notes in the margins of the Qurans in the prisoner's library. Xavier reported it and had his men remove the Qurans."

Pritchard's head bows. "Well, apparently some of them thought that removing the Qurans meant sending them to the incinerator, not just taking them out of circulation and sending them up the line of command."

I frown. "Okay."

Pritchard finally turns and looks at me. "You don't get it. Burning a holy book is enough to start a jihad over there."

Oh no. My stomach sinks. I'm starting to get where this is going.

"Some Afghan workers on base saw the Qurans in the incinerator pile and pulled them out, half-burned." He closes his eyes. "They told the Afghan guard and went to the press. The entire country started rioting. The airbase itself was taking a constant barrage of petrol bombs and stones. One of the Afghan soldiers the Americans were training within the gates started shooting American soldiers before being shot down. Another threw open the gates to the rioters. Seven American soldiers died at that site alone. Some of the other rioters had bottles of acid."

I step back, a fist to my mouth, but Pritchard's not done.

"Xavier shouldn't have even been there." He shakes his head, devastated eyes beseeching mine. "He was stationed inside the detention facility. But as soon as he realized what had happened and that the facility was surrounded by protestors and rioters, he immediately went to the front lines of the air base's defenses."

He drinks down the rest of his water like it's a shot glass. "Damn fool."

I look toward the door. "Hero," I whisper. Then I look back up at him. "But none of it was his fault."

His father laughs darkly. "Try telling him that. He blames himself for not stressing to those under his command how holy documents should be treated. For not walking the Qurans personally to HQ after he discovered them." He gestures toward the door. "For living when other men died. You heard him."

I look out the window. It's raining even harder now and lightning flashes, illuminating the dark sky. It should only be near twilight, but with the storm, it looks to be full dark.

Where is Xavier?

Is he having trouble with the horses?

I cross my arms and then stop and look down, surprised like I am all the time by my suddenly larger stomach.

Oh, sweet little baby. What hell did your father live through? And what torment does he still go through daily, blaming himself for things he had no control over?

I go to the window and look out, trying to see if I can get a glimpse of Xavier between the flashes of lightning that are coming at regular intervals. Thunder cracks almost as quickly.

God, the storm must be right on top of us.

But it's not so loud that when the gunshot rings out, both Pritchard and I don't know it for exactly what it is.

20

"Oh my God!" I shout and throw open the door.

Pritchard is on my heels but I don't wait for him as I sprint into the darkness. Mud sucks at my boots with every step I take but I press on.

What the hell *was* that? Who would have a *gun* out here?

Xavier. Xavier has a gun.

Did a wolf or bear get close to one of the horses? But I would have thought in a storm they'd hole up, not come near a house. Unless they got their directions all screwed up and—

As I get closer to the stable, I hear the most bone-chilling noise.

It's a scream, but not human.

It's a horse.

I run even faster. I throw open the barn door. The lights are on and all the horses are stomping madly, but Xavier's not there. The opposite door is open, though, and slanting sheets of rain pour into the stable.

I sprint through the barn, the light making me squint after the darkness, wiping water off my forehead. Only to hit the wall of water once I burst out the other side.

The horrible horse scream greets me again once I exit the stable, and that's when I see a sight that will forever haunt me.

Not fifteen feet in front of me is Xavier facing off with Samson, holding a pistol straight out in front of him while Samson rears up on his hind legs.

"No!" I scream and run forward.

I'm not sure if I mean for Xavier not to shoot the horse or for Samson not to land and trample Xavier.

Either way, Xavier looks over at me and his entire demeanor changes. He lowers the pistol and races toward me.

"What the hell are you doing?" He shouts, shoving me behind him as he faces Samson. I can barely hear him above the rain. "Get back in the house."

"What's going on?" I shout back. "Why do you have a gun?"

Samson rears up once more and then settles, stamping and shuffling backward. It's only then that I see Sugar moving along the side of the pasture fence not far away and—is she limping?

What the hell happened out here? Did Samson hurt her?

Xavier keeps his body between me and Samson, all the while facing the horse. With one arm on me, he shuffles us backward toward the barn, with the other, he lifts the gun at Samson again, jaw like iron.

When Samson takes a step toward us, he cocks the gun.

"Stop it!" I shout, grabbing his arm holding the gun. He immediately lowers it and turns on me, lifting me over his shoulder and walking briskly for the barn.

As soon as he gets me inside, he puts me down on my feet.

"Don't you *ever* put our baby in harm's way like that again!" he shouts at me. "What the fuck were you thinking? Are you a fucking idiot? How many times have I told you not to approach a horse when they are upset or you aren't in control of the situation? That horse could have killed you both!"

I stand tall and strong in front of him even though he towers over me and is screaming at the top of his considerable lungs. "Put the gun down," I say calmly.

It's only then that he realizes he's been waving a loaded gun at me while he rants. He freezes and I can see the absolute horror as it hits him.

It's like he just shuts down.

An inhuman calmness takes over.

He lowers the weapon and uncocks it, then clicks the safety on and puts it in the back of his pants. We're both soaking and breathing hard but suddenly his breaths even out like he flipped some kind of switch.

"I should have gelded Samson as soon as I got him on the property. Keeping him as a stallion for even a few months was a foolhardy and sentimental decision." He speaks in such a monotone that he sounds like a robot. "He broke out of his paddock and mated with Sugar, injuring her in the process. I should have foreseen something like this happening. I failed her just like I failed so many before."

"Xavier," I start but he cuts me off.

"It's not safe for you to stay here."

"What?" I exclaim. "That's ridiculous, we'll get Samson gelded and—"

He gives a hard, decisive shake no. "The problem isn't Samson. It's me. I fail those who rely on me. And the consequences..." His jaw goes tight and his sight distant like he's seeing something far beyond the stable. After a moment he refocuses. "I thought with this place... If I could just control enough factors, if I could train them *correctly* from the *start*..."

He looks around at the stable and for the briefest moment I think I see longing enter his eyes before they go dead again. "But no. First Hellfire. Now Sugar. I'll always fail them." Then he looks at me. "God forbid anyone entrust a human to me. It was bad enough that I already endangered you and the baby when I cut out after Hellfire." He shakes his head. "Leaving you to do all the work, you could have lost the baby, but did I even consider that? No." His eyes are darting everywhere. Unfocused. "You'll leave with my father tonight."

My mouth drops open. "I will *not*." I laugh out a disbelieving scoff. "You're insane if you think I'll—"

Suddenly he's whipped the gun out again, only this time he's pointing it at his own head.

"Xavier!" I scream.

He unclicks the safety and cocks it. "I'm having a hard-enough time believing I deserve to be in this world at all. I should have died that day in Afghanistan. Those men were killed right in front of me because of something *I* caused. It should have been me."

"Xavier, stop it! Put the gun down! We're going to have a *baby*," I cry. Tears pour down my cheeks. Oh God, how can he be saying these things? How can the man who's stronger than anyone else I know believe this of himself?

"I can't hurt anyone else," he whispers, desperation entering his voice. For a brief moment, I can see the man I love breaking through this deadened façade he's trying to portray. "Especially not you or our baby."

"Give me the gun, Xavier." I try to swallow my tears. "We had a fucked-up start, okay? I'm not going to romanticize it. You bringing me here like you did was majorly fucked up."

He nods like I'm making his point for him. I shake my head vehemently. "But getting to know you, to *love you*—it's been the best thing that's ever happened to me." I can see in the way his eyes shutter and his face closes down that I'm losing him again so I press on.

"I always thought that submission meant weakness. I grew up thinking the only way I'd make it in the world was on my own because no one was ever going to help me, not even my own father. I never believed I could belong anywhere. I had to be strong on my own terms, always, 24/7. I could never let my guard down for even a second."

I take a step toward him when I see what looks like the slightest bit of hesitation on his face. Am I getting through to him? Oh God, please let him hear me. "Do you know how exhausting living that way was? I didn't even realize it until you started breaking down my walls and showing me a different way." I have to make him understand. He *has* to understand. "You showed me how lonely and empty a life is without real connection. We're wired to connect. But that's only possible if we open ourselves up to trust. And God," tears course down my cheeks, "that was so goddamned terrifying, I fought you tooth and nail every step of the way. Making myself vulnerable enough to trust you? To trust anyone? After what my mother did to me? Or even Dad, how he pushed me away my whole life, even though he thought it was for my own good? You gave me the gift of learning how to trust. And now I'll be able to pass that on to our son or daughter."

"Don't come any closer," Xavier says, blinking rapidly. His hand holding the gun starts to shake so badly I'm terrified he'll accidentally pull the trigger. "You're stronger than me. You always were. I knew it from the start." His voice is strained, like every word is gutting him. At least I'm not talking to a zombie anymore.

I shake my head, taking another step toward him. "I'm sorry I didn't see how much you've been hurting. We can work through this. You have to trust me now."

"Stay back!" he yells, his eyes wide and neck so taut with tension all the veins are standing out. "I hurt everyone around me. I swore I'd protect you! And I will. Even if it's from myself."

Oh my God— "No! Okay, give me the gun and I'll go." Something is seriously wrong with Xavier. And it's bigger than me or logic or maybe even love, a poison that's been warping his perception of himself and the world ever since what happened in Afghanistan. Right now the only priority is to get that gun away from him. "I'll go with your father. We'll leave. Okay? Just give me the gun. I can't leave without knowing you're going to be okay."

Behind Xavier, I see his father step forward from behind the horse stalls. He raises a finger over his lips as he approaches his son from the back.

"I'm doing what you wanted," I try to soothe. "I'll go. But you have to give me the gun. I won't leave unless you give me the gun."

His dad is almost to him. Just a little bit closer...

Xavier shakes his head rapidly back and forth and I see tears forming at the edges of his eyes. "You and the baby have to be safe. From me. This is the only way." His finger twitches on the trigger.

"Xavier, no!" I shout.

His dad lurches forward in the same moment as the shot rings out.

21

"Push! You're doing great. Just give us another good push!" the perky twenty-five-year-old blonde nurse encourages.

"I fucking hate you!" I shout and then bear down. "Fuuuuuuuuu-uuuuuuuuuuuuuuuuuck!"

"Oh, you're a feisty one," Perky Nurse enthuses. Her actual name is Kristi or Kelly or something. "Your baby is going to need all that wonderful energy as soon as he comes out."

Oh my God, this woman is unflappable, no matter how many obscenities I shout at her. Turns out the first words my son hears in this world are going to be the four-letter kind because, yeah, pain brings out the potty mouth in me.

Which brings a pang that feels almost as wrenching as the pain currently splitting me in half because I can just imagine his father leaning over me and growling, "Language."

But little Dean's father isn't here.

I think Dean is a good name.

Pritchard told me that Xavier always hated how fancy the first names in their family were. So Dean sounded like a good, simple, solid name.

Not having Xavier here to meet his son when he's born, I can't, it's just—

Oh shit, here comes another one.

"Where is my goddamned motherfucking epidural?"

"You know you're too far dilated at this point for an epidural," Perky McPerky Fuck reminds me. "Now push. You're almost there."

"Oh shit, oh shit, oh *shiiiiiiiiiiit*!!" I yell then take a breath and push while the pain rips through me. The doctor holds one ankle while the other's in the stirrup.

"He's crowning," the doctor announces. "Keep pushing."

"Fucking fuck!" I scream.

"That's right, Precious! You scream your head off."

What? How did—?

But it's him. Xavier's here! He's not supposed to get out of the PTSD treatment facility for another three weeks but he's here. In a fresh gown and ridiculous cap and mask they make people wear to be in the delivery room.

"How are—" I start to ask but then I'm racked by another contraction.

"Push, Precious." He comes to my side and grabs my hand. "I love you so much."

Tears explode down my cheeks. With how hard I'm pushing, no body fluid is graceful at the moment. Is he really here or is this some pain-induced hallucination?

I haven't laid eyes on him for three months. When his father tackled him, the gunshot went askew into the ceiling of the barn, thank God. But it was enough to convince Xavier to submit himself to a treatment facility his father had found in upstate New York.

After a few weeks, he had something of a breakthrough and got clear-headed enough to realize just how much he'd almost lost. Then he became so dedicated to getting better, he took the doctor's suggestion to really commit to the intensive inpatient treatment program— one that had no contact with the outside world, to my dismay. In our last conversation, he promised he would come out and be the man that I and our son or daughter deserved.

"I'm so fucking sorry I couldn't tell you those words before. I love you and I love our son. Precious, we're about to meet our son." He laughs and sounds so young and *free*. I blink through my tears to look up at him. He's never been more gorgeous to me. His blue eyes have tears glistening at the edges, too. "Because of you. Because of how fucking amazing you are."

The doctor asks Xavier if he wants to take my other ankle. He looks to me and I nod.

I can't take my eyes off him as I push.

"He's crowning," the doctor announces. "Keep pushing."

I grit my teeth and push. Xavier squeezes my ankle. "Precious, he's almost here. Holy Christ, you're doing it! Our son. Our son!"

His eyes flip back and forth between me and watching for our son.

"One last big push," calls the doctor.

"You can do it," Xavier encourages. "I love you. I *love* you."

I take a huge breath and then push with every bit of energy I have. When that's gone, I borrow the rest from Xavier who's infusing me with his strength through his touch.

And I push our son into the world.

EPILOGUE

"Dada, Dada." Dean toddles across the stable to Xavier as soon as he comes in with Samson. "Horsey! Up! Up! Horsey!"

I laugh as I run forward and scoop Dean into my arms before he runs straight into Samson's giant hooves.

All the horses are good around Dean. As soon as the baby was born, the first thing Xavier did when we got home from the hospital was immediately start doubling down on training the horses on their halt commands. He trained them in every conceivable situation with dolls and with recordings of baby cries, squeals, and shouts. Every hour that wasn't spent with us was spent out with the horses.

He had loops of baby noises on repeat in the stable while he groomed them, rode them, put them out to the paddock or pasture for the day—you name it, there was a non-stop baby soundtrack on.

The vet, Hunter, had helped out while Xavier was away and I was pregnant by lending us Carlos, his intern for the summer. Carlos stayed at the resort rent free and took care of the horses in the morning and evening after his rounds with Hunter. He was still with us after we got home from the hospital and the baby-soundtrack about drove him crazy. He constantly wore ear plugs. I think he was more than happy to say goodbye to us when his time with Hunter was done and he went back to the city for school.

At the facility where Xavier spent several months, they worked with him on his need to control every little detail of a situation. He continues to work on it but argues that training horses is still about constant repetition. He has biweekly calls with his doctor to discuss boundaries.

And if you think it means he's given up his love of discipline in and out of the bedroom when it comes to me, think again.

Case in point:

"Mommy's looking a bit hungry, don't you think, big boy? I think it's time to take her in and feed her."

Yep, while occasionally I get to feed myself, most meals still come from his hand.

And yeah, I kind of love it now.

"Horsey!" is Dean's response.

Xavier scoops Dean out of my arms and hefts him up to Samson's long nose. Dean immediately starts to blow in Samson's nose. Samson blows back and Dean lets out a peal of giggles. He does it again and gets the same response. It's become a game between them.

I roll my eyes. Dean's only twenty-two months old and is already horse crazy. I rue the day he actually starts riding. Naturally, Xavier is already talking about getting him a small pony.

Which shows how far he's come because there's so much you can't control when it comes to animals. He about had a fit when I wanted to get back on a horse four *months* after giving birth.

While there have been some bumpy moments, overall, things have been wonderful. The time at the clinic finally helped Xavier face his demons. His nightmares are only very occasional now and he's able to talk about them in a way he wouldn't before. The clinic helped him begin to believe that what happened at the air base *wasn't* his fault and to work through his survivor's guilt and his PTSD.

His relationship with his parents? Well, that's still a work in progress. Pritchard still lives in DC for most of the year, but he and Xavier's mom fly out every couple months to spend time with their grandson. Pritchard and Xavier have even managed to have a few civil conversations when I wasn't present to referee.

My dad? We talk almost every day over Skype. We have a vacation to the Maldives planned for later this year, the first time I'll see him since it all began and the first time he'll get to meet his grandson face to face. Does it suck he has to live in exile all his life? Yes. But at the same time, what he did wasn't a victimless crime. While a lot of the people defrauded by him were rich Wall Street assholes, there were plenty of regular folks who lost their pensions, too, in his scam.

At least I'm protected by Xavier's father's name. And the fact that no one else knows where Dad is and he stays disappeared. In the meantime, he enjoys fishing every day and has taken up pottery and painting.

I'm sad he'll never get to know his amazing grandson beyond talking to him on a screen a few minutes a day. But my focus is on my new family.

Family. Something I never thought would be an important part of my life at all. And now it's everything.

Progress all around.

"Okay, time to say bye to horsey," Xavier says.

Dean starts to whine but Xavier just gives him a look. The *serious dad* look.

Ugh, that never works for me. Probably because whenever I look at my son who is an absolutely *adorable* tiny, little version of his father, I'm always far too tempted to give in to him. And he knows it and now tries to manipulate me and game the system. Smart little punk.

Ha, who am I kidding? He's not little. He's in the 99th growth percentile for his age. He was a ten-pound baby to start with. About tore me in two. Xavier actually had a reason for being concerned about me riding. Well, not being *that* concerned, but it did take me longer than average to heal.

I told him he had another thing coming if he thought I was birthing an army of his kids. Maybe *one* more. Well, that's what I say until I see Xavier with Dean and I'm like, damn, I want a passel of these.

We'll see.

"How'd the interviews go?" I ask as we head up toward the house.

Xavier nods. "Good. There were several I think will be a good fit. We can start taking on more horses as soon as we get them on board and familiar with how we do things here."

I glance back at the stables and my heart does a little twist. We've been talking about expanding the rescue for almost a year now. We have the land, the facilities, and, now that Xavier's inheritance has come through, the resources to take on more needy horses.

The only thing we lacked was the manpower. The big house had been originally built as a lodge, so we've done some remodeling to get the six small one-room suites on the first and second floor ready to take on residents again. We'll live on the third floor and share the common areas on the first.

I couldn't be more excited to take on this new chapter in our lives. It breaks Xavier's heart every time he's had to turn down taking in a horse because we just didn't have the set up to take on any more.

His heart is so big. I love watching him with our son, too. He's so tender and patient.

Dean drops his head on Xavier's shoulder right before we get up to the house, his pudgy little cheek flattening in a way that's so goddamned adorable I feel like my heart's gonna split straight down the middle. His eyelids flutter and then close.

"I think it might be time for someone's nap," I whisper as Xavier opens the back door to the kitchen. Which is good because we're supposed to go to Hunter and Janine's later and it'll go much better if Dean is well rested. They've become close friends over the past couple of years. Even if Janine can be a bit hard to take sometimes.

She's more than a bit bitter about living out here in Wyoming. Hunter was being generous when he explained the situation that day when he came for Hellfire. I try to be a friend to her, but frankly, both Xavier and I feel bad for Hunter. Xavier's solution is for Hunter to invest in a good riding crop. I rolled my eyes at that suggestion. I hope that they're able to either work it out or, as hard as it might be, decide to go their separate ways. I don't see the point in them continuing to make each other miserable like they are now.

"Naptime. My thoughts exactly," Xavier says, bringing me back to the moment. He steps inside with Dean. "Let me just run him up to his room."

He does just that, walking smoothly so he doesn't wake the kiddo up. Not much chance of that. One good thing about living on a farm, Dean spends his days running around outside so he always naps and sleeps hard at night.

I set up a late-afternoon lunch while Xavier's upstairs. Just some sandwiches and chocolate pudding I whipped up earlier. I cut the sandwich into squares.

Then I take off all my clothes and position myself on the plush cushion at the foot of the head chair.

It's rare to have the resort all to ourselves like this. After Carlos left, we've continued hosting volunteers to help out so we can take on even more horses in need. But Caroline, our current intern, is visiting family for a couple weeks, and I intend to take full advantage of the time alone.

"He went down easy, no problem at—" Xavier's words freeze in his throat when he sees me. "Well, what do we have here?"

"Your pet is awaiting her meal, Master."

A low growl is all I get in response. His feet scrape across the kitchen tile as he prowls toward me.

"Is that right?" His voice is low. Predatory.

He sits in the chair in front of me. "I've missed playing with my favorite pet. It's been far too long."

I swallow hard, my sex clenching as moisture gathers. "Yes, Master."

I think he'll start with the sandwich but instead it's a glob of pudding he shoves in my mouth.

"Suck," he commands, voice harsh.

I suck for all I'm worth.

He hisses out a low breath.

And then he does something rarely does. I hear the sound of his buckle being undone and then, my head still down, I see his pants drop to his ankles.

My breath gets short in anticipation. Usually these dinner games always end with him dragging me upstairs. To the bath or the bed.

I wait for his finger to descend with more chocolate.

Instead, his chair scrapes on the tile as he shoves backward from the table. He grabs my upper arms and pulls me forward.

"Suck," he growls.

And that's when I see he's coated the tip of his long, glorious cock in chocolate pudding.

I don't need any more encouragement. I lean forward, about to eagerly gobble him up when I hesitate at the last second.

Instead, I extend the tip of my tongue and lick the chocolate just from the very tip of his slit. He hisses and his cock bobs toward me.

My core starts to melt at seeing his reaction and my sex gets even wetter. If I was wearing panties, they'd be soaked. Tentatively, I lick all around his crown.

Teasing licks.

Tasting then retreating.

"I said, *suck*," he says.

But when I continue to nibble and smear my lips with chocolate and his essence without ever fully taking him into my mouth, he simply sits back in his chair and watches me through hooded eyes.

The only way I know I'm affecting him at all is the occasional hitch in his breathing and the way his cock jumps every so often under my torturous explorations.

"Goddammit," he finally whispers, and I realize his fingers are white-knuckled on the side of the chair.

Only then do I bob my entire head down on his cock and swallow him so deep I'm choking on him. But I love it, knowing I'm driving him absolutely insane after the long session of teasing him.

I massage his balls as his hands come to my hair.

I think he's going to hold me down while he starts pumping up and down into my throat, but instead, no, he's getting my attention to lift me off of him.

I raise up, a little confused.

"Ride me, Precious."

His pupils are blown with lust and that's when I realize his cock is longer and harder than I've almost ever seen it.

"Oh," I whisper as he lifts me by my waist and settles my aching sex down on his huge cock.

"Oh God, you're hung like a horse."

He laughs—that low, throaty chuckle of his that I adore.

"Not quite," he says, "which I bet you're grateful for. Now hush and let me love you."

I meet his eyes and I swear, if there were any corner of my heart this man hadn't already conquered, yeah, I'd be a goner right here, right now. As it is, I lost all of myself to him a long time ago.

He holds me, chest to chest, impaling me so deep that with every thrust he hits that *spot*. I gasp and he kisses me, swallowing it.

"I love you," I whisper between kisses.

"Love you too, Precious. Forever and always."

∽

Continue Reading for a Preview of *Cut So Deep,* a dark romance Available Now

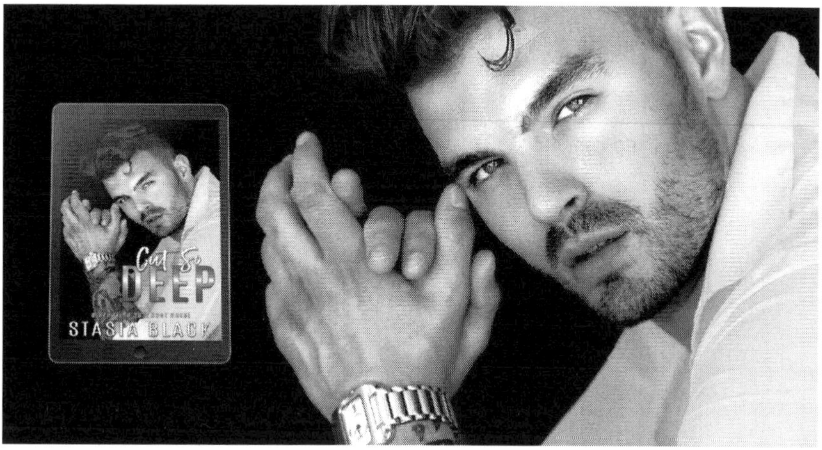
Cut So
DEEP
STASIA BLACK

PREVIEW OF CUT SO DEEP

CHAPTER 1

Bryce Gentry of Bryce Information Technologies doesn't look up from his computer when I enter his huge corner office. Even though I know for a fact his secretary buzzed him to tell him she was sending me in.

Just from his profile I can see he's as good-looking as the online pics I saw last night when I was researching the company. Blond hair, aquiline nose. Long face and squared jaw, like a model. Not that I was paying that much attention last night. Kinda hard when Charlie kept trying to climb into my lap and bang his favorite rubber spoon on my nose. All the while yelling, "Mama! Mama!" to get my attention.

Try telling a two-and-a-half-year old that Mama needs her me-time on the laptop or you're both going to get evicted by the nasty landlord. Yeah. I shudder even thinking about Mr. Jenkins. He doesn't even *try* to pretend he isn't staring at my boobs, no matter if Charlie's with me or not. At least Mr. Jenks-a-lot waited till he caught me alone to tell me to get the rent to him by Friday or come around to some 'alternate forms of payment.' Said while blatantly rubbing at the crotch of his pants.

I stretch my neck and shake out my hands. *Focus Callie.* All that shit just means this interview is more important than ever. Which leads to the mantra I've been whispering over and over to myself all morning: *Don't fuck this up. Don't fuck this up.*

"Mr. Gentry?" I finally venture. Maybe he didn't hear the secretary when she buzzed him or notice when I came in. The wall separating his office from the reception is that cool futuristic glass that can frost and unfrost at the touch of a button. It frosted over as I opened the door. I thought Mr. Gentry had control of it, but maybe I'd been wrong and that had been the secretary as well. Am I an idiot just standing here like a stalker and he doesn't even realize there's anyone in the room with him? "I'm here for the Personal Assistant interview?"

A grunt is all that greets me in return. I stand awkwardly and look down at my shoes. I immediately frown. Shit. I polished them last night but the left one has a giant scuff down the side. They're just crappy knock-off pumps, but I thought they'd at least last the interview process. I've been desperately job-hunting all month ever since the lawyer's fees and rent and student loan repayments have started stacking up too high.

Especially when another custody hearing is looming. My stomach cramps just at the thought, even though it's the last thing I need to be focusing on right now. But God, the money. It's why I'm here. The money has to come from somewhere. Waitressing gigs aren't cutting it, no matter how many hours I work.

And after a month of job hunting, interviewing with no callbacks, turning over every damn rock possible, this is my last shot—and for a job I'm only remotely qualified for. Personal Assistant. I can do that, right? Assist a person. I'm great at thinking on my feet, helping out where needed. And I know computers and robotics. Well, I've taken classes about them anyway...

I look around the pristine room and swallow. The space isn't like the others I've interviewed in. It looks almost like one of those futuristic sets for a movie. Everything is white, glass, or chrome—the floors, the ceiling, the chairs, the desk. It's all so... immaculate. Perfect.

At least I *thought* I was qualified for the job. My hands squeeze into fists but I quickly relax them again. The listing didn't say the PA job was for the freaking *CEO* of the company. And to say that I engaged in a little... *creative truth management* on my resume would be putting it kindly. But doesn't everyone? And if I can actually pull this off... there wasn't a salary listed, it said full details would be offered at inquiry. But damn, who hasn't heard of Gentry Tech? We talked about Gentry Tech products all the time in my classes at Stanford and studied research this man developed. God, this could be the break I've been looking for.

If I don't fuck it up.

Bryce Gentry finally shuts his laptop with a loud clap and looks up at me. For a second I'm startled, just staring at him. He really is attractive, but with a Parisian suave vibe more than an overly muscled All-American football player way. No, he's sleek. The kind of guy you imagine standing in the shadows. Mysterious. Maybe smoking a cigarette. Although the blond hair does throw off the image a little. He's *really* blond, like me. And younger than I would've thought. I'd guess he's in his thirties, but just barely.

"Miss...?" He waves a hand in my direction and I hurry forward, realizing I've just been standing here stupidly instead of introducing myself like a normal human.

Damn it, Cals. Don't fuck this up!

My legs feel wobbly. I've probably only been waiting about five minutes, but it's felt like fifty. God, I hope I don't have obvious sweat stains under my pits already. I put on my extra-strength deodorant this morning, didn't I?

"Miss Cruise. Calliope Cruise." I smile enthusiastically and hold out my hand across his spotless white desk. "Or Callie. You can just call me Callie."

Awesome, way to come across like a bumbling idiot. I just can't believe I'm meeting him. And interviewing in person with him. Although it makes sense, if it's him I'd be working directly with.

Bryce Gentry's eyes finally make their way to me.

But they don't make it all the way up to my face. My excitement deflates. His gaze lands firmly on the real estate that is my chest. Of course. Never my face.

I keep my hundred-watt smile though. It doesn't falter even a few degrees. I don't know why I thought for even a few moments it would be different with this guy. Fortune 500 company or not.

You don't do the beauty pageant circuit without getting accustomed to men ogling you at every turn, even when you're only in the running for Miss *Teen* California. Not when you sprout double D's at fourteen.

He snaps out of it a lot quicker than most, at least. I slide my resume out of my faux leather folder and hand it to him.

I keep that smile plastered as I take a seat in the chair set across his desk from him. Then I jump in head first. "I was very excited when I saw the personal assistant job opening and the chance to work here. Bryce Information Technologies is at the cutting edge of short-range drone technology." Ugh, I want to punch myself. Why am I rambling about shit he already knows about his company?

I pause only to take a breath before refocusing my pitch, "I have extensive experience in public relations and communications. I also have a background in computer science, specifically machine learning and robotics, and I will dedicate myself to this job one hundred and ten percent."

I only realize that I've been slowly leaning further and further over his desk, all but entreating him as I finished my spiel. Shit. Don't look like you're begging, look like you're offering him an opportunity he can't afford to miss.

I pull down the edges of my suit coat and sit up straighter. "In short, I know I can be an asset, both to this company and to you personally."

Mr. Gentry stares at me with an unreadable expression for several moments, his head slightly tilted. Shit. What is he thinking? And does he have to be so handsome? It's worse now that I'm closer. Even his haircut looks expensive, trimmed short at the sides of his head and perfectly edging into the longer hair on top. His face is shaved totally smooth though. The kind that makes you want to run your fingers across to see if the skin is as soft as it looks.

Shit. I'm weirdly staring at his face. And his hair.

I look away even as beads of sweat break out on my brow. Am I smiling? I smile. Shit, that probably looks weird. I just started smiling all the sudden. I drop my lips into a straight line. Dammit. That probably looks even weirder. I wasn't smiling, then I smiled, then I stopped again. What. The. Hell. Am. I. Doing? And what is he thinking?

He finally looks away from me only to glance down briefly at my resume. His mouth twitches. Was that a good mouth twitch or a bad mouth twitch?

"Background in Computer Science, you said? I'm to assume that's from the undergraduate courses you listed, by name." His eyebrows go up.

His deep voice doesn't sound mocking, but I don't see that there's any other way to take it. I sit up straighter in my chair. "Yes." My voice is firm.

"But you never actually finished college." His eyes are brown. They meet mine. I still don't know how to take him or his words. I can't read him. Dammit. Even if he's mocking me, I still have to fight for this.

"I understand that it might not be *conventional* to list an unfinished degree in the educational experience area, but those courses are relevant to the work this company does." I hold my trembling hands together and hide them in my lap. "For example, in my advanced robotics course, we studied the real-time reaction simulation algorithm you and Jackson Vale developed while at MIT. You were only students, but you pushed the state-of-the-art years forward from where it had been." Good. My voice is coming out confident. I sit up even straighter, if that's possible. Fake it till you make it, right?

I continue. "I'm only on a short hiatus from Stanford, with just a semester left. So it's not that I never completed college," I smile a winner's smile, "it's that I'm about to finish and for now I'm just after some real-world experience." He doesn't have to know that with a toddler and a constant need for steady income, the thought of tackling my last twenty-one credit hours of college has been too overwhelming to even consider.

"Real-world experience." This time the lip twitch is definitely a smirk. *Bastard*. It's a struggle to keep my face open and pleasant, but I do it.

He glances back down at my resume. "Such as *The Bridge Bar & Grill*? And *Hooters*? I assume that's where these communication skills you touted were developed?"

Fuuuuuuuuuck. I knew I should've left *Hooters* off. But if I had, I'd have no work history before a year and a half ago. I worked at *Hooters* for three years, from when I turned eighteen till I was twenty-one. I had to hide it from my parents when I was still at home and going to community college for my first couple years before transferring, but it was the only place to earn any real money in our podunk-freakin' town. Plus, I was an assistant manager by the end. That counts for leadership skills.

I feel my cheeks heating up, but when I look at Bryce Gentry, his eyes aren't where I'd have predicted they'd be. He's not looking at my double D's again. He's staring straight at me. In the eye. It's like for the first time in the entire interview, he's looking at *me*.

I don't care if he's being an ass and judging me like everyone else in my life has. I keep my voice confident. "Look, I did what I had to do to get out of the tiny-ass town where I grew up. No one there ever amounted to anything special. That wasn't going to be me."

He doesn't have to know that I've already learned my lesson the hard way that I'm not a special fucking snowflake. I was an idiot with all my big dreams and princess wishes.

All I want now is to be able to pay rent and keep custody of my son, Charlie—and all *this* bastard needs to know is that I want this job and I'll do anything to get it. "I know how to work hard and do whatever it takes to get the job done."

One of his eyebrows lifts and there's challenge in his face. "Will you really, *Callie Cruise*?" Even the way he says my name is clearly mocking. My name has never sounded blonder than it does coming from his lips. "Will you really do *whatever* it takes?"

My jaw thrusts out. I can take what this guy dishes. "Absolutely."

He smiles an easy, carefree smile. "Then open the front of your shirt and take out your tits."

"What?" I choke out.

Some of his easy demeanor drops. A challenging glint enters his eye. "You said you'd do whatever it took. Do you need this job or don't you?"

I— I—

I cannot *believe* this. This is— I can't— how can this be happening in the 21st century? After Harvey Weinstein and Matt Lauer and Me Too? Yeah my assets have gotten me work, and tips, and I know that we live in a shady world where bosses still ogle their employees. But this? This man—so respected in his field, just asking so blatantly for me to... to...

Bryce Gentry waves his hand as if dismissing me. "I really thought you wouldn't be so squeamish considering your work history." He looks completely uninterested now.

I stand up, ready to spit fire at him. "I'm not a fucking prostitute!"

He stands up as well, his interest from a moment ago reappearing in a blaze. His hands are closed fists on the table as he leans over.

"Good," he says, his voice low, brown eyes blazing. "Because I don't want a fucking prostitute. If I wanted a fucking prostitute, I could hit East San Jose any time after dark. I want you, with your big titties, your gorgeous smile, and the fact that you know what a simulation algorithm is. But," he flashes a smile, and I swear it's straight from the devil itself, dimples and all, "I really do need to see the headlights in person."

I can only just stare at him. I don't even know why. This isn't the first time I've been propositioned like this. Well, all right, it's certainly never been exactly like *this*.

This office just looked so classy. Bryce is so handsome. He could have any woman he wants. It doesn't make sense.

He comes around the desk toward me and I take a step back. He holds up his hands and sits on the edge of the desk.

He's got an easy smile back on again, like we're having an everyday conversation. He seems kind of schitzo that way, moving between intensity and a California laid-back vibe. I don't know which one is really him, or if either are. If this guy is showing any of himself at all. This is clearly a game to him, and I don't know the rules.

So much is at stake for me. What am I going to do if I don't get this job? How am I going to afford a lawyer? For half a second, the panic threatens to choke me. I know from the little my ex, David, told me that his (supposedly *ex*) wife is wealthy—yeah, I found out after he broke up with me that he wasn't divorced after all, just separated. Another juicy tidbit in the train wreck that was my relationship with Charlie's dad.

And now I can barely afford an ambulance chaser type lawyer. I can't let them take Charlie. I work two jobs as it is, but it's not enough. Not enough. I look up at Bryce and he's just sitting there on the edge of the desk, staring at me, that easy, expectant expression on his face.

Shit. Shit, shit, *SHIT*. Are my options really to expose myself to Handsome Boss Man or suck off sleazy landlord Mr. Jenks-a-lot? I shudder even thinking about the second option. And that would only get me one month's rent. As opposed to what?

God, Callie, you think showing your tits to Boss Man this once is gonna be the end of it? Don't be stupid. This is just the audition. My mind scrambles for other options when I see Bryce start looking impatient again.

Oh, screw it.

I start opening the buttons on my cheap blouse. I'll figure the rest of it out later. If Bryce tries something I can't handle, I'll just start screaming. His secretary is on the other side of the glass wall, for Christ's sake.

I glance up at Bryce again. The easy smile is gone and the intensity is back. Instead of my chest though, he's watching my face. I look away, behind him at the distant Bay Area skyline. It's a magnificent view. I can even see the Golden Gate Bridge in the background. *Float away, Callie. You remember how this works, don't you? Just float away and let him do whatever he wants to your body.*

I'm at the last button. I let my shirt fall slack.

"Hold it open." Bryce's voice has gone deep.

I keep my gaze firmly on the window as I pull the shirt to the side. It's still tucked into my pants. I have to tug to get it loose enough so that it pulls all the way around the curving edges of my breasts. I look at the floor, but watch Bryce with my periphery vision.

I can always run if he makes a move toward me. But will I?

Shit. I don't know how far I'm willing for this to go. I need this job. That's the only reason my breath is getting quicker. Right? I'm putting on a performance.

"Pull the cups of your bra down. Sit those fat luscious tits on top of them." There's a rasp to his voice now. Damn. Have I heard a man's voice like that anywhere outside of a movie?

My breath hitches as I push down the left cup and pull my breast out.

"Mmmm, that's right," he says low. "Look at that nipple. So pink and pretty and getting hard just listening to my voice."

Shit. I look down. My nipple is hard, but it's not from what he's saying. It's not. It's just cold in here. That's all. *That's all.*

Right, maybe I could believe that. If I weren't sweating. What is *wrong* with me? After everything? After—

"Look at me, Callie." My name doesn't sound stupid or immature coming from his voice now. "Look at me, in the eye."

And I do. My eyes all but snap up to obey and meet his gaze. He doesn't have his hand on his cock like I expected. His hands are braced on the desk and he's just watching me. Watching my face. Can he see how short of breath I'm getting? Did he see how I just twisted my legs together?

No. Oh my God, this is *not* turning me on. This is all so wrong. I'm disgusted by this. By this whole situation that he's putting me in. I swore I'd never be in a position like this again. *Ever again.*

"Now pull out your right tit," he says in that deep, growling voice of his, so low it's almost like it's mesmerizing me. That's what it is. I'm not doing this entirely consciously. It's some kind of spell he's got me under.

"That's riiiiiight," he says slowly. "Pull out that pretty titty, and then roll the nipple in your fingers. Grab both your breasts and rub them. Grab them like you do when you're touching yourself."

This is the most embarrassing thing I've ever done in my life. But I do it. I grab my breasts in both hands as he watches.

"That's right, twist it." He speaks through his teeth. "Like that, that's right my pretty girl. Massage them. Gently at first. Eyes on me."

I swallow even though my mouth is the driest it's ever been in my life. He slowly moves from the desk. I see it but I don't pull back. He's closer. Just a step away.

"Now I want you to pull a little rougher. Squeeze your nipple between your thumb and forefinger."

I do it.

He's so close I can smell him now. Cologne, aftershave, I don't fucking know what it is or how to describe it. But it smells manly and I can feel the warmth radiating from his hard chest.

And right then and there I decide that *no*, this is not like what happened before. It's my choice to be here. I could leave if I wanted. I could jump off this desk and bolt for the door.

But as I pant even harder—oh God, am I really panting now?—I know that for better or worse, I don't want to go yet. And not just because of needing the money. There's a telltale heat that's started in my stomach. It shoots to the place between my thighs and my panties. My cheap cotton Walmart underwear are wet. I can't— How can—?

Mr. Gentry leans in and I think he's going to touch me. But even though he's so close my hands holding my breasts are near enough to brush his chest, he only runs his nose along my cheek, never actually making contact. Like he's scenting me.

"Are you wet, pretty girl?"

Oh my God. I can feel the heat in my cheeks. He can't smell *that* from all the way up here, can he? My hands freeze on my breasts.

Everything freezes. What the hell am I doing? How did I get myself into this situation?

But Bryce Gentry doesn't freeze. He moves again, this time shifting around behind me. His breath is hot in my ear as he reaches around me from behind. His hands cover mine over my breasts. "Yes, you're perfect. A perfect little slut, just for me to take out when I want to play."

At the word *slut*, he pushes my hands gently away and squeezes my nipples.

What the—? *Slut?*

The haze of everything starts to clear. This is fucked up. I came here for an interview. An interview for Christ's sake. What the hell is he talking about? He's calling me a slut and talking about me like I'm a toy. And what, is he thinking he's hiring me, as like his personal sex assistant or something—

But *shit*, that feels *good*. He's started nibbling with teasing bites at my ear while he's still massaging my breasts. God, how long has it been since I've felt this? I haven't been touched in so long. I can't even remember the last time.

It's not just hot between my legs, it's fucking pulsing down there. I need— I mean, God, I need—holy shit—can I come from just this alone? Someone playing with my breasts?

But he's not just playing. I mean, every guy I've known has just been a mauler. They get all excited about my big boobs and just start yanking on them. But this guy is like a virtuoso. I bet sex with him would be insane. Because that's what he wants, right? That's where this is leading? He wants a Personal Assistant he can fuck when he wants?

He'll just keep me up here in his office, push a button, and I'll come in and blow him or he'll fuck me or something? I'd said I'd never get this low, never degrade myself... but if it could feel like this?

I can't help the high-pitched whine that comes out of my throat. Fuck. I'm almost there. And it's been so long. So long...

I can't think. Oh God, if he would just touch me there. Maybe I could touch me there. He'd find that hot, right? And that's what this is about? Sex? What would it feel like if he was sucking on my nipple instead of just playing with his fingers? His face is so smooth-shaven, but even the thought of his tongue—

Another whine comes out of me, and he sucks and bites at the back of my neck.

Holy *shit*, that's hot.

I'm so close. So fucking close. He's gotta know. But he's not doing anything about it. Fuck it. I put my hand down the front of my pants. A girl's gotta get it done sometimes.

"That's right, my dirty girl," he hisses in my ear. "Make yourself a little whore for me."

His words should disgust me. They should *not* be turning me on even more as my fingers find my clit.

"Show me how bad you want this job. Make yourself come." His voice lowers, but the words are intense.

His grip on my breasts continues the same massaging pressure, but he's twisted my body slightly sideways so he can see my face. We're looking eye to eye and all traces of the nice guy fall away as he sneers, "Dirty bitch, I want to see your cum face, you trashy fucking bimbo whore."

The breath is knocked out of me at the nastiness of his words. And in the same instance, I come harder than I ever have before in my life.

Continue reading *Cut So Deep,* Available Now

Want to get my free short story collection not available anywhere else, news about upcoming releases, sales, exclusive giveaways, and more?

Get Stasia's News

ALSO BY STASIA BLACK

DARK MAFIA SERIES

Innocence

Awakening

Queen of the Underworld

LOVE SO DARK SERIES

Cut So Deep

Break So Soft

Hurt So Good

THE MARRIAGE RAFFLE SERIES

Theirs to Protect

Theirs to Pleasure

Their Bride

Theirs to Defy

Theirs to Ransom

STUD RANCH STANDALONE SERIES

The Virgin and the Beast: a Beauty and the Beast Tale

Hunter: a Snow White Romance

The Virgin Next Door: a Ménage Romance

ABOUT THE AUTHOR

Stasia grew up in Texas, recently spent a freezing five-year stint in Minnesota, and now is happily planted in sunny California, which she will never, ever leave.

She loves writing, reading, listening to podcasts, and has recently taken up biking after a twenty-year sabbatical (and has the bumps and bruises to prove it). She lives with her own personal cheerleader, aka, her handsome husband, and their teenage son. Wow. Typing that makes her feel old. And writing about herself in the third person makes her feel a little like a nutjob, but ahem! Where were we?

Stasia's drawn to romantic stories that don't take the easy way out. She wants to see beneath people's veneer and poke into their dark places, their twisted motives, and their deepest desires. Basically, she wants to create characters that make readers alternately laugh, cry ugly tears, want to toss their kindles across the room, and then declare they have a new FBB (forever book boyfriend).

Printed in Great Britain
by Amazon